Glass House People

KATHRYN REISS

HARCOURT BRACE & COMPANY
SAN DIEGO NEW YORK LONDON

Dedicated to my grandmother, *Mabel Catherine Reiss,* and to the memory of my other grandparents, *Elsie May* and *William Earl Kauffman,* and *Edmund Lewis Reiss*

Thanks, also, to *Clifton Raphael* for the use of his name!

First Harcourt Brace paperback edition 1996

Library of Congress Cataloging-in-Publication Data
Reiss, Kathryn.
The glass house people/by Kathryn Reiss.—1st ed.
p. cm.
Summary: Sixteen-year-old Beth and her brother discover that their mother has been estranged from her sister and the rest of her family because of the mysterious death of a man both sisters loved.
ISBN 0-15-231040-1 ISBN 0-15-201293-1 (pbk.)
[1. Family problems—Fiction. 2. Brothers and sisters—Fiction.
3. Interpersonal relations—Fiction.] I. Title.
PZ7.R2776Gl 1992
[Fic]—dc20 91-26850

Text set in Simoncini Garamond
Designed by Lydia D'moch
A B C D E F G H I J D E F G H I J K L M (pb)

Printed in the United States of America

Life, like a dome of many-coloured glass,
Stains the white radiance of Eternity.
—Percy Bysshe Shelley, "Adonais"

May

❦❦❦❦❦❦❦ Summer came early that year. Everyone agreed that the heat was uncomfortable already. Weather forecasters predicted that as the summer went on things would become worse. Fans whirred on high in all the bedrooms in the house on Spring Street.

The couple in the big front bedroom had kicked off their sheets and fallen asleep at last, peacefully unaware of the silent activity in the other bedrooms.

In the corner room down the hall, the young woman sat in an armchair with a sketch pad on her lap. She used a thick black stick of charcoal to sketch from memory and in minute detail the face of the man she loved. She was smiling as she shadowed his cheeks and with deft strokes added a sparkle to his eyes.

In the small pink bedroom the younger girl lay staring at the ceiling, an open romance novel facedown on her stomach. She was feeling slightly smug because the story in the paperback book simply could not compare with her own real-life romance. She stretched out her long legs, adjusted one shoulder strap of her baby doll pajamas, and felt a little shiver of excitement tingle at the back of her neck despite the warm breeze from the fan, as she imagined her own next chapter.

The young man typing on the sunporch left his desk to sit at the window. He chewed thoughtfully on the plastic cap of his pen as he stared out at the stars. His eyes widened for an instant as he thought he saw a meteor streak across the night sky. Then there was another—and immediately another. It was astonishing. It was a whole parade of shooting stars just for him! He took off his glasses and polished the thick lenses on his T-shirt. Then he replaced the glasses on his nose and sat watching, chewing the pen, waiting for more. But nothing happened. And after another minute the faint glow from the tails of light faded away completely.

1

They had been on the road for six whole days—motel after motel for three thousand miles. On the map it looked a snap—just a nice long blue line stretching across the country. But off the map it was mountains and desert and rivers and plains, all the way from California to Pennsylvania. Beth Madigan sat in back most of the way, glaring at the map.

She glared at the back of her mother's head, too, just visible over the top of the headrest. Sometimes if she glared at someone hard enough, that person would start to fidget, feeling the power of her eyes. But her mother was impervious. At sixteen, *Beth* should have been the one having an identity crisis, not her thirty-seven-year-old mother. With all Beth's carefully made summer plans on hold and God-knows-what ahead, not to mention the mammoth zit about to erupt on her chin, she was *entitled* to a crisis of major proportions.

Beth pressed her cheek to the window, felt the heat of the glass on her skin despite the air conditioning, and thought about Ray, all those thousands of miles back there in Berkeley. He'd be working in the glass shop all day and teaching the evening class after hours. She longed to be with him. For a moment the smooth pane of glass against her cheek became the soft flannel of his shirt as it had felt on her skin when he'd hugged her good-bye. Then the flannel became glass again, as hard and unfeeling as her mother.

She glanced from the window to the red head of her brother, Tom, next to her mother in the front seat. Poor Tom. He was entitled to a crisis or two of his own—his zits were worse than hers, he'd never even had a girlfriend yet, and he was going to miss the computer camp he'd been so excited about. Fifteen was a prime age for crises, too. But since their mother had chosen this summer to "get her act together" (as she insisted on putting it), no one else mattered. Beth sighed heavily, then leaned forward and tapped her mother on the shoulder.

"Can I drive again, Mom?"

"Thanks, honey. But we're almost there."

Beth slouched back and slipped on her earphones, turning up the volume on her Walkman until the beat drowned out the Lite Rock tapes her mother insisted on listening to. She stared out the window.

Their old, battered car had cruised the highways between Berkeley and Philadelphia for six days now. Beth's mother, Hannah, normally so scatterbrained, drove with a strange intensity, piloting the car smoothly, relentlessly back east, back to the hometown she hadn't seen for twenty years. Beth, who had passed her driver's test soon after she'd turned sixteen in March, had driven whenever she could persuade Hannah to relinquish the wheel. Driving gave her something to think about other than what awaited them at the end of their journey.

Most of the six days on the road Hannah seemed determined to keep hold of the wheel, as if holding it tightly gave her some kind of courage. And since Tom got carsick unless he sat in the front and looked straight ahead, Beth was stuck most of the time in the backseat with Romps, their old schnauzer, and all the bags and piles of junk that wouldn't fit anywhere else.

She read one cheap detective novel after another as they crossed the mountains and the deserts and the plains, until the plots blurred into a single, predictable murder with one half-baked solution.

When her tape ended, Beth pulled off the headphones. "You'll really like Philadelphia," she heard Hannah telling Tom. "We can take a day or two and explore the historic district. I haven't seen it since I was a child."

"Didn't you go there a lot when you lived at home?" asked Tom.

"Not really. I don't think you ever really see the touristy things if you live in the place."

"Yeah, like how we never ride on the cable cars—even with San Francisco right there."

"I took you and Beth when you were little," said Hannah. "But I guess you don't remember."

Beth thought she recalled riding on a cable car with her mother. She remembered wearing a jacket with a red hood and holding tightly to her mother's hand on one side and to the hand of a man on the other. That might have been her father. Or was he already dead then? She remembered the house they lived in when she had that red jacket. It was a big, rambling house just over the hills from Berkeley, with a sagging front porch and chickens in a pen in the back. The man could have been her father or any other member of their communal household. Now she and Hannah and Tom lived in an apartment in Berkeley right near the highway. Her mother had finished high school through a correspondence course she'd begun when Beth and Tom started school, and she now worked as a general secretary in the English department at the university. Beth tried to help out by buying her own clothes and lunches at school with the money she earned at Glassworks, the stained-glass shop where she'd met Ray.

"This is it," Hannah said suddenly, turning the car onto the exit ramp. "This is really it! Oh, my God, this is it!" Her hands gripped the wheel so tightly her knuckles shone white.

"Hey, guess what, Mom," said Tom.

"What?"

"This is it." His voice was dry.

She frowned at him. "I still don't think you and Beth know what this means to me, to go home again after all these years."

"Guess not."

Beth didn't say anything. There was nothing to say. Of course she and Tom didn't understand what "going home" meant to their mother. But how could they? Hannah had always been silent on the subject of her family. "I left them when I was seventeen," she'd told Beth and Tom once. "Didn't even stay to finish high school. I was miserable living there, and they were happy to see me go. I've never wanted to go back. There's no reason to go. I can't relate to them. I don't expect I'll ever see them again—and that's fine. People don't have to stay with the families they're born to, you know. People can build their *own* families. It's better that way." That had been when they were still in the big house on the other side of the Berkeley hills. Hannah had wanted to stay with the people she'd chosen as family—especially after Beth and Tom's father died. Even a few years later, when the group house broke up and the three of them were alone in the little apartment, Hannah remained adamant: "In the end, we each have to make our own way in the world," she told Beth and Tom. "Never look back."

Beth had noticed that each day, as the car sped further east, Hannah became increasingly nervous and tense. She talked more and drank coffee nonstop as she drove. Once at a rest stop she bought a pack of cigarettes and lit one, puffing hard. Beth and Tom stared in amazement. "You don't smoke, Mom!" Tom exclaimed.

Hannah's voice trembled as she lifted the cigarette for another long draw. "I do now." Then she looked up at the surprise in their faces and threw the cigarette down with disgust. "No. I won't let them get to me! I swear it!"

That was when Beth got the feeling there might be some trouble ahead.

Now Beth stretched her long legs out around Romps and rubbed his ears. The little dog settled himself across her legs, his gray muzzle resting on her stomach. She scratched him automatically, and he moaned a little.

"Mom? Romps sounds weird."

"I'm sure he's fine," said Hannah, glancing over her shoulder. "Is your seat belt fastened, Beth? You know it isn't safe without—oh, look!" She broke off and pointed out the window. "There's the Waverley! That was the movie theater we'd go to every other Saturday. Imagine—it's still here!"

"How extremely thrilling, Mom."

"And that's the candy store—I can't believe it's still in business!"

"Fascinating. Awesome. I don't think I can stand it."

"Oh, Beth." Hannah sounded wistful. "I wish you'd take an interest. This is where I grew up! And it's going to be our home for the summer. We would have come here years ago, if I'd had my act together then."

"I liked your old act better. And I wish you'd let me stay with Ray. He said it would be fine. He has plenty of room in his apartment You know, Mom, I had my whole summer planned out perfectly, and now it's totally wrecked!"

"Honey, we've been through this a hundred times. You're too young to be left behind while I'm on the East Coast—especially with a man ten years older than you."

"Look, please don't start in about Ray again. Mom, when you were only a year older than I am, you ran away from home and got married!"

"Yes, I know." Hannah's voice was soft. "But I see now I was wrong to do that. I was too young. In any case, it's time to go back. I need to. And more important, you need to meet your grandparents. They're getting older. They won't be around forever."

That was the new Hannah speaking. The one with the identity crisis. The old Hannah had no regrets about anything. Beth preferred the old self-assured one, the one who had always taught her, "Move forward. Never look back."

This was looking back in a big way right now.

The car veered sharply to the right. "Whoops!" cried Hannah. "Almost missed the turn! This is it, kids. Spring Street. Here we are!" Her voice was happy, but Beth caught the nervous tremble in it.

Romps moaned again. He was panting, pink tongue hanging loosely.

Despite the indifference she longed to assume, Beth craned her neck to see out the window. After six days of fast food and cheap motels where they had to smuggle Romps in after dark, she welcomed a real house. She welcomed any change of scene from the never-ending stretch of highway. Soon she would be meeting her grandparents, her mother's parents. Henry and Clara Savage. Her mother had been Hannah Savage when she last saw them. Beth figured it was no wonder her mother had run off to get married—anything to change a weird last name like that!

Beth leaned over Tom's shoulder to watch out the front window as their car passed the houses on Spring Street. Another moan from

Romps made her look down at the seat. He was still panting, so she pulled him onto her lap. Then he heaved. The quick turn onto Spring Street had been too much for him.

"Oh, Romps, *no!*" She tried to push him off in time but could not. He heaved again, his eyes rolling back miserably. And all his lunch, as well as the ice cream cone Beth shared with him at their last rest stop, frothed out onto Beth's stomach. "Mom! Help!" she cried as the stench of partially digested dog food filled the car and the hot vomit soaked through the thin fabric of her T-shirt.

Hannah pulled the car sharply into a driveway, cut the motor, and whirled to look at Beth helplessly. "Oh, no! Not now!"

"Get him off me!" Beth shrieked. "I can't stand it!"

She heard a gurgling sound from the front seat, from Tom, and the thought flitted across her mind that he was about to throw up, too. But then she saw he was laughing, and she snarled at him, furious. "I'll kill you!"

"Beth!" said Hannah. "And Tom! Please! We're here. Hurry, let's get you out and cleaned up somehow. Quickly! I don't want them to see us like this. After twenty years!" Her voice trailed off as the porch door opened and a heavy, white-haired woman stepped out.

Beth felt the sudden panic in Hannah's intake of breath.

"Sorry, Mom. Too late." Beth shoved Romps to the floor, craning her neck to see the woman coming nearer. And she sensed, without actually seeing it, the sudden guilt in her mother's face.

"Hanny? Hanny Lynn?" called the woman in a high, brisk voice. "Is that you?"

Hannah slid out of the car and hurried toward the porch. "Mama? It's me!"

Beth was trying to mop up the vomit, and so she couldn't stop Romps when he struggled out of the car and leaped joyfully up the porch steps. He thrust his vomit-covered nose eagerly against the older woman's legs in welcome.

"Down, boy!" shouted Hannah, pushing the dog away. She hugged her mother. "It's me, Mama."

"So I see." The woman looked distastefully at the stain on her pant leg and wrinkled her nose. "I see."

"It's been too long, Mama." Hannah shoved Romps away again and looked toward the car. "Beth! Come get this animal."

Great, Mom, thought Beth, still mopping at

her T-shirt with the green bandanna she'd had tied in her hair. *I'm half-dead from the smell, and you expect me to . . .* But she smiled politely as she walked to the steps, Tom behind her, her glance taking in the stone house at the side of the narrow driveway, the large front porch, the thick flowering bushes that shielded the house from the street. "Hello, Grandmother? I'm Beth."

"Hello, dear." The voice was cool, the glance appraising. Beth wondered what the woman was thinking. "And you, young man? Are you the other one?"

Tom ran up the steps behind Beth. "Hi. I'm Tom. Nice to meet you."

Beth glanced at him with surprise. He sounded so composed and mature. She herself felt suddenly ill at ease—though that could be explained by the vomit covering her T-shirt. She didn't often meet relatives stinking like a sewer. Actually, she'd never met any relatives at all.

Grandmother nodded at the door. "The first order of business is baths for everyone, I think. And then we can say all the right things and so on."

Hannah followed Grandmother into the

house without a backward glance. Beth and Tom, left on the porch, shrugged at each other. Romps, who had relieved himself against the rosebushes in the side yard, trotted onto the porch. Beth tied his leash to the leg of one of the wrought-iron porch chairs and patted his head before entering the dim interior of the house. "Stay," she whispered. "Good boy. I'll be out to clean you up soon."

Hannah was standing at the foot of the stairs, just inside the front door. Beth nearly bumped into her. "Ohh," Hannah sighed. "It hasn't changed here, not really. It's still just the same."

"Well, what did you expect?" Grandmother pressed Hannah's arm.

"Where are Dad and Iris?"

"Upstairs," said Grandmother. "Your father's been very weak in the legs since his stroke. Stays in bed a lot, though the doctor says he should exercise more."

"He'll be fine again, though, won't he, Mama?"

"We'll talk about everything later. Let's get your girl cleaned up first and bring things in from the car."

"But is he very sick?"

The older woman sighed. "Let's just say your letter was very welcome. Gave him something to get better for."

"Oh, Mama!"

There had been several manifestations of Hannah's identity crisis, but the two biggest changes in her life were her decisions to apply to colleges and to get back in touch with her family in Philadelphia. She'd shown Beth and Tom the letter she was sending and showed them the one she got back the following week from Grandmother. Hannah's letter had begged forgiveness and said she wanted to see them and could they get together soon. Grandmother's letter said that Hannah's father had suffered a stroke and that Hannah and her kids might want to consider visiting before anything worse happened to him. There had been several phone calls back and forth as plans were made for their summer trip. And Beth could see now that her mother was struggling with all sorts of guilt feelings—like maybe her father wouldn't have had a stroke in the first place if she hadn't run away from home twenty years ago? That sort of thing.

Tom hurried back out to the car to bring in some of their suitcases. Beth and Hannah followed Grandmother upstairs. Beth was starting to feel dazed and nauseated from the smell of the vomit that saturated her shirt. Now that she was out of the air-conditioned car, the heat of the late afternoon pressed around her and made her feel weak.

The stairs were steep and narrow. She ran her hand along the polished wooden railing as she climbed. On the landing a fragile wooden knick-knack stand held porcelain figurines and some tiny china cups and saucers. The stairs continued up another shorter flight to the right—the heat increasing as they moved up—and then Beth stood in the long, dim hallway. Grandmother led them down the hall into a small room with faded pink-flowered wallpaper. Hannah's smile trembled. "Oh, Mama! It still looks the same. After all this time."

"Not because we're sentimental, I assure you," said Grandmother in a tight voice. "But we don't have money to redo the house every time someone moves in or out."

"Of course not! I only meant—well, it's just funny to see the room again. Like stepping right back in time."

"Well, it's yours. Take it or leave it. You can sleep on the couch if you prefer."

"Oh, no. I'll be fine in here."

Beth hovered near the doorway. Her mother saw her and grimaced. "You're a sad sight," she said, taking a suitcase from Tom. "Here, take this suitcase and go get a bath. The bathroom's just there, across the hall."

"There are fresh towels for you on the back of the door," offered Grandmother as Beth moved across the hall with her suitcase.

Soon Beth had cool water running into the tub. She rubbed herself all over with the thick bar of scented soap, then washed her hair, delighting in the fragrant suds. She loved baths and hadn't felt really clean these past six days of the trip, with only dripping showers at the motels.

Beth dried herself with a thin, faded green-and-white towel, then hung it carefully back on the hook behind the door. She dug in the suitcase until she found a clean pair of track shorts and a not-too-rumpled T-shirt and dressed. She felt hot and sticky again almost immediately. As they'd driven east, the air had grown hotter and heavier with each state. Her mother had told her about the horrible humidity of eastern summers, but Beth hadn't understood till now how limp such thick air made things feel. She dragged a wide-toothed comb through the abundant auburn tangles of her hair and noticed it was much curlier in this heat than it was back in Northern California.

The mirror above the sink was cloudy in the upper left-hand corner and spotted with age. Beth opened the medicine cabinet and stared at the bottles of aspirin, tubes of God-knows-what, little bottles of iodine, yellowed toothbrushes. Everything looked so old, so permanent, so much a part of old people's lives. Only the tube of Crest looked new.

She tried to imagine Hannah as a sixteen-year-old in this house. She would have stood right here before this mirror, putting on makeup or brushing her teeth, but Beth couldn't picture it. Nothing about this house seemed remotely connected to her mother.

"Gotta go, gotta go," chanted a voice softly outside the door.

Beth swung the mirror shut guiltily and hurried to open the door.

"I thought I was doomed," said Tom, pushing past her.

"Wait a second!" Beth balled her soiled clothes up in a towel and picked up the suitcase. "Where's Mom?"

"In with the old man—'Grandad' to us—

and Aunt Iris. Big front room at the end of the hall." He pushed her toward the door.

"Where should I put this?" she hissed at him, pointing to the suitcase.

"Top of the stairs. Can't miss it." The door closed firmly; the lock clicked.

The hallway was empty. Through the door at the end of the hall, Beth could hear voices—her mother's and a man's deep rumble. Then a woman's shrill voice, not Hannah's or Grandmother's, rose angrily. "You've no idea what I've suffered!"

Beth hurried down the hall in the opposite direction to the room at the top of the stairs Tom had said was hers. She closed the door behind her and dropped her suitcase on the floor with a great thud, standing silently, an empty feeling spreading through her. Who had suffered? What was going on?

She looked at the room dully, taking in the high old bed, the dark, curved-front dresser with the heavy mirror on the wall above it. Hannah had said her family had owned this house for generations, and the furniture attested to this fact. It was all old and solid. Under the single window was an old-fashioned sewing machine and a little low stool. The walls were papered with a yellowed pinstripe pattern. The feel of this house was so different from the apartment in Berkeley, which was light and airy and furnished with the wicker and glass and Native American print fabrics Hannah loved. Beth tried again to picture her mother living here and failed. She caught sight of herself in the mirror and stared at her wild mane of curly hair. She was out of place here—her track shorts and thin, bare legs seemed almost indecent.

Then Tom opened the door to her room and walked in.

"Hey, don't you ever knock?" she asked, surprised at the way her voice came out sounding shaky. Actually, she wasn't sorry to see him at all.

"I sleep out here," he said, crossing the room. She noticed for the first time that a door led out to a little sunporch. She followed him into the adjoining room. It had windows on three sides.

"You're lucky," she said. "It's a little cooler out here." From down the hallway they could hear the muted hubbub of angry voices.

"They're waiting for you," Tom told her, flopping onto the narrow bed against one long screened window.

"What are they like?"

"Go see." He unzipped his suitcase and pulled out some computer manuals—his favorite reading material these days.

Steeling herself as if for an ordeal, she walked down the hall. Outside the door at the end, she hesitated, then knocked.

Hannah opened the door immediately, relief shining in her face. "Here she is, Dad! Here's Beth!" And Beth was pulled into the darkened, air-conditioned room and found herself standing next to one of the two high old beds that took up much of the floor space. The cool air felt wonderful after the close heat of the rest of the house. Beth breathed in deeply, as if hoping to cool her body from the inside out.

A lanky old man lay under a sheet, his head propped up on pillows, a pile of books and magazines, topped by wire-rimmed glasses, at his side. He fumbled for the glasses, picked them up, and peered through them, then replaced them carefully and held out his hand. "Beth, is it?"

"Hi." Beth leaned over to embrace him, wondering whether she would hurt him. His grip was strong, though, as he hugged her shoulders, pressing her down to sit on the edge of his mattress. He wore a pale blue pajama shirt with the sleeves rolled up to reveal long, thin arms, fuzzy with dark red hair, the color of her own. The top of his head, however, was totally bald and covered with tiny, blurred age spots. His eyes were as blue as her own, and Beth hoped hers were as piercing.

"So, you're Beth. Hear you had an accident with a dog. I'm your grandad. Glad to meet you at last."

"I'm glad to meet you, too, Grandad," said Beth. She smiled at him and felt her mother beam at them both.

"Hope you'll come up often to talk with me, you and that brother of yours. Don't get downstairs much anymore. Same old company gets boring. You know."

Beth nodded sympathetically, then started at the sound of a dry cough from the corner of the room.

"Oh, hello! I'm sorry—I didn't notice you!" Beth felt her face flush, and even as she spoke the words, she knew she should not have said exactly that.

"Most choose not to notice me, so I'm quite used to it," said a voice from the dim corner by the closet. A figure sat stiffly on a straight-backed chair, looking awkward and uncomfortable. "But eventually I'm introduced."

"I—I'm Beth," said Beth, glancing to her mother for help. But Hannah merely stood by the door, her eyes on Grandad.

"Oh, don't carry on, Iris," said the old man from the bed. "Stick yourself back where nobody can see you and then complain when they don't. Come on out where the girl can see you. Or do you want her to creep back there to shake your hand?"

Beth hurried to the corner even as the woman was struggling to rise from her chair. Beth had thought she was old—possibly even older than Grandmother—but now saw with a shock that the woman was not too much older than her own mother. And she was terribly thin. She grasped the hand Beth held out as if to shake it, but then clutched tightly and heaved herself to a standing position.

"I used to have red hair, too," she rasped, peering at Beth and running bony fingers through her wisps of graying hair. "Not that you'd ever know it now. Red hair, long and curly, just like yours. Poor Hanny Lynn always wished her hair looked like mine. Didn't you, Hanny? Remember the dye—that time? Mama was furious when she caught you."

Was that beer she smelled on Aunt Iris's breath? Beth waited until Aunt Iris steadied herself, then she pulled away and moved back across the room to where Hannah still stood by her father's bed.

"You always did want hair like mine, Hanny, you know you did. You wanted a lot of things I had."

"Yes," sighed Hannah, turning to look at her sister. "You're right, Iris. I sure did. But since then I've learned to live with my mousy brown hair and even like it. And, of course, I've got Beth's and Tom's beautiful red hair to look at!"

"I'm not talking about hair, Hanny Lynn, and you know it."

"Come on," said Hannah brightly, turning back to her father. "Why don't we go downstairs and let Dad get some rest?"

"That's right, girls," said Grandad. "I'll be fine up here. Feeling better already." He picked up a paperback that lay facedown on the sheet next to him.

Beth followed Hannah out of the room, then

turned back once to tell the old man she would come up later and talk to him. But she stopped short at the sight of Aunt Iris.

Aunt Iris, supporting herself by clutching the post of her father's bed, was starting to follow Beth and Hannah. But the going was slow because she was so impossibly thin and frail, and because her left leg was shorter than the right by a good three inches.

Before dinner Beth and Tom hosed Romps off and took him for a long walk down the dusky streets. The houses were close together in this neighborhood, with neat green yards and borders of flowers along the driveways. They had a well-tended, cared-about look, Beth thought. Different from their apartment building in Berkeley, where neighbors came and went at all hours, and no one had any time or place for gardening. Tom stopped suddenly and grabbed her hand, then dragged her over to wait in line behind a gaggle of tiny children at an ice-cream van with a jangly bell parked at the side of one narrow street.

Beth held Romps firmly while Tom paid for two fudge bars. "Shall I faint now or later?" she asked when he handed one to her. "I didn't think old Mac *ever* spent his allowance." She'd nicknamed him Mac when he first started raving about the Macintosh computer he used at school. "Aren't you still saving for a computer? What's the deal?"

"No deal." He shrugged and looked away. "I'm just celebrating being out of that house."

"We've only been there a few hours."

"Yeah, but don't you feel it?" He reached for Romps's leash. "It's like—I don't know. I just can't believe Mom grew up there. Freaks me out."

"That's another first," Beth teased. "Nothing freaks out old Mac. He's fearless as only a computer wizard can be." She stopped teasing when she saw his face. "Listen, what's wrong? I mean, Aunt Iris is bizarre, but—"

He shrugged. "Never mind." Then, pulling on Romps's leash, he started running. "Come on, boy! Let's go!" They raced away, leaving Beth to lick her fudge bar alone.

Beth was glad they had been able to bring Romps along on this trip. When she was six and they still lived over the hills, someone had dumped the schnauzer runt off at the porch. All the commune children had helped care for him, but he'd favored Beth. And so when Hannah left the house a few years later, everyone agreed the dog should go with Beth. He had been her constant friend. When Hannah first told them of the plan to return to Philadelphia this summer, she said Romps would have to stay behind in Berkeley with a neighbor. But Beth had put her foot down. If she wasn't going to have any other friends around this summer, she was *at least* going to have her dog. And Hannah gave in once she saw the look on Beth's face.

Beth wandered after Tom and Romps, enjoying the sights of a real neighborhood again after so many nights with only motel parking lots to stare at after dinner. She heard the swish of wheels on pavement and turned to see a slim, dark-haired girl about her age roller-skating toward her, eating a frozen yogurt bar. She braked neatly in front of Beth and flipped her long hair over her shoulders.

"Hi. You must be new around here."

"That's right. But just for the summer."

"You don't look very happy about it."

"It wasn't my idea to come."

"I'm Monica Clements," the girl said, finishing her yogurt bar and wiping her fingers on her shorts. "I'm fairly new around here, too. Just since January. Maybe we should start a club."

Beth looked at her with interest. "I'm Beth Madigan. We're staying at my grandparents' house on Spring Street."

"I live around the block, next to the Waverley." She shook her hair back again. "Where are you from?"

"California. We live in Berkeley—across the bay from San Francisco."

"I went camping in Yosemite once," Monica said. "And then we went to San Francisco for a few days. It was foggy."

"Yeah, but at least it's never humid like this!" Beth held her arms away from her sides. "I'm dripping."

"You get used to it." Monica bent down to adjust her roller skate. She stood up again and threw back her hair. "Listen, I work every day, but maybe we can get together when I'm off and do something, if you're going to be around all summer. It's pretty tame around here, but there are movies."

"That would be great!" Beth smiled at Monica with relief. Things wouldn't be so boring if she had somebody to do things with.

"I've got to go now, but I'll have time on the weekend. Wait a sec," Monica said, and skated up to the little window of the ice-cream van.

She borrowed a pen from the vendor and scribbled on a paper napkin.

"This is my phone number," she said, handing the paper to Beth. "Give me a call when you want to get together."

"Great!" Beth took the slip of paper. "I'd give you my phone number, but I don't know it yet. We just got here this afternoon."

They said good-bye, and Beth watched Monica roll down the street, admiring her skill. For all that roller skating was a big deal in California, she'd never been able to skate more than a few feet without crashing onto her knees.

Beth started walking around the block after Tom and Romps and caught up to them on the corner. They were still panting from their run. "Time to go back, you crazies," she said.

Tom chewed on his ice cream stick. "Romps likes long runs. What's your hurry?"

"We'll be late for dinner and Mom will be mad. You know she's trying to make a good impression." She took the dog's leash and set off with Romps prancing at her heels. "Come on. Mom's a basket case already." Tom shrugged and moseyed along a good ten paces behind.

• • •

At dinner Beth found herself only picking at the food, hoping Grandmother wouldn't be insulted or think she didn't like it. Maybe the fudge bar had taken away her appetite, or else the heat had. There was an enormous spread—a real feast—on the table, but Beth didn't want any of it. Maybe, Beth thought briefly, Grandmother meant to welcome them with food rather than words, for most of what she'd said so far had been cool and distant.

Tom ate steadily. Hannah kept complimenting Grandmother on the delicious chicken stew. It was thick with vegetables and had big, fluffy squares of dumplings floating on top. Grandad ate his dinner upstairs in his air-conditioned room. Beth watched covertly as Aunt Iris carefully picked half a potato, one tiny piece of chicken, and five peas from the stew tureen, and then plucked a single tomato wedge from the salad bowl. She arranged the food in a circle on her plate. She adjusted each pile with her fork, making sure the different kinds of food were equidistant from each other. She nibbled with her head down, finishing quickly, then washed down the scanty portions with gulps of beer.

"It's been ages since I've had chicken potpie," said Hannah. "This is really a treat."

"I make it often, you know," said Grandmother. "You could have come back at any time."

Hannah was silent. Iris passed the heavy tureen of stewed chicken to Tom.

"Thanks, Aunt Iris."

"I like to see a young man eat," she said. "I hope you and your sister aren't picky eaters." She filled the tall glass by his plate with beer. "There you go."

"Oh, Iris—Tom's too young to drink—," began Hannah, but Tom cut her off.

"Thanks a lot!" He seized the glass and drank deeply. "Don't worry, Mom."

"Tasty, isn't it?" asked Aunt Iris.

Hannah ignored the smile her sister bestowed on Tom. "There's plenty of time to drink when you're older, Tom. One more sip and that's it."

"Oh, Mom. It's only one glass. I'm grown-up enough."

"He's right," said Aunt Iris, her voice cold. "What were you doing when you were around his age, Hanny Lynn? You thought you were plenty grown-up then, didn't you?"

Hannah set her fork down gently. "I did,

then," she said. "But maybe I've learned something since. Tom's only fifteen, Iris. I'd hate to see him or Beth grow up too soon." She removed the glass of beer from Tom's place and poured him some ice water from the pitcher into a clean glass.

"What's with the beer, Iris?" asked Grandmother. "You haven't touched alcohol in ages!"

"Hanny Lynn's here now." Aunt Iris's voice was succinct. "So I drink."

Then no one said anything else, and Beth remembered how her mother had lit that cigarette at the rest stop during their journey. She continued picking at her meal until everyone else had finished. After dinner she volunteered to do the dishes, knowing her mother would be pleased and surprised. But her true reason was she wanted to be alone so that she would not have to talk to anyone else. When Tom offered to help, she shoved him into the living room with the others.

From the kitchen, Beth could hear Grandmother pumping Tom for information about their life in California. Her questions made it clear she believed only degenerates and movie stars lived on the West Coast. Beth could hardly make out Tom's answers; he spoke in a murmur.

But Grandmother's questions were loud and sharp, almost as if they were not meant for Tom's ears, but for someone else's.

"So you were born in a commune, hmm? It couldn't have been an easy life for a child. I've read about those cults."

"No, Grandmother," he said. "It wasn't a cult—it was like a group house. There were three families and one or two couples without children, and we all lived in a big house and shared the space and the work. That is, the adults did. We kids had a great time just playing. It seemed like there were acres of space! We moved away when I was little, anyway. I don't remember all the people—"

"Too many folks coming and going, eh? Hard to keep track of?"

"Well, no—"

"But there hasn't been much in the way of family life for you, has there, way out west? With your father getting himself killed racing around in those sports cars they all drive out there, and your mother taking up with—"

"Mama!" interrupted Hannah.

"Taking up with anyone who would put up with two little kids." Grandmother's voice continued inexorably. "Such a shame, I always felt, two little kids growing up in day care, while their mother was off doing God-knows-what—"

"Off working, Mama!" Hannah's voice, sharp now, cut in. "Stop talking nonsense. I had to work, and I've worked hard. Tom and Beth were always well cared for."

Grandmother's voice was even sharper than Hannah's. "Are these children of yours on drugs, Hanny? Most kids today are—especially in California. I want you to make it clear to your children that there's to be no running around with drug dealers here. They both look like they're on something right now!"

Beth nearly dropped the cup she was drying. She set it on the counter and moved closer to the door to listen.

"Mama, please! You know nothing of my life, how hard it's been to manage on my own. You have no idea what my children have been doing, what their interests are—nothing!"

"And who is to blame for that, Hanny Lynn?"

"I am! I know it! I accept that blame. But Beth and Tom are good kids. They're just exhausted now, poor things. That's all. We've been on the road for days."

"That girl of yours," pressed Grandmother, her voice rising over Hannah's. "You make it clear to her there's to be no running around with boys here. She seems mannerly enough right now, but then you always seemed that way, too. Like mother, like daughter, I expect—"

Her voice dropped, and Beth moved back to the sink and plunged her hands into hot, soapy water. She scrubbed the stew pot with long, angry strokes.

Then Tom was beside her, grabbing up a dry tea towel. "I'm helping."

"Sure," she said, moving over. Who could blame him for not wanting to sit in the living room with them?

"You know what gets me?" he asked in a low voice.

"What?"

"The whole time Grandmother was going on about how badly we've been brought up, tears were falling down her face. And old skinnybones was sitting back in her corner in the dark—and she was *smiling*, Beth! Grandmother was crying and Aunt Iris was smiling the whole time."

Carrying Romps, Beth went up to bed early. It was true, as her mother had told Grandmother, that she was exhausted from traveling. But she wanted to be alone more than anything. The days on the road had afforded her little privacy—cooped up in the car by day and still together with her mother and Tom in a single motel room by night. It would feel luxurious just to stretch out on top of the bed, all alone, and write in her journal.

She'd kept a journal for four years now, since she was twelve, and was already on Volume Eight. She wrote down daily events, dreams she remembered when she woke up, and plans for her future with Ray, when she'd be out of high school and would stop feeling so much like a kid next to him.

She also made sketches of stained-glass windows she hoped to make someday when she got her own studio. She usually worked at the kitchen table in their apartment or after hours at Glassworks. Jane Simmons, the owner of Glassworks, offered her and Ray space to do their own work on their own time. She was impressed, she'd told them, with the artistic promise both of them showed. Ray was a professional in his own right already, Jane Simmons said. And Beth was a rising star.

She lay on the lumpy bed in the hot bedroom and thought about that now. She liked the sound of those words: "Rising Star." Maybe that would make a good name for the shop she and Ray would have. She'd call him in the morning and see what he thought. Tell him they'd arrived safely, too.

She heard her mother, Aunt Iris, and Grandmother on the stairs and then in the upstairs hall outside her door. "It's so nice to be back," Hannah said. "I'm glad you've let me come back."

"You're our daughter, Hanny Lynn," said Grandmother simply.

"Yes—but I didn't know whether I'd be welcome."

"There's a lot of water under the bridge now. Still, families need to stick together." Grandmother's voice grew fainter as she walked down the hallway to the bedroom she shared with Grandad. "Families ought to take care of each other. Good-night now."

"Good-night," Hannah said. "And good-night to you, too, Iris."

Aunt Iris started to laugh. The hair on the back of Beth's neck prickled.

"That's a good one, Hanny Lynn. That's a good one!" laughed Aunt Iris.

"I don't know what you're talking about,

Iris." Hannah's voice was tight. "I'm going to bed."

"Doing what you're good at, hmm, Hanny?" The laughter became a cackle. "Glad to be back in your own little bed—or would you really rather be all tucked up in the Lodge?"

"Shut up, Iris."

"That's what I thought."

"I am perfectly happy to be back in my old room."

Aunt Iris's shrill laughter skidded under Beth's closed door. "Ha! Oh, right, Hanny Lynn. That's rich! You'd rather be in that little single bed when you could be in the big double bed instead? All cozy and warm with the man of your choice? And we know who that would be, don't we? Don't we just!" This time her laughter seemed more like sobbing to Beth, who sat up tensely on her bed, eyes riveted on the door.

"Iris, I'm telling you—" But Hannah lowered her voice to a whisper, and Beth couldn't make out the words. Then, after she heard the clicks of two bedroom doors closing, Beth got out of bed and tiptoed to the sunporch to see what Tom thought of the exchange in the hallway.

But he was crashed out on his bed, still in his clothes, with the fan on high and aimed directly at him. His curly hair, the same color as Beth's, flipped up and down on his forehead in the current of air. He was snoring gently and, clearly, hadn't overheard a thing. Beth unplugged his fan and took it back to her room. She stood it on the radiator under the window and directed it at her own bed.

The bed had an old smell, and the mattress dipped uncomfortably in the middle, holding Beth like a hammock. She'd left the door to the sunporch open so that the night air coming through the screens could circulate freely between the two rooms. She heard creaking as Tom rolled over in his narrow bed, and she was glad she and Romps were in a big double one, bumps and all.

A double bed. What had Aunt Iris meant by saying Hannah must really want to sleep in the double bed? Which double bed? And what was the Lodge? Beth turned on her side, scratched Romps's ears, and reached for her journal on the nightstand. As she opened the diary to begin writing, she tried again to picture her mother living here as a girl. She couldn't.

As if thinking about Hannah had summoned

her, the bedroom door opened slowly and Hannah stepped in. "Are you awake, Beth?" she asked.

"Yes." Beth slipped the journal under her pillow.

"Romps has to sleep outside in back, honey." She stroked the dog. "Is Tom awake?"

"Nope."

"Yes, I am," he said groggily, standing in the doorway. "Beth stole my fan. I can't sleep without that fan."

"Well, I'm glad you're awake. I want to talk to you both."

Tom threw himself across Beth's bed, and Hannah perched on the side. "So, kids," she said. "Shall I ask what you think of this place?"

"Better not," muttered Beth. "We might tell you."

"Oh, Mom!" Tom struggled to keep his voice low. "This is going to be awful. Why didn't you tell me how weird everybody is?"

"Your grandparents aren't weird," Hannah defended them. "Grandad has been ill, and Grandmother—well, she's been sad, I think, for the past twenty years. I hurt her much more than I ever realized by leaving home."

"I don't blame you for leaving," said Beth.

"I'd run pretty fast if I had a sister like Aunt Iris. I just don't see why you wanted to come back."

Hannah leaned back on the bed. "Coming back isn't easy for me, Beth. After so long. But it was suddenly something I knew I had to do You keep saying I'm having an identity crisis, Beth, and maybe you're right. But I feel as if things fell into place for me this past year. I realized I've been on the run for a long time, and yet I haven't been really happy doing what I do. Dating men who don't mean much to me, working at a job I don't enjoy, living just about as far from my family as I could get and still be in the same country . . . At least I've had you kids! You mean so much to me, both of you. But I want things to change for me."

"I know, I know," said Beth. They had heard this before. It was all her mother had talked about the last few months. She was going to stop the casual dating she'd been doing for years and start spending her time studying. She had applied to Mills College in Oakland, only a few miles from their apartment, and was accepted to begin in the fall as a new freshwoman. She planned to major in English and get a job working for a publishing company once she'd received her degree. And she wanted to repair the broken bridge back to Philadelphia and see her family again after twenty years.

"Why did you leave in the first place?" asked Tom. "Was it because of Aunt Iris?"

Hannah twirled a lock of her soft brown hair. "I've told you before. I left home just before I turned eighteen. I wrote immediately and told them that I was all right and that I was getting a job and that I didn't want anyone coming after me, hauling me back home as a runaway. I knew that once they were sure I was safe, they'd leave me alone. They wanted me gone as much as I wanted to be gone—well, let's just leave it at that for now. There were problems, and I didn't want to stay and wait for them to work themselves out. I didn't think there was any way they *could* be worked out."

"But now you think they could have been, is that it?" asked Tom.

"Not really. But I do think I probably shouldn't have left when I did. I was angry and hasty. You both must know what it's like to do things you regret later, and then not want to change things because you're too proud."

Tom nodded, but Beth just lay back staring at the ceiling. There was an interesting crack up there. It looked like the outline of a man's head.

"Well, I wanted to get out, and the place to go seemed to be California. I took all my savings out of the bank—it wasn't much, just a few hundred bucks—and bought a train ticket. I figured I'd get myself some kind of job when I got to San Francisco. But instead, I met your dad on the train. We—well, we fell in love."

"On the train?" asked Tom.

"Oh, well, it was the sixties." Beth said dryly. "You know: love and peace? Dad was a hippie type. You've seen the pictures."

"It was the early seventies," corrected Hannah with a smile. "But you're right. We fell in love—I was so young! We were both just babies."

Beth pictured Ray's face, his thatch of straight blond hair falling over his forehead. Her mother hadn't been too young to fall in love at seventeen. Neither was she, at sixteen.

Her dad had been young, too—only nineteen—when he'd met Hannah on the train. Beth knew this because, although Hannah rarely spoke about her life before she left Philadelphia, she loved to tell stories of the adventures she'd had with their dad. He was from New York and was planning to move out to California, where, he said, the action was. Hannah was ready for action, too, she said, so they got married when their train arrived and worked at odd jobs in San Francisco until finally, a year later, they ended up in the group house with a dozen other young people. Both Beth and Tom had been born right there—not in a hospital but attended by the resident midwife—surrounded by their parents' friends in the old house with the sagging front porch.

But then, when Beth was five and Tom was four, their dad and two friends from the group house had been killed in a car accident. The three young men had been drinking their homemade brew, Beth and Tom knew, and their dad had been at the wheel when the car smashed through the guardrails and careened off a highway overpass in San Francisco late one night. He was only a dim memory to Beth now, though the pungent smell of a wood fire could conjure the feeling of strong hands holding her up to watch a bonfire in their backyard. She knew his face only from photographs.

"I married for love," Hannah said now, "but I really shouldn't have been away from my family that young. I was ready to fall in love—maybe I was desperate for it. And I was, as I said, on the run. That's never the best way to leave home. I thought about that a lot this past year—the way I left. I'd die if either of you kids left me that way. And I knew I had to get in touch with my parents again. Can you believe I never told them about you kids, never told them when your dad died—? Nothing."

"But you've never told us what you were so mad about, Mom. You'd have to have been pretty furious to stay away so long." Tom was asking an old question. Beth waited to see if this version of the answer would be any more informative.

Hannah just shrugged. "I was having a hard time. We all were. And the twenty years just seemed to fly by. When you stay away that long, going back seems impossible, and you rarely even bother to think about it. But then, as I've said, I started wanting different things for myself this past year. A new life. College. And connections again."

"As you've said and said and said," muttered Beth. The conversation seemed to be moving, as it had so often back in Berkeley these past few months, toward Hannah's lecture about the

Necessity of College. Beth had heard it often and resented every word. It was fine with her if her mother decided to go to college. Fine! Let her get her bachelor's degree and a master's degree—even a Ph.D., if that's what she wanted—but let her leave Beth out of it. Beth had her own plans, ones her mother once had approved of—even encouraged. These plans didn't include college or law school or degrees from anyplace on earth. She wanted to own a stained-glass shop with Ray and live with him. They'd have an apartment above the shop and work together and teach classes and have loads of time just to enjoy each other. Leave it to Tom to carry out their mother's new goal for her children; he could become a college-educated computer wizard. But Beth intended to keep her hands busy with glass patterns and tools, not computers and books. She was exhausted now and wanted only to write in her diary and sleep.

"What's wrong with Aunt Iris?" asked Tom, and Beth forced her eyes open again.

"Oh, well, polio," said Hannah. "And something else, now. I'm really shocked to find her so emaciated. I'll have to talk to Mama about her. Find out when this started. But she had polio as a child, one of the last cases, I think. She's ten years older than I am and had it before I was born." Hannah laughed sadly. "I was always jealous of that limp, if you can believe it! Mama absolutely fawned over Iris because of it. And I always felt left out, just because I was normal. You wouldn't know to look at her now, but Iris was gorgeous. Long red hair, a beautiful figure. Next to her I was a mouse. She was an artist, too—maybe you get your talent from her, Beth. After she finished school she stayed home and painted. She actually sold a few oil paintings and won a state competition. She was working on paintings for an exhibit in Philadelphia the summer I left. God—she had everything. It didn't seem fair."

Beth digested this information in silence, comparing Hannah's description to the Iris she'd met that afternoon. How bizarre!

Hannah stood up. "I'll let you two get to sleep now. We can talk more tomorrow. I hope—" She hesitated. "I hope you won't mind too much being here. It's only for the summer."

Tom unplugged the fan and stumbled back onto the sunporch with it. The springs creaked as he flopped down onto his bed. Beth resolved to steal it back as soon as he started snoring.

"Mom?" She caught Hannah's hand to detain her. She lowered her voice. "I heard Aunt Iris out in the hall earlier. She said something about the Lodge—about how you wished you could sleep there instead of your room. What's the Lodge—some sort of summer home?"

Hannah grew pale under her suntan. She stood motionless next to Beth's high old bed, then shrugged slowly. "The Lodge? Why, that's just this room, sweetie. That's all."

"This room?" Beth stared at her. "What do you mean, 'that's all'? What's the big mystery, then? I'll change with you if you want to sleep in here."

"No!" The word was almost a gasp. "No, that's okay. My room is just fine. Just where I want to be. Iris was kidding."

Oh yeah? Beth remembered her aunt's sharp, hysterical laughter. She burrowed down under the sheet, fingering her diary under the pillow. "But why was this room called the Lodge?"

"Oh, just because Mama and Dad used to rent it out to lodgers—you know, boarders," said Hannah, her voice now rather vague and tired. "Just for extra income. No big deal at all."

She left then without another word, taking

Romps with her. But as Beth lay in the valley of the mattress, the sheet tangled around her sweaty legs, she felt sure her mother was lying, that the Lodge had been a great big deal after all.

2

Beth awoke to the chatter of birds outside her open window. She lay listening for a moment, then turned her attention to other sounds. Tom was snoring. Downstairs the screen door to the porch banged. After another minute she heard a car start up. Tom's snoring broke off abruptly.

She waited until he came creeping through her room. "I didn't want to go down alone," she greeted him. "Hang on a minute till I get dressed."

He went sleepily down the hall to the bathroom, and she jumped out of bed and into her shorts and oversized T-shirt. When she looked out into the hall, she saw that her mother's and Aunt Iris's bedroom doors were shut. The door to Grandmother and Grandad's room at the end of the hallway stood open. Tom came out of the bathroom and followed her down the narrow flight of stairs.

The living room was empty. No one was in the kitchen, either, but Beth found a note on the counter.

Hanny Lynn,

I've taken Dad to his physical therapy appt. There's plenty of food. You and the children just make yourselves at home.

Mama

"No wonder Grandmother's fat," said Tom from the doorway to the dining room. "Look at this spread!"

Beth pushed in behind him and stared at the round table. She could make a wonderful stained-glass window based on the feast before her. It would be round like the table itself, with panels to represent all the different dishes of food. Ray liked it when artists came up with new ways of using glass, not just making the same designs of flowers and birds. There were boxes of cereal and a white-glazed jug of milk on the table, a platter of bacon, another of fried potatoes, a plastic pitcher of orange juice, and a huge urn of coffee. Beth lifted the lid of a warming pan and found half a dozen fried eggs and something that looked like square sausage patties.

"That's called scrapple," Tom told her. "I saw a whole brick of the stuff in the fridge."

"I think I'll pass," said Beth, eyeing it doubtfully.

They piled their plates. Although Beth hadn't been able to eat last night with the family around the table, she found herself starving now. She gobbled an egg and drank some juice, calculating in her head the time difference between here and Berkeley. She would call Ray at eleven o'clock—just before he left for the glass shop. After watching Tom devour square after square of the scrapple, she tried some for herself. It was delicious, she found with surprise. Fatty and sausagey—not the kind of food they ate much at home. Her mother was into health food and had all sorts of herbs and beans sprouting in pots in the kitchen. They hardly ever ate meat.

Beth had two pieces of scrapple and another egg on toast, and while she ate she told Tom about what she'd heard Aunt Iris say about the

Lodge the night before, and what their mother had said about how they'd taken in lodgers when she was a girl.

"Totally weird," he muttered, munching toast.

Usually Beth didn't confide much in Tom, but she had the feeling that she might need an ally while living in this house. She was also getting the feeling that something creepy had happened here once. And it seemed to her that with Hannah back home now, something might happen again.

"What do you think went on here, Tom? Why is Aunt Iris so mad at Mom?"

He pushed his plate away. "Do I know? I'm just praying the time flies by so we can get out of here."

But he sat at the table with her a while longer, mulling over what the Lodge might have to do with Aunt Iris's hostile behavior. When they heard footsteps in the hall upstairs, they both stopped talking at once and listened.

"Mom's getting up," whispered Tom.

But then they heard the uneven shuffle and knew it was Aunt Iris. Without speaking, they jumped up from their chairs, carried their plates to the kitchen sink, and slipped out the back door into the driveway.

"We'll take Romps for a walk," said Beth, and she went to untie the dog from the elm tree in the backyard, where Hannah had staked him last night.

"Yeah," agreed Tom as they set off. "A nice long walk. And I mean long."

They started around the block, past the corner where the ice-cream van had been the evening before, down to Penn's Pike. There were a few children on tricycles on one of the side streets, but otherwise the neighborhood was quiet. When they passed the Waverley Theater, Beth looked for a house that might be Monica's, but there were only shops. Beth made a mental note to phone Monica later that day to set up a time when they could go see a movie. It seemed a good strategy to stay out of the house as much as she could.

When they returned from their walk, they could hear voices upstairs raised in argument. Their mother's sounded angry: "I don't know what you mean, Iris!"

"Mom's up," said Tom.

"Tell me about it." Beth climbed the stairs. Her

grandparents' bedroom door was closed now, and the angry voices rang from inside. She stood in the hallway for a moment, fighting the impulse to creep down the hall and listen outside the door. Ray had laughed at her once and said it was a sign of her youth that she liked to snoop. Still, it was hard to resist such an impulse when her own mother was yelling only a few feet away. "I absolutely refuse to live under a cloud anymore!" Beth heard Hannah cry and knew her mother wasn't talking about the weather.

But she clenched her teeth and went back downstairs, wandering aimlessly through the rooms of what was to be her home for the summer. The whole house was as tidy as her best friend's room back in Berkeley. Beth hadn't thought anyone in the world could rival Violet for being the neatest neatnik, but possibly Vi had met her match in Grandmother. Everything was scrubbed and polished. Not a speck of dust anywhere. The pillows on the couch were plumped up and smooth, as if no one ever sat down. All signs of the breakfast feast in the dining room were gone already, and the round table gleamed with polish. Beth's house tour took her through all the rooms—living room, dining room, kitchen, and pantry—and even down to the basement.

It was cooler down there and as orderly as the rest of the house, with shelves along the walls stacked full of canned food. At first Beth thought they must be earthquake provisions, but then she remembered that there weren't any quakes here. She figured that Grandmother must have been born during the Depression years and had pack-rat tendencies, always wanting to stock up in case hard times came again.

In a corner of the basement Beth saw a stack of white canvases and shoe boxes. This time she forgot about Ray's criticism and, after wiping cobwebs off the top box, lifted it. Inside she found dozens of tubes of oil paint. She opened the second box and found watercolors, thin paintbrushes held in bunches with rubber bands, and palette knives. She replaced the box tops thoughtfully, then turned to rummage through the stack of canvases. But voices in the kitchen upstairs stopped her before she'd brought them out into the light, and she turned guiltily away.

• • •

The first week passed quietly, though the tension between Aunt Iris and Hannah seemed to deepen. Beth called the number Monica had given her several times, but a man's voice on an answering machine said no one was home. She left her grandparents' phone number and a message reminding Monica they'd planned to see a movie sometime. Then she waited.

She waited, too, for a letter from Ray. She had sent him a postcard each day of their journey across the country and a long letter the day after they'd arrived in Philadelphia. She'd given him the address of the house on Spring Street even before she left Berkeley and hoped there would be at least one letter waiting for her. As yet she had received nothing. And she had phoned him every day—twice some days—but heard only a cheerful message on his answering machine saying he would be home later. Sometimes she called just to hear his voice.

At least there was Grandad. When she wasn't taking Romps on long rambles around the neighborhood, Beth slipped upstairs to visit him. Grandad lay in his bed most of the day with the door closed and the air conditioner on high. His room was the most comfortable in the house, and she'd settle in the chair near his bed with relief at escaping the heat of the other rooms. Before she sat down, though, she always checked to make sure Aunt Iris wasn't lurking in one of the corners.

Grandad asked Beth to tell him all about her life up to this point. "It's a shame we've missed knowing each other all these years," he said, and although she waited for stronger criticism against her mother, none came. So Beth told him what she could remember of their years at the group house and spun long tales of her adventures at school and with her best friend, Vi, who was one of triplets—three sisters, all with flower names. Jasmine and Rose were an identical pair, but Violet looked different. Beth told Grandad how she and her friend had been inseparable, almost like sisters themselves, until she'd met Ray last year.

Then she launched into the wonderful story about Ray—the expurgated version.

"This Ray," Grandad asked, "he works after school?"

"No, Ray's out of school. He's the full-time assistant to Jane, who is the owner. Ray's a fantastic artist who teaches the glass classes on weekends." She explained about her art classes at school and how her teacher, Mr. Hunter, had said she showed—in his words—"great promise" when her class spent a few weeks learning to cut and shape glass for small stained-glass windows. He had suggested she take stained-glass classes at Glassworks, and that's where she'd met Ray. The first class was on Saturday afternoons, but she soon moved on to the more advanced workshops two evenings a week. Then she started working at the shop after school as well.

She told Grandad how she felt about Ray and about her plans for their own glass shop. Grandad said it sounded like a fine idea to go into business, but he hoped she wouldn't stay in a relationship with an older man. "That sort of thing never works," he said.

"Look at Princess Diana and Prince Charles! He's twelve years older than she is." She never believed the supermarket tabloids' accounts of trouble in that fairy-tale marriage. "Ray's only *ten* years older than I am!"

Grandad just shook his bald head.

What Beth didn't tell Grandad was the important stuff. The stuff about how Ray made her feel. How he looked in his light blue work shirt with the sleeves rolled up, the hairs on his strong arms glinting in the yellow lights over the worktable. The turn of his fine wrists as he held a glass cutter, the strength in his long fingers as he carved clean shapes from the colored panes. How he bent his head in concentration over his work, straight yellow hair falling over his forehead; how his eyes lit up when he saw her watching and his face broke out in that huge grin, white-toothed and happy. How he called her "Babe" in a voice that could make her tremble. She had dated a few guys at school before, but nothing about them had reached into her heart the way Ray did. Nothing about them made her want to throw herself into their arms and never let go. Nothing about them had her planning for a joint future. Only Ray had that power.

On other days, Grandad would tell stories from his childhood. Even Tom, bereft of his computer, often sat with Beth next to Grandad's bed and listened. He told Beth once that Grandad's stories were the only things keeping him from going crazy in this old house with all these old people. Beth agreed it was the same for her.

Grandad's stories were mostly about his boyhood during the Depression. His father had died when he was only nine, and his family had been so poor that he and his two brothers had to stand by the train tracks in hopes of picking up the pieces of coal that dropped from the coal cars as the trains chugged by. They'd use the coal in their stove to heat the little house where they lived. Tom took notes in a thick spiral notebook while Grandad spoke. He told Beth that once he got back to a computer, he'd write everything out. He already had a title for the book: *Out of the Coal.*

When Beth and Tom asked for stories about when their mother was a little girl, Grandad would grin and scratch his bald head. "That's an easy order," he'd say. "Hanny Lynn was the star of a lot of stories around here." Stories about how four-year-old Hannah stole a chocolate bar from the candy store and hid it in her little toy stove up in her room. And how she'd been spanked and made to return it when Grandmother found it the next day. How Hannah and Aunt Iris had once, during a three-day raging snowstorm, pretended that the little sunporch, where Tom slept now, was a boat. The two girls slept out there, ate meals out there, and basically, said Grandad, got along much better than they normally did.

"You mean they normally fought all the time?" asked Tom.

"Well, they didn't have much in common. Mostly stayed out of each other's way. You know, with Iris ten years older, they just didn't have many of the same interests." And then he grew quiet.

Grandad's reminiscences covered only so many years and no more. Beth couldn't get a single story out of him about Hannah when she was a teenager or when she left home. When Beth pressed him, he frowned. "Those were the dark years," he said once, his face grim. "Nobody wants to be reminded now." And Beth and Tom didn't dare press any harder. At least not then.

If they weren't up with Grandad, Beth and Tom spent a lot of time that first week sitting out on the glider swing on the front porch. Tom finished his computer manuals and read *The Lord of the Rings.* Beth read the last of the mysteries she'd brought from California and then sketched some ideas for future stained-glass projects. She designed a window for her shop with Ray—a big rose-colored heart floating in a night sky dotted with stars (she'd use clear prisms for the stars) and the name of the shop etched inside the heart: Rising Star. She would have to ask her mother if anyone would mind her working on it here this summer. It would fill in all the boring hours. The cool basement would make a good workplace. She'd have privacy down there. She went up to her room for her diary and wrote down a list of the colors of glass she would need for the project.

She stepped out of her room into the hall, planning to go downstairs to look up the names and addresses of Philadelphia glass shops in the phone book. But when she saw that the door to Aunt Iris's bedroom was open, she stopped. Usually the door was closed. Beth looked inside, catching her breath when she saw Aunt Iris in a chair facing the window. Like the rest of the house, the room was spotless, with gleaming oak furniture. Out the window Beth could see Romps's elm tree with the rope swing still hanging from one branch as testimony that little girls once played there. The chair where Aunt Iris sat looked rigid and uncomfortable. There was a narrow single bed made up with a white bedspread, the corners and sides tightly tucked under the mattress. Beth thought it looked like a hospital bed. There was a large dresser next to the window, with a frame rising from the back, where once a large mirror had hung. But now the frame was empty, holding nothing but blank wall.

There were no books in the room and no television. No signs of anything personal lying around. What could Aunt Iris do in there all day? Beth edged toward the stairs, halting in midstep as Aunt Iris rose from her chair and limped to her dresser. She stood in front of it, her arms braced on its surface, leaning toward the wall. Toward the space where the mirror should have been hanging. Beth turned to hurry downstairs, but Aunt Iris's brittle voice stopped her.

"Elisabeth."

Beth whirled around, but Aunt Iris was still standing facing the wall. How could she see her when there was no mirror?

"I was—um—just going down to look up something in the phone book," she said. "And then I'll see if Grandmother needs help getting dinner." She shifted from one foot to the other.

"Very charitable of you. But my mother needs no help concocting her mountains of food."

Beth waited a moment, but Aunt Iris didn't turn around or say anything else and, grateful, Beth hurried down the stairs.

She went straight to the little mahogany phone stand in the corner of the dining room and checked the phone book quickly, jotting down an address. Then she slipped out the front door onto the porch. Fresh air—she needed fresh air. And she needed Ray!

Hannah was on the porch, alone in the glider, kicking sporadically with her toe to keep moving. "Hello, sweetie," she said when she saw Beth.

"Well, if it isn't the prodigal daughter." Beth's voice sounded weak.

Hannah patted the glider seat. "Come listen to these course descriptions! Mills has a lot to offer."

"I need to write a letter to Ray."

"Just for a minute, honey. It's fascinating!"

So Beth sat next to her mother and listened indifferently as Hannah read from the catalog about English courses and economics courses and botanical excursions into the Sierras. "They have a wonderful art department, Beth," Hannah added. "Maybe you could apply to Mills next year and we'll be students together!"

"Lay off, Mom." Beth kicked the porch floor to set the glider in motion again. "Listen, there's a glass store on Wannamaker Road. Can I borrow the car and go there? I want to buy some glass."

"Poor Beth. Are you going crazy? We'll ask Grandmother if you can set up a little studio somewhere. Then we can get the glass tomorrow. It's a good thing you brought your tools."

She wouldn't be caught dead traveling without her tools. "I don't see how you lived here, Mom. Or wasn't it so deathly dull here when you were young?" She saw her mother's frown and amended: "Younger, I meant."

But Hannah's frown deepened. "Deathly dull!" She snorted. "Oh, that's rich."

"What's rich?"

"It was so exciting around here, Beth, that I ended up having to leave."

"What do you mean?"

Hannah shook her head and began turning the pages of her catalog again.

"Come on, Mom! Can't we forget some of this closed-mouth secrecy stuff? If I have to live in this house for the whole summer, at least I should know what went on here."

"You need a course in logic," said Hannah. "And I thought you liked mysteries."

"Only in books, Mom!"

Hannah sighed. "I know it must be frustrating

for you and Tom. It's just—it's just that I don't know what to tell you."

"How about the truth?" Beth asked. "For starters. Is that so hard?"

"Well, what if I don't know the truth? For starters."

Beth bit the inside of her mouth in frustration. "Look, I asked if it was so deathly growing up here. And you said—"

"I know, I know." Hannah hit the porch floor with her toe and sent the glider shaking back and forth. "I said that was rich—because, well, because it's ironic. Deathly! It's because our lodger died that I ran away."

Beth twisted a strand of long red hair in her fingers. Despite the heat and humidity of the afternoon, she felt a sudden shiver pounce between her shoulder blades. But she kept her voice light and casual. "Come on, Mom. I want the whole story."

Hannah turned to Beth. "The whole story? I don't know the whole story, Beth. I know only my own version—and you'll hear something different from everyone else. That is, if you can get them to talk about it. Oh, it's bound to come out sooner or later. And I guess I would rather you heard my side first."

"Your side?"

Hannah sat back on the glider. She pushed mightily with her toe again and the swing rocked wildly. "It's a long, awful story."

"I can take it."

Hannah lowered her voice, and Beth had to lean against her to hear at all. "Iris had a boyfriend once, Beth. He was our lodger. A wonderful, handsome, loving, *perfect* man named Clifton. There! I never thought I'd be able to say that name again without crying."

"You mean because he died?"

"Oh, Beth! Because I loved him, too. And he loved me—he was only marrying Iris because he had said he would—before he fell in love with me. He pitied her, you know, because she limps."

"Why didn't you two just run off together?"

"I told you! Because he felt sorry for Iris. Everybody always felt sorry for poor Iris! But"—and here Hannah bent close to Beth's ear, her breath hot—"then Iris found out. She found out he really loved *me.*"

"Then why did you run away, Mom?" Beth felt a shiver along her backbone again. "I mean, it was too bad for her, but, so what?"

Hannah's voice was the merest breath of

whisper against Beth's cheek. "So? So I thought Iris killed him, Beth."

"You *thought?*" Beth gasped, and the sound was a shot in the stillness of the porch.

Hannah sank back against the glider cushions, limp. "But she blamed it on me." Her voice was still a whisper. "I couldn't stand it—believing all the time she'd murdered him herself. I had to get away from here."

"Mom—" Now Beth could barely find her own voice. She stared at her mother. Hannah's face was pale, and the hands she had folded loosely in her lap were trembling. "What about your parents? Didn't they stand up for you?"

"Mama's always taken Iris's side," murmured Hannah.

"But we're talking about *murder!* I mean—" She broke off abruptly. "Unless—oh, Mom! You don't mean that Grandmother believed what Iris said? That *you* killed that guy—Clifford?"

"Clifton." Hannah looked up from her hands, and Beth was shocked by the pain in her face. "Yes, Mama believes I killed Clifton. Daddy took my side then—but I don't know anymore."

Beth's imagination leaped into action: There would have been guns going off—where?

Maybe out in the backyard at midnight. And Hannah had gone out in her nightgown to see what the noise was. And then she found Clifford, no, Clifton, dead! Shot through the heart—and no one there but her and the body. And then Iris came running out, and she told everyone that *Hannah* must have shot him. . . .

"Well, I hope you told them you had nothing to do with any murder!"

"Of course I did," said Hannah. "I did nothing but defend myself for weeks, but I knew I couldn't keep on living in the same house with people who thought I was guilty. They had no proof of anything—the police were never involved—but my life was miserable. I don't know if you can imagine, Beth. I *loved* him. I had to get out. I knew when I left that they'd see my escape as confirmation I had killed him, but at the time I didn't care. I left a letter telling them I was innocent and that I thought they were all perfectly horrible for driving me away."

"I should hope so! I'm surprised you ever came back at all!"

"Oh, well," murmured Hannah. "Things change."

"Things don't change *that* much!" said Beth staunchly.

"They do, sweetie. I've had twenty years to do a lot of thinking. And now I'm not too sure about anything anymore. That whole time is so fuzzy in my head—I guess I'm able to come back now precisely *because* I'm not sure about anything anymore."

"What do you mean, Mom?" Beth's voice rose wildly. "What are you talking about?"

Hannah sighed wearily and stopped the glider. "I mean that I've started wondering whether Iris was right. That's all."

"That's *all?*" screeched Beth, but Hannah walked slowly back into the house, and the screen door closed behind her.

Beth jumped off the glider and raced after her mother, grabbing her elbow just as Hannah started up the stairs. "Tell me what you mean, Mom!"

"Sshh!" Hannah tore her arm out of Beth's tight grasp. She looked apprehensively over the banister down into the empty living room. The sounds of running water and voices from Grandmother's soap opera filtered up the stairs from the kitchen. "Wait until Tom comes home from his walk," she whispered more gently. "We can talk later."

Beth's whisper was harsh. "You didn't kill

anybody! How can you even think such a thing?"

"Later, sweetie." And she continued up the stairs, leaving Beth on the bottom step.

Beth sat on the low swing under the elm tree and clutched the blue pen tightly. She tried to keep the swing steady by bracing her feet on the grass. She balanced her notebook carefully on her lap, a fresh sheet of scented notepaper on top.

Dear Ray,

Oh, why haven't you written? I am going totally crazy here without you! This household is driving me up the wall. Grandad is up in bed most of the time, and Grandmother is in the kitchen cooking mounds of food while she watches soaps on a little portable TV—it's one of the rare modern things in the house. Everyone eats here the whole day long—I'm sure I'd be gaining tons if I ate all the starchy, meaty things she serves. Funny thing is, I hardly ever feel hungry anymore.

Maybe I'll end up a skeleton like my Aunt Iris. She looks almost as thin as this girl I knew in school who was hospitalized last year with anorexia. But that sad girl never gave me the creeps the way Aunt Iris does. It's not just the skin and bones or the aunt-from-hell raspy voice—it's more a kind of horror. Like, why did she let herself GET this way? And is it catching?

My mom sits around all day planning her brilliant college career. And Tom just mopes and goes on long walks with Romps. Everyone around me seems like a stranger. And I've got this sick feeling in my gut because I need to see you, and you're not here! Talk about melodrama!

But it isn't just melodrama—it's real. And let me tell you, it doesn't help that the man I love hasn't called or written and is three thousand miles away! Oh, Ray, I long to hear from you. Please write NOW!

Love,
Beth

After dinner, Hannah led Beth and Tom upstairs and motioned them into Beth's room. "We can talk here," she said, closing the door.

Beth and Tom flopped down on the bed, and Hannah sat next to them. For a long moment no one spoke. Then Tom cleared his throat. "Beth's been telling me some really bizarre things, Mom."

"I'm going to tell you two a story, okay?"

"I get nightmares if I hear scary bedtime stories, Mom," said Tom in a fake baby voice.

Hannah pleated the sheet between her fingers and began softly. "It's the story about Clifton Becker. He was twenty-seven when he came here. A few years out of college and gorgeous. Curly blond hair, a body like a Greek statue—"

"But with arms, I hope," said Tom, then fell silent when no one laughed and Beth glared at him.

Hannah's voice was dreamy. "He came to live here in this room. We rented it out for extra money. The other lodgers had been single women—one was a nurse at the hospital, the other was a secretary someplace, I don't remember. They seemed old and boring. But then Clifton came—and everything changed around here." Hannah's eyes swept the room, seeming not to see it as it was now, with Beth's books piled on the dresser, her clothes draped over the chair and the sewing machine, but as it once had been.

"Yes, this was Clifton's room. He had studied biology in college but wanted to be a writer. He worked at the zoo doing all sorts of odd jobs as assistant to the zookeeper—and then spent the evenings and weekends working on his novel. I'd always ask him to let me read parts of it, but he kept telling me to wait until he could give me an autographed copy. So I'd sneak in here sometimes when he was at work and read it! I've always wondered what happened to that novel. It was really good—science fiction. After he died, no one wanted to go through his things. We left everything until his parents came to collect it. He had a big typewriter out on the sunporch—a funny old-fashioned one that he used at night. I could hear it across the hall in my room, and it would keep me awake. He asked me once if it bothered me, but I told him no. I liked to hear it, you see. Liked knowing he was so close."

There was a long pause. Clifton was suddenly real to Beth, as was the girl who had been Hannah, listening late at night from her room down the hall. The room seemed full of Clifton's presence. When Hannah did not resume her tale but sat picking at a piece of lint on her shorts, Beth prompted her.

"So you got to like Clifton, Mom?"

"Like him?" Hannah's head rose; her voice was startled. "Oh, Beth! I loved him more than

I've ever loved any man. More than I loved your father, even."

"Sounds like a major crush, Mom!"

"Beth! It wasn't a crush! No one could ever compare! Clifton was a—a god."

"Then what's all this about how maybe you killed him?" asked Beth in a low voice.

"You couldn't have!" said Tom. "You thought all those years it was Aunt Iris—and you must have been right. You wouldn't think she killed him, if you didn't think there was a good reason to believe it!"

Hannah held her hand up sharply. "Sshh! I don't want anyone to hear us talking like this. I did not say I killed Clifton. I said Iris has always said I did, and I've come to wonder whether I might have after all. It was hard to tell what really happened."

"Come on! You'd *have* to know if you had killed someone, Mom!"

"No, Tom. Not the way it happened."

Beth stared at her mother, and the memory of a dream she'd had as a child popped into her head—a dream about driving on a country road with her mother at the wheel, and suddenly knowing she was going to steer the car right off the road and over a cliff. Beth had grabbed the wheel and tried to jerk it out of her mother's hands, but Hannah was stronger than Beth and held on tight. Beth cried out, "Mom! You'll kill us!" But when Hannah looked at Beth she was laughing wildly, and the crazy look in her eyes told Beth that killing them was exactly what her mother had planned all along.

She pushed the dream away and tried to listen to what Hannah was saying now.

"I know this is coming out all garbled, but if you two would just sit quietly and let me talk, I could explain what happened—what I think happened. And then the subject is closed. Absolutely and forever. It's nothing to do with you two. Okay?"

They nodded. Hannah twined her fingers together. "Well, then. I fell in love with Clifton. I was only seventeen, and he was engaged to Iris. But it wasn't long before I learned he loved me as much as I loved him! And then two things happened: Iris found out he loved me instead of her, and Clifton vowed he would marry Iris as he had promised in the first place."

Hannah drew a deep breath and continued, her glance moving around the room, never once resting on Beth or Tom. "I've never been more upset in my life. Maybe you can imagine. . . . Anyway, it was a summer night—in August, a hot, humid night just like this one—and there was a horrid scene. My parents were furious at me and Clifton for, as Mama put it, 'carrying on behind Iris's back.' Iris was insane with jealousy. She said he had betrayed her. But he was so gallant—he insisted he would stick by his promise. Iris screamed she was going to kill me. Then she screamed she was going to kill *him.*"

Hannah paused, and her eyes came to rest, at last, on Beth and Tom. "Clifton was angry, then, too. My parents sent him away that night—told him he couldn't stay. He got his things packed and was standing right out in the hall. As I said, it was late at night. I felt I'd die if he left. I ran out into the hall after him, actually followed him down the stairs onto the landing. And then there was Iris, like a madwoman, rushing down at us, screaming. And Mama and Daddy were there, too. God, they were angry. Daddy was yelling for Iris to be sensible, to calm down, and Mama was screaming at me to get back to my bedroom and that I'd been the cause of all the trouble in the first place." Hannah's shoulders sagged.

"Oh, Beth, Tom—I can still see us all so

clearly in my mind at that moment. Five people crowding onto that tiny landing. There I was—grabbing at Clifton to hold him back—and there was Iris—trying to shove him along even faster than he was already going, shouting how she was going to kill us both if we ever looked at each other again. And there was Mama—reaching out to pull me back upstairs—and there was Daddy—trying to get Iris to let go of Clifton. All those hands reaching out . . ."

Tears were falling fast now, dropping from Hannah's wide eyes onto her knees. Beth and Tom sat silent, tense. Suddenly Hannah stood up and flung open the door into the hall. She left the room and, wordlessly, they followed. She slowly descended the short flight of stairs to the landing. She rested her hand on the fragile knickknack stand as if to steady herself and pointed down the long flight of stairs. "There," she whispered, her voice trembling. "He fell down there and cracked his head on the radiator. He died instantly."

Beth stared down the stairs, imagining the accident, then flicked a glance down over the banister into the living room to see if anyone was listening. The room was empty. She lifted her heavy hair off her neck.

"I'm sorry, Mom. That is *so* awful."

Hannah sank down to sit on the top step. Her voice was so low they had to crouch to hear. "I had to leave, you see. Everything was so confused. When I tried to remember exactly what happened, it seemed to me that Mama had already pulled me back—that Iris's hands were on him when he fell. I've always felt it would be like her to have pushed him and then blame me for it. But now—I just don't know. We were all there. All our hands were close to him—too close."

She stood up and dusted off her shorts, even attempted a smile. "But there's no proof of anything. That's it. That's the story."

Beth escaped to the basement in the morning and spent most of the day down there. It was dim and cool and private. She had permission from Grandmother to set up a space for her glasswork in the corner near Grandad's workbench. The bench was as neat and tidy as everything else in the house, with screws and bolts and nails all labeled in neatly arranged glass jars. The surface of the workbench was so smooth and polished that Beth knew Grandad hadn't worked at it for a long time.

She had brought her equipment from home and unpacked it now: butcher paper for tracing patterns, glass cutter for shaping the glass, grinder and protective goggles, coils of lead and zinc, soldering iron, copper foil, etching solution and tools. After arranging her work space, she moved to the corner where she had found the stack of canvases. The first one she pulled out was a portrait of Grandmother as a much younger woman. She was thinner, with soft brown chin-length hair and only a touch of gray. Her eyes were gentle. There was no signature, but Beth thought she knew who must have painted this. The second canvas was a still life—and Beth had to smile. It was the morning feast from the dining-room table, almost exactly as Beth had seen it that first morning and envisioned as a stained-glass window. There was the plate of fried potatoes, the platter of scrapple and eggs, the pitcher of orange juice, the jug of milk—all painted with an attention to detail that seemed lighthearted, as if the artist were amused, too, by the overabundance. The other paintings were varied: some were portraits, some were still-life compositions of fruits in baskets or flowers from the garden. Beth stared a long time at one of her mother. Hannah's brown hair was long and straight, parted in the middle. She wore a leather thong around her forehead and tied in a knot at the side. Her eyes were mischievous, the eyelids bright with blue eye shadow, her smile smirky. Beth could almost hear her begging the artist to hurry up and get on with it. There was a full-body portrait of a much younger Grandad wearing a work shirt and shorts, crouching over a cookstove. The blur of green around him suggested a forest.

Beth flipped through all the canvases, stopping now and then to peer at one more closely in the dim light. The last one made her gasp with delight, and she pulled it out and carried it over to the high window. It was a painting in oils, in bright and glorious colors that still looked wet even after so many years. Beth had to smile as she looked at it—there was such a happy feel to it—not so much in the subject matter of the picture, which was a group of islands in a stormy sea, all minutely detailed—but in the atmosphere. The painting told a story of delight in every brush stroke.

As she studied the painting, Beth imagined how fantastic it would look in glass. She knew she would never be able to work in all the details of the islands, but perhaps if she etched some of them she might at least convey the mood of joy and mystery. There were castles and princesses and all kinds of astonishing animals right out of a legend—lions with two heads, bears with the faces of dragons. Up in the sky were stars and planets and little rockets. Colorful flags flew from the turrets of the castles, and on the largest flag was a single, mysterious word: "Notfilc."

Beth knew who the artist had to be, though all the canvases she'd seen were unsigned. She checked this painting for the signature anyway, and this time found it down in the far left corner—a little blue flower floating on the crest of a wave in the stormy sea. An iris.

Who ever would have believed that Aunt Iris could paint such a joyful picture? Beth realized suddenly that *this*, not the sign for her shop with Ray, was the project she needed for the summer. She wanted, no, she *needed,* to see this painting rendered in stained glass. She wondered if she should ask Aunt Iris's permission before beginning her work to make the window, but something told her Aunt Iris would say no, and Beth knew she couldn't bear that. Beth had a feeling about this project that she wouldn't, if someone had asked her, have been able to express in words at all, but it felt to her as if suddenly, in all the gloom of this house, a little light had been switched on.

Beth was going up to bed that night with her arms full of clean, folded laundry. When she reached the little landing, she couldn't help but stop and turn to stare down at the iron radiator on which Clifton Becker had cracked his head and died. She often found herself stopping there since hearing Hannah's story, as if compelled by some outside force to imagine the grisly scene. She held her awkward bundle of laundry tightly now as she imagined him falling backward—imagined him fighting to catch his balance after someone's hands—surely Aunt Iris's hands—shoved so angrily. Had he known she meant to kill him? Beth clutched the pile of laundry. Surely it *had* been Aunt Iris.

The pile of clothes sagged to the left, and Beth turned swiftly to prevent it from toppling. A pair of tightly rolled socks tumbled down the stairs, coming to rest under the radiator. She groaned.

"Never mind, Elisabeth. I'll bring them up for you." Aunt Iris stood at the bottom of the stairs, peering up at Beth. She carried a tall glass of beer in one hand, and she held it carefully aloft as she crouched to retrieve Beth's socks.

"Oh, thanks, Aunt Iris."

Aunt Iris struggled to her feet with the socks in her hand. She set her beer on the windowsill for a moment while she unrolled them and peered at them closely—white running socks with a band of pink around the ankle. "Sweet," she said, picking up the beer again. "Very little-girly."

Beth turned and headed up the short flight from the landing to the upstairs hall. She kicked open her bedroom door and allowed the tall pile of laundry to fall onto the bed. Then she went back out into the hall to collect her socks from Aunt Iris. Aunt Iris was still making her way up the stairs. She gripped the banister with one white-knuckled hand, the other hand holding the glass of beer. Beth's socks she carried draped carefully over her shoulder.

"Here, let me take them," said Beth, reaching for the socks as her aunt stepped into the hallway.

Aunt Iris staggered past her. "Little-girly socks! I used to have some with lace around the ankles, I remember. I was about seven years old then and cute as a button. Everyone would tell you. I had long red curls like yours, only much nicer because I didn't let them hang in my face like that. I wore ribbons."

Beth glanced down the dark hall and bit her lip. Everyone else had gone to bed. Her aunt's voice was rising—the effect of the beer?—and Beth hoped she'd wake someone up. Despite Beth's discovery of the joyful canvases, she didn't like being alone with Aunt Iris. Far from the person who had filled a canvas with a magical world, Aunt Iris seemed now a person who filled the whole house with an invisible fungus. Carefully, Beth moved away from the stairs. No sense in letting history repeat itself.

"Thanks for getting the socks," she murmured, reaching out to take them off her aunt's bony shoulder.

But Aunt Iris flinched away. "Wait a minute. Come with me," she said hoarsely and lurched toward her bedroom. Beth followed reluctantly.

Aunt Iris set her glass carefully on the dresser, then lowered her body onto the bed.

"So, you think I'm ugly, do you?" She grabbed the socks off her shoulder and waved them in front of Beth "Ugly because I can't wear little-girly things like this without drawing attention to my big, crippled feet? Well, let me show you something, pretty Elisabeth."

"I don't think you're ugly!" cried Beth, alarmed. "I never said anything! I just want my socks."

"Your socks!" And she eased herself off the bed and crossed to her neat dresser, yanking open the top drawer. She withdrew a pair of thick beige stockings and dangled them at Beth. "See these? Support hose, that's what they are. Ugliest things on the face of the earth. But they help the circulation. And they don't clash with my shoes."

Beth couldn't help glancing down at her aunt's feet, heavily encased in sturdy black shoes that laced to the ankles. The left one had a thick platform attached to it.

Aunt Iris dropped the support stockings back into the drawer and rummaged in another drawer. She withdrew a thin folder. "I want you to see this, Elisabeth. You think you're so pretty! I just want you to see this."

"But I don't, Aunt Iris! I don't think I'm pretty at all! I hate that my hair is so red and bushy, and I always get zits, and I'm flat-chested—"

"But you have perfect feet," interrupted Aunt

Iris. "Like your mother. And you probably think you're entitled to have whatever makes you happy, just like your mother does. Do you take whatever you want, too? Even if it doesn't belong to you?"

Beth backed toward the door, goose bumps rising on her arms despite the heat and humidity of the summer night. "I don't know what you're talking about, Aunt Iris. You can keep the socks if you want them so much."

"I want you to see this. See who this crippled old skeleton once was!" She flipped the folder open in front of Beth's nose. And Beth felt her eyes widen.

A lovely red-haired young woman in her late twenties with long curls pulled back from the temples to cascade over her shoulders stared out from a studio photograph. Two realizations struck Beth at the same time: This was a picture of Aunt Iris, and this was also very much how she, Beth, would look in another ten years or so. And with those realizations came an immediate sense of horror—horror that the pretty woman in the picture had become the dreadful woman in front of her now—and delight—delight that she herself might indeed grow out of the pimples and even the flat chest

"It's a beautiful photo," she said at last, very softly. "I like the way you wore your hair."

Aunt Iris snapped the folder shut. "I just wanted to show you what she ruined, that mother of yours."

"What do you mean?" Beth's back was against the door now, but she felt compelled to hear what came next. It would be so easy just to open the door and run—she could outrun Aunt Iris, no sweat.

"I mean this." Aunt Iris's beery breath hit Beth's face. "That was my engagement photograph. I had just about everything a girl could want. I had good looks, good health, and a wonderful man in love with me." She paused and drew a long, choked breath. "But there was more. I had more. I had a twisted foot and a shriveled leg—and he loved me anyway." Her voice grew darkly bitter.

"And I also had a little sister. No big deal, no beauty. Only seventeen and skinny, with mousy hair and a nothing body. But she had feet—and legs that worked properly. And you know what she did with those legs, don't you, Elisabeth?"

Beth just stared at her.

"She walked in and took him! She took my

Clifton! She forced herself on him, and made him betray me—betray our love. Oh, my God, I remember it all so well!" Big, round tears were trickling down Aunt Iris's sharp cheekbones.

"Oh, Aunt Iris." Beth reached out a tentative hand and touched the woman's shoulder. Aunt Iris flinched away.

"She stole him! But in the end, she couldn't have him, either. And do you know why? Because he still wanted to marry *me.* He begged me to forgive him for letting that worthless sister of mine seduce him. And I would have done it, married him anyway. But she—she couldn't stand the thought that I'd get something she wanted! She had to ruin it all for me. If she couldn't have him, she wanted to make damn sure I couldn't, either!"

Aunt Iris moved to the bed, sobbing, and fell onto it. She dragged her fingers through her scraggly hair. When she raised her head she stared at Beth as if surprised to see her still standing there.

But Beth felt rooted to the spot. Her voice came out weak and shaky, but she had to ask. "So, what happened?"

Aunt Iris sat up and hugged her arms around her skeletal body. She was sobbing. "She killed him, Elisabeth! She pushed him right down the stairs. She swore at the time she'd kill both of us—but she hasn't managed to get me. Not yet."

Beth closed her eyes for a second as panic welled in her throat. The memory of her dream about Hannah and the car and the cliff pressed behind her eyes. Then she spun for the door, yanked it open, and ran for the hall—a sound like crashing waves pounding in her head. *Not Mom! No!* Aunt Iris was wrong! Aunt Iris was lying—

"Elisabeth." Aunt Iris's hoarse rasp called her back, and Beth stopped, heart hammering, just outside the door to her own bedroom. "Here are your socks."

Finally Beth lay in bed. She had not even brushed her teeth or performed any of her usual bedtime rituals. No zit medicine. No leg lifts, no diary writing. She huddled under the sheet, strangely cold in the summer heat. Tears stung behind her closed lids, but she fought them back. Her eyes flew open at the sound of Tom's connecting door opening, and she hastily shut them again and tried to breathe regularly so he would think she was sleeping. She didn't want to talk. She could feel him standing at the head of her bed, even with her eyes closed.

"Beth? I know you're not sleeping."

She remained silent, willing him to go away so she could cry in privacy.

"Look, if you were sleeping, your eyelids wouldn't be twitching like that. Eyelids only twitch like that if you're awake or if you're in very deep sleep. I did a report at school last year, all about sleep. You know? Sleep patterns. There's this thing called Rapid Eye Movement. REM, it's called, and it means that your eyes move rapidly when you're deeply asleep and dreaming. But you can't get to that stage till you've already been asleep for about twenty minutes, which you haven't, so why don't you just sit up and tell me about it?"

Beth sat up, tears spilling. "Leave me alone."

"No." His voice was surprisingly firm, and Beth peered at him from her curtain of hair. "I heard everything."

"Everything?"

"Everything she was saying to you. Aunt Iris. She was drunk, you know, Beth. Don't forget that."

"I—I know." Beth sniffed and reached for a

tissue from the box on her bedside table. She blew her nose noisily. "So, were you listening at the door or what?"

"Didn't need to." Tom sat on the edge of the bed. "The windows of her room are open and so are the windows on the sunporch. It's right next door! I couldn't *not* hear. I was going to rush in and save you if she turned, you know, violent."

His voice was firm and sounded grown-up. Beth peered at her brother and thought he might turn into someone she could lean on, someday. She blew her nose again and tucked the tissue under her pillow. "Well, she didn't touch me. But what do you think about what she said? Do you think Mom *could* have done it—pushed that man?"

"Of course not! Don't ever think such a thing! She isn't the murderous type."

"And Aunt Iris is?"

"Probably."

"But Tom—" Beth hesitated. It chilled her to know Aunt Iris was in the next room—it chilled the air she breathed. And yet there was something even more chilling. "You heard Mom. She herself said she doesn't remember exactly what happened—"

Tom sat on the edge of the bed, frowning fiercely. "No! Don't even think it! I don't believe it for one second. And you'd better not, either!"

She regarded him for a long moment, surprised at the tremble in his voice. Then she realized he was trying to mask a fear that left him dizzy. He changed again before her eyes—from the person she might be able to lean on back into old Mac, just her younger brother. She put on her most reassuring voice. "I never said I suspected Mom, did I? I'm just saying it's strange. I don't think Aunt Iris was lying tonight. I mean, I think she really *believes* Mom pushed that guy! There's something really weird about all this. We know Mom wouldn't have pushed him, right? But what if Aunt Iris didn't, either?"

Tom's eyes were round. "Then someone else did?"

"I don't know. I wonder how we can find out."

He scowled. "You've read too many detective books this summer. There's no way to find out what happened here so many years ago."

"Maybe not." But Beth suddenly felt cheered at the prospect of trying. An aggressive attempt to clear up the past and settle once and for all what had happened to the lodger might be better than living here with all the undercurrents. "Don't you want to uncover family skeletons, Tom?"

"She's uncovered already," muttered Tom. "Over in the next room. And remember, Mom said the other night that the subject was closed. Absolutely and forever. That's what she said."

Beth stared up at the crack on the ceiling. She'd thought earlier it looked like a man's head. But now it resembled a winged insect. "How do you solve a twenty-year-old mystery?" she mused to herself. "Oh, Tom—wouldn't you love to be able to turn yourself into a fly on the wall and go back in time to see what *really* happened here?"

Because the June heat drew such crowds, Clifton had been staying later and later each night to clean up before heading home from the zoo. There was so much garbage to pick up from the picnic areas, he couldn't believe it. People were such slobs. And it wasn't just kids, either. He couldn't count anymore the times he had watched adults toss cotton-candy cones, paper cups still half full of melting ice and orangeade, and hamburger wrappers into the bushes, onto the paths, or even right into the animals' pens. It was disgusting.

He took solace in the fact that evening would bring him back to the Savages, to their spotless home. He rode the train back from the zoo, then caught a bus. Normally the walk from the bus stop to the old house on Spring Street, where he had lodgings with the family, was his chance to daydream, to unwind after a long day. His daydreams generally focused on the novel he was writing—well, trying to write—at night up in his room. The plot was great—better than any of the science fiction junk he'd ever read. The classic writers had nothing on him. Even his favorite writers, Jules Verne and Isaac Asimov, paled beside him. When he sat down at his old typewriter out there on the little sunporch that came with the bedroom, he entered a world of time travel, space exploration, new planets discovered around new suns, and thrilling tales of war. Clara Savage, his landlady and soon-to-be mother-in-law, often had a very hard time pulling him out of that world when dinner was waiting on the table. Lately, of course, concentrating on that other world had become more and more difficult.

Who would have thought he would fall in love! And with such a beautiful, fascinating woman! He still couldn't get over it. He had once believed there could be only one person in the whole world who was truly right for him—his soul mate, his anima. And he believed he had met her while he was in college.

She'd been a waitress at the café near campus, not a student herself, but a seeming waif—a thin, pale beauty named Abby, who had few connections and lived, as he did, in a rooming house near the campus. He had been twenty. She swore she was eighteen, but she looked fifteen. He hadn't complained. They'd dated for two years, until he graduated and felt ready to marry her. But two years hadn't changed Abby a bit; she still looked fifteen, was still elusive and vague when he tried to pin her down to a date when they could be married. He had complained bitterly then. After all, he was quite a catch, wasn't he? Not rich, of course, but a great writer, which was nearly the same thing—he would be rich in a few years' time, once his books started to sell.

One evening two weeks before Christmas, after they'd finished dinner together in the café, Abby handed him a present. She made him promise not to open it until Christmas. He agreed to wait. Then, suddenly, she'd said she had to go and left him sitting there in the café. He finished his dinner, then went back to their rooming house. But Abby wasn't in her room. He figured she must have gone out for a walk—she didn't really have any other friends that he knew of—but, although he waited until quite late, she didn't return. He remembered the present she'd given him and decided to open it then and there.

It was a collection of science fiction time-travel stories he had been eyeing in a bookstore the previous week. And there was a letter enclosed:

Clifton,

I really do care about you, but I don't *want to marry you. I'm leaving Philadelphia. Don't worry about me. Good luck. I will look for your books.*

Abby

His first thought was that she hadn't even signed the note "Love, Abby"—just "Abby." His second thought was that she clearly was not his soul mate after all. Soul mates just didn't run off like that. So he never thought of trying to find her. As Christmas drew nearer, he half-expected a card from her, but none came, and after that he rarely thought of her. He immersed himself in his writing, working at odd jobs to support himself. A few years later his rooming house began to seem crowded, full of students much younger than himself, and he decided it was time to find a new place. He'd moved into the house on Spring Street and met Iris. And thoughts of Abby never crossed his mind again.

Talk about soul mates! He was drawn to her from the start, but his first Christmas with the family had been the turning point. As the holidays approached, he noticed he was spending less and less time at his writing and more time sitting with her over coffee after dinner. Iris was eager to hear about all the new plot twists, and eventually he began reading her each chapter as he finished it. Yet he found it hard to concern himself with the good people (or villains either, for that matter) of the Planet Notfilc—"Clifton" spelled backwards, but he doubted anyone would notice—when he could sit by the fire and watch the twinkle of tree lights with lovely Iris Savage. What a great name, he'd told her. A savage flower. It sounded like it should be in lights somewhere or, at the very least, on the cover of some stormy gothic romance. He told her he'd decided to work in a princess modeled on Iris as a tribute to her. She laughed—that soft, sweet laugh that caused a curious, sensual prickle along the back of his neck. (Abby had never caused him to feel such a thing!) And he began to think he'd found his true soul mate at last.

On Christmas Day he kissed her for the first time—and learned that it was her first kiss. He wasn't surprised; she had led a very sheltered life. Her parents were too protective by far, he felt. And Mrs. Savage, maybe as a reaction to Iris's childhood bout with polio, was extra-indulgent and lavished attention on the girl. Mr. Savage, on the other hand, balanced his wife's excesses by favoring the little sister.

Clifton and Iris had fallen in love at the very moment they opened their gifts: she'd given him a ream of thick, top-quality typing paper, new typewriter ribbons, and, best of all, an original oil painting—her interpretation of Notfilc. She had used him already to pose for several portrait sketches, one of which she later did in water-color, but he liked the landscape best of all. In it she'd brought out more of the real Clifton than the portraits showed. The colors in the painting were glorious and clear. Bright blues and purples in the sky, with silvery stars and shimmery spacecraft. The planet itself was a series of red-rock lava islands dotting a stormy green-and-blue sea. The details on the islands were amazing: On each one some chapter of the novel unfolded. There was a laser-beam sword fight between the hero and villain on one, a sumptuous feast to celebrate the capture of the Evil Overlord on another, the dark castle where the lovely Princess Siri was held captive on a third, the lairs of the Notfilckian Beasts on the fourth. The painting was signed down in the left-hand corner with a single delicate blue flower—an iris. She told him she had been working on it for weeks, every day, while he was at the zoo. He told her he hoped the Christmas painting would someday become the cover of his novel. Then they would both be famous.

He had given her an expensive jasmine perfume and—more intimate—bath oil of the same fragrance. (Although he searched everywhere for an iris fragrance, he'd found only rose and lemon and jasmine. The jasmine had seemed the most sexy. He hoped she got the message.)

Funny how her leg didn't bother him. She was so ashamed of it, and he believed her mother did more harm than good by insisting Iris be treated specially because of her handicap. Not much more of a handicap than his own weak eyesight, really—Iris could move around as well as anyone; maybe she went just a little more slowly. But she told him about her childhood, how she'd been coddled because of her limp and how she was always made to feel different.

She had already decided she would never marry because of it—Who could possibly want her? she'd asked him.

He could only shake his head over such nonsense.

An early April evening on the front porch had been special in more ways than one: Yes, he had asked her to marry him—but first, before he drew the little ring box out of his pocket, he had moved his hands down her soft body, caressing it through the light spring dress she wore. They had had little physical contact except kisses, and he hadn't minded. He knew she was inexperienced, and he knew why. The caressing on the porch that evening was, in fact, not so much for his satisfaction as for hers—as a way to show her he loved her, and that the withered leg didn't matter to him at all. He leaned down and lifted the hem of the fashionable maxiskirt she wore—he remembered the day she shyly confessed to him how happy she'd been when long skirts became as stylish as the miniskirts she refused to wear. He lifted the hem, drew the skirt up slowly, folds and folds of soft, bright cloth, up over her knees. He pretended not to hear her quick intake of breath, nor the little sigh with which she let it out when he bent over her and kissed her thighs, her knees, and ran his kisses all the way down both legs, down to her toes. He lingered no longer over the shapely leg than he did over her withered calf and twisted left foot.

They didn't speak of what he had done, but just held each other tightly for a long time. He could feel her heart beating. And then he produced the ring. He loved the way her voice squeaked when she said, "Oh, yes!"—and loved her delighted laughter, the laugh that made him tingle. They had then told her parents and phoned his, and everyone said theirs was a perfect match.

He could hear Hanny Lynn's favorite Rolling Stones song blaring from her record player upstairs as he reached the house and jumped up the four stone steps onto the big porch. He whistled along with the guy who couldn't get no satisfaction, then laughed at how inappropriate that lament was to his own situation. He felt immensely satisfied—especially with the good news he had for Iris. The scent of boxwood from the bushes mingled with the warm smell of chicken potpie wafting from the kitchen inside, and he hurried through the screen door, eager to join the family—soon to be his own—at the dinner table.

"Here's Clifton, Mama!" Iris moved across the living room, her limp more pronounced at the end of a day than in the morning, and embraced him. He buried his face in her soft, fragrant hair, then turned her face up to his, hungrily seeking her mouth. She had a dab of blue paint on one cheek.

"You've been working," he said, tangling his fingers in her red curls.

Iris broke away after a moment, grinning. "I'll show you later. But now it's time for dinner."

"You mean that kiss wasn't sustenance enough?" asked a sarcastic voice, and Clifton and Iris turned together to see Hanny Lynn, the younger sister, smirking at them from the landing halfway up the stairs. "It looked like you two were practically down each other's throats."

"Go turn off your music, Hanny Lynn," said Iris coolly. "You're to set the table now." And she walked back into the kitchen, where she had been helping her mother.

Clifton followed her. "Can I do anything?"

"You can throttle Hanny Lynn, if you want."

"Men out of the kitchen," said Mrs. Savage,

playfully snapping her dish towel at him. "We have everything under control."

Clifton was relieved; he had never learned to cook. The memory of the ruined roast—his sorry attempt at a special dinner for Iris one evening last winter when her parents and Hanny Lynn had been away at a high school open house—still embarrassed him. Iris had laughed it off and told him he'd just have to find a wife who could cook. Well, he had found her!

Their wedding was set for the beginning of September and dinnertime talk these days centered around bridesmaids' gowns, flowers, and whether or not the wedding cake could be chocolate. Iris loved chocolate, but her mother insisted wedding cakes must be white.

"How about white cream frosting, Mama," said Iris. "And chocolate cake inside—nobody would know until it was cut!"

"Oh, Iris, honey. You don't want to be untraditional, do you? You want the wedding to be just perfect—let's not fuss about details."

Iris smiled across the table at Clifton. "Okay, Mama. Whatever you like."

"Hey, whose wedding is this, anyway?" asked Hanny Lynn, pushing her peas around on her plate with distaste. "Yours or Mama's?"

"Mine, of course," said Iris. "But Mama and Daddy are paying for it, remember. And the cake doesn't really matter. What matters is that Clifton and I love each other and are going to spend the rest of our lives together. Maybe Mama is right. Keeping old traditions alive is a fine way to start a marriage."

Hanny Lynn rolled her eyes. "Excuse me," she said and pretended to retch over the side of her chair onto the floor.

"That's enough, young lady!" Mrs. Savage threw down her napkin angrily. "Your displays of temper are going too far. I expect more adult behavior from a seventeen-year-old."

Hanny Lynn opened her mouth to retort, but Clifton caught her eye and winked at her. She subsided, coloring. Clifton wasn't surprised this time at her blush; he had noticed it several times lately when he spoke to her—or even looked at her. He wasn't sure what it meant but supposed she was just going through a stage or something. Hanny Lynn might be okay when she grew up, but now she was a gangly, long-legged kid, and an ill-mannered one at that. Certainly nothing like her older sister!

Henry Savage, Iris's father, began talking

about camping again. He had this idea that he and Clifton should go backpacking alone—get to know each other, he said. Up in New England somewhere, some national park. Clifton didn't want to be rude, but he didn't want to go camping anywhere. And yet Iris's father was set on going. "A fine way to get to know each other better," he said. "I've always wanted a son, someone to rough it with." But Clifton didn't like roughing it. He liked soft beds, home-cooked meals, all the modern amenities of what he called the Good Life. Camping in the backwoods didn't appeal at all, though he hesitated to give this as his reason for declining. Maybe his weak eyesight would count him out—it had been the reason he'd escaped the draft, after all. Instead, he told Mr. Savage how much he would miss Iris in the backwoods—which was true, of course—and how he couldn't take the time off from work.

He'd hoped the subject of camping was closed, but tonight Mr. Savage was going strong again.

"I'll hunt out the photos after dinner," he said. "Show you the ones from my trip with my college roommate. Years ago, but the area up there is unchanged even today. Bear and moose right where you can see them! The snapshots will give you a sense of the beauty of the wilderness. Maybe even Iris will decide she wants to go."

"I really am sorry, Mr. Savage." Clifton smiled. "I'd love to see the photos, but I really think a trip will be impossible this summer. I have to keep working right up until the wedding. And then"—he dropped his secret—"as soon as we get back from the honeymoon, I'll be starting at the paper."

Mr. Savage put down his fork. "The paper? What paper?"

"Oh, Clifton!" squealed Iris, jumping up from the table to hurry to his side and envelop him in a warm hug. "You got the job? That's super! Why didn't you tell me when you came in?"

"What job?" asked Mrs. Savage. "Oh, tell us right now, you sly boy!"

That had been the single problem. Iris's parents didn't feel his job at the zoo was enough to support him and Iris both once they were married—and he had to admit they were probably right. He wouldn't want to keep living here with her family once they were married, even though he enjoyed being the lodger. The zoo was a good enough job most of the time for a writer—simple work that kept his mind free to plan further chapters of his novel. But the money was barely enough for a single man, so he had gone out hunting for something else.

He grinned at their eager faces—that is, all eager except for Hanny Lynn's face, which was carefully indifferent.

"Tell us, dear," urged Mrs. Savage, and he did.

"I'll be working at the *Philadelphia Inquirer*. I'll be a copy editor at first, to start. But I like to write my own stuff, you know, and I hope I'll eventually be able to do a science column or something. The starting pay isn't great, but it's more than I'm making now and enough to pay for our first apartment."

"Oh, darling, that's wonderful!" Iris's eyes shone, and she hugged him again before limping back to her place at the table.

"We always knew you'd take good care of our Iris," said Mrs. Savage.

"But it is good to hear *how* you'll manage to take care of her," added Mr. Savage.

"Anyway, I'm sorry about the camping," said

Clifton, adjusting his glasses on his nose. "But it really doesn't look possible now. Maybe next summer, if I get a few days off." He'd have time before then to read up on fending off moose and bears. For all his love of wild animals, he liked them best in cages.

Mr. Savage nodded, reaching for the potatoes. Mrs. Savage passed Clifton the salad. Then, as soon as everyone had finished, she left the table to bring her homemade cherry pie in from the kitchen.

"That's beautiful," Clifton said, sniffing. "A masterpiece."

"Mama always makes masterpieces," said Iris proudly.

"Well, she certainly did when she made you!" he rejoined, and everyone smiled—everyone but Hanny Lynn, that is, who sat staring sullenly at her dinner plate.

After dinner Clifton and Iris sat on the glider, his foot tapping gently to keep the swing moving. She leaned against him, her legs tucked beneath her on the cushions, and he twined his fingers in her long curls, wrapping the soft strands around and around his fingers.

"I'm so happy, darling," Iris said softly. "Being with you is so perfect it almost scares me. I keep thinking something might happen—"

"Sshh, don't be silly," he said, and parted her lips for a kiss.

"Just listen to those tree frogs," she murmured. "And smell that boxwood. I think for the rest of my life, whenever it's June, I'll remember this moment, being here with you like this—with our whole life together before us."

He kissed the top of her head where it was nestled under his chin. "I bless the day I answered that ad in the paper: 'Lodger Wanted. Large bedroom with sunporch. Free board in exchange for yard work.' It didn't say that my soul mate would be waiting for me here! Oh, Iris, babe—we're going to be so happy!"

They rocked gently in the dusk of the summer evening, relaxed and content with each other's company. Soon Mr. and Mrs. Savage joined them on the big front porch, he with his newspaper and she with her knitting. Iris joked it was a baby blanket for the first grandchild. Their talk was lighthearted: more congratulations on Clifton's new job with the *Inquirer*, more wedding plans, comments on the garden—how lovely it looked this summer since Clifton had pruned back the bushes and planted wild-flowers.

No one missed Hanny Lynn, who lay across her narrow bed upstairs in her hot little bed-room, sobbing as if her heart were broken.

3

At first Beth began visiting Grandad mainly to get away from the other members of the household, but after the first week her devotion was real. The days took on a pattern: She spent nearly every morning with Grandad, sitting by his bed and matching wits over word games and card tricks. She passed solitary afternoons down in the basement working on her stained-glass window. Only the evenings were difficult, when the family met around the dinner table or out on the porch, the tension among them thick and silent and angry.

It seemed a morning like any other when Beth came in and sat in the blue chair next to Grandad's bed. They did the crossword puzzle from the *Philadelphia Inquirer,* Beth marveling as always at Grandad's speed. He must have memorized the dictionary at some time in his past, she'd decided.

When they finished the puzzle, Grandad reached for his pad of paper and a pen. "Now here's a brainteaser," he said. He wrote a sentence on the page and drew a box around it. "What do you make of this?"

She took the pad.

All sentences within this square are false.

"What do you think, Beth? Is it true or false?" Grandad lay back on the pillows, watching her with anticipation while she studied it.

Being with Grandad could be as easy and companionable as spending time with Violet at home. He *was* older, certainly, and had weak legs since his stroke—although Beth suspected that he kept to his bed more for the refuge of the cool, peaceful room than out of necessity—but his personality was what counted, and that was something old age hadn't altered. Here he was, living in a house full of tension, with a wife he rarely spoke to and a daughter more puzzling than any math trick, and yet he just made the best of it by being funny and smart and reasonable about things. He kept well informed about current events by reading two newspapers a day and three news magazines each week. He read all the best-sellers. He ordered travel books and maps from catalogs and studied them as if planning a major trip—he could have almost as much fun, he told Beth, traveling in his head as he used to have on his big camping trips. They talked about almost everything. The only subject that seemed taboo was what had happened to Clifton Becker. Grandad always changed the subject when she brought up that name.

Beth read the sentence in the box again, trying to work it out. If all sentences in the square were false, then this one must be false because it was in the square. That seemed clear enough. "The sentence is false," she said. "Just like it says."

"Ah." Grandad smiled. He quirked one eyebrow.

There had to be a trick to it or Grandad wouldn't be grinning like that. She pondered the sentence again.

"Okay," she said after another minute. "It says that all sentences in the square are false, right? And that is a sentence itself, so it has to be false." Then she paused and looked at him. "Oh, no! But if the sentence is false, then what it *says* has to be false, too, and if it's saying it's a false sentence, that must mean it's really a *true* statement." She frowned back at the pad. "But it *can't* be true, because all sentences in the square are false!" Her voice rose to a wail.

Grandad chuckled. "You've got it! It's a paradox, Beth. A built-in contradiction—what the ancient Greek philosophers called an antinomy."

She tossed the pad onto the bed. "So you mean there *is* no answer? But that's not fair! How can we ever know what's true or false?"

"The philosophers grappled with just that question and never figured it out, either." He cocked his eyebrow at her. "Maybe it doesn't matter."

She hoped she had inherited even an ounce of his style.

She leaned back in the blue chair. "I have a

riddle for you, Grandad." It was one Ray had told her. Though Ray laughed them off as childish, he was secretly just as big a fan of light bulb jokes as Beth was.

Grandad set aside his pad and pen and leaned back on the pillows. "Okay, shoot."

"How many psychiatrists does it take to change a light bulb?"

"Go on, how many?"

"Only one." She grinned. "But the light bulb has got to *want* to change!"

He rolled his eyes.

"Listen, I've got another one! How many Californians does it take—"

She was cut off by pounding footsteps out in the hallway. The bedroom door burst open and Hannah raced into the room, her hair loose on her shoulders and her eyes wild.

"Mom!" Beth jumped up from her chair. "What's wrong?"

"I don't care! That's it—that's the end!" yelled Hannah. She ran to the window and pressed her palms flat against the glass.

"What is it, Hanny?" asked Grandad, pushing off his sheet and struggling to get out of bed.

Hannah stared at them over her shoulder.

"We're out of here, that's what. I just can't stay another minute in this house. I won't! Not with Iris here. Not another second!" Her trembling voice rose. "Beth, go start packing—immediately!"

"Whoa, Hanny Lynn!" Grandad walked haltingly over to her. "Come on, of course you mustn't leave. Your mother and I are so happy you've come back and brought the children. We need you—please. Have you and Iris had another fight? Is that it? Is that it, Hanny?"

"Is that it?" she mimicked him with tight sarcasm. "Of course that's it! When has it ever been any different?" She balled her hands into fists and pounded them against the windowpanes.

"Mom!" Beth ran to her, sure the glass would shatter. "Watch out!"

Hannah whirled on her. "Just go start packing! If we don't hurry, we'll never get out alive. She'll see to that!"

Beth had seen her mother angry many times, but occasionally there was a quality to the fury that frightened her. This was one of those times. Hannah didn't seem quite herself. She beat the panes of glass, her face contorted.

"It was a mistake to come back here," she

hissed suddenly. "This house is contaminated! It's *haunted!*"

Beth stepped back, her stomach churning with dread and something else that, strangely, might have been embarrassment. She headed for the door.

Grandad had his arms around Hannah, murmuring to her. She was shaking her head so wildly that her straight hair fanned out off her shoulders. At the door, Beth paused, afraid her mother might shove him away, afraid he would fall. But after a moment's fierce resistance, Hannah threw her arms around him, sobbing brokenly.

"I'm sorry, Daddy, I'm so sorry!"

And as quickly as that, the storm was over. Beth knew there would be no need to pack now.

"Well, how about if you be Watson and I be Holmes," suggested Tom, tearing the husk off the ear of corn he held and tossing the ear into the large pot Grandmother had given them. "Already we have two versions of what happened from Mom and Aunt Iris."

"I'm older," said Beth. "I'll be Holmes." They sat on the back steps, glasses of cold lemonade standing beside them in dark, wet circles on the gray stone step. She kept her tone light. She didn't want to tell him about Hannah's outburst upstairs. It just made things seem even weirder. She could hear voices from inside the house now—high, low, quarrelsome—and tried to ignore them. The hedge around the yard grew wild, effectively shielding the stone house from the street, but through its insulating tangles Beth could make out the summer sound of lawn mowers.

Tom tossed another ear into the pot. "Anyway, I have an idea. How about we ask Grandmother and Grandad for their versions of what happened? You deal with Grandmother, and I'll tackle Grandad after his nap. Maybe they *did* notice something else."

"Like a stranger lurking on the landing that night?" Beth snorted. "Anyway, I've already tried to ask Grandad and he clams up like—like a clam."

"Maybe you're not going about it in the right way. You're too blunt. You've got to be sneaky. You know, get him talking about something else and then work the conversation around to Clifton Becker." He drained his lemonade.

"Got it all figured out, hmm?" Beth curled a husk around her hand. "I guess I could try again with Grandad. But *you* tackle Grandmother."

Tom scowled. "No way, Holmes. She thinks I'm a drug addict."

"Oh, she does not."

He grinned. "Come on, Beth. Remember my sensitive nature! My youth!"

She menaced him with the last ear of corn, then began shucking the husk onto the pile. He picked up the pot when she was done and carried it up the steps to the kitchen.

"I'll take Romps for a nice long walk, and you can get started," he offered.

Beth followed Tom inside, banging the screen door behind her. Old Mac never had been known for his generous spirit. On the other hand, why *not* interview Grandmother? It wasn't as if Beth had anything else planned. It wasn't as if life in Philadelphia were thrills-a-minute exciting. She had phoned Monica again after leaving Grandad and Hannah, but the answering machine answered, and a man's voice told her no one was home just then and she should leave a message. Weren't these people ever home? She'd cleared her throat and said that it was just Beth, the girl with the fudge bar, calling yet again, and would Monica *please* call her as soon as she came home, if she ever did come home? She decided this was the girl's last chance.

Grandmother was perched on her stool in the corner between the stove and the counter. Her white hair curled in wisps around her face from the summer heat. She had a pie pan full of sliced peaches on the counter at her side and was carefully cutting strips of pastry out of the dough on the floured board in front of her. She looked up when Beth and Tom entered, and she wiped her floury fingers on the faded apron she wore over her housedress.

"Thank you. Put the pot on the back burner, Tom. We'll have the corn for lunch."

"What are you making?" asked Tom.

"It's pretty obviously peach pie," said Beth. "And it looks yummy, Grandmother. But what are you doing to the crust?"

"It's a lattice-weave crust, my girl. It takes time to do, but I've got enough of that on my hands. And if a pie is worth making, it's worth making well. Like most things, I think." She bent back over her work.

Beth was uncomfortably aware that interviewing someone didn't happen naturally. How was she supposed to change the subject gracefully and start being sneaky to get the information they wanted? Would it be too horrible if she casually asked straight out: "So, who do you think killed Clifton Becker?" She didn't have the nerve. She glanced at Tom for help, but he just shrugged and moved toward the door.

"Well, I'm off," he announced. "Unless you'd like me to stay and help, Grandmother?"

The old woman did not even look up from her careful cutting. "The kitchen is no place for a boy. Why don't you take that dog with you? He's been lying out there under the tree all morning."

"Good idea, Tom," said Beth sarcastically as he bounded past her to get Romps's leash from the hook in the pantry.

"I don't hold with men in the kitchen," Grandmother said firmly to Beth as the screen door slammed. "Men have more than enough to occupy themselves with elsewhere. I'll set him to work later pruning the hedge."

Beth didn't bother to tell her that Tom was a better cook than their mother and that Ray made the best guacamole this side of Mexico. She herself had little patience with kitchen work, and little practice, preferring to cut glass rather than pastry dough.

She washed her hands at the sink. "Let me help, then."

Grandmother frowned. "Can you cook? Hanny was always a terror in the kitchen. We tried to teach her, Iris and I. But she had no natural gift—couldn't do any more than read a recipe book." Grandmother snorted. Then she peered at Beth. "There's more to good cooking than following a book. There's intuition—and instinct."

Beth nodded and reached for an apron on the hook by the refrigerator. She might as well look the part of the intuitive chef working by instinct. "I really do want to learn, Grandmother. Let me in on the family secrets."

"You can be in charge of rolling out the crusts," directed Grandmother, handing Beth the rolling pin. "Use just enough flour on the board to keep the dough from sticking. Too much flour makes a crust crumbly." She divided the dough into three equal balls. "We'll be making three pies."

Beth positioned herself at the cutting board and started pressing the soft dough of one ball awkwardly with the rolling pin.

Grandmother peered at her critically. "Don't just mash it around like that. You need to *roll* it out. Smoothly. Here, let me show you." She climbed off her stool and took the rolling pin from Beth's hands. "Like this"—and under her touch the floury mass became a smooth, thin circle ready to go into the pie pan. "See? Just like that."

"No problem," said Beth. She tried again and this time managed to spill half the flour from the board onto the floor. "Oh, sorry!" She rushed to the sink for a cloth.

Grandmother sighed. "Well, I guess you take after your mother. Hanny Lynn never learned to make a pie, either."

"Mom hasn't had much time for pies and cakes," Beth said, defending Hannah. "But she makes great salads."

"California food," sniffed Grandmother, perching on her stool again. "If she weren't out at work all the time, she could learn to cook. She should be at home where she can bring up her children properly. She needs to be married—and stay married. None of this changing your mind all the time, dating different men, running around like chickens without heads."

Beth scraped a wad of dough off the rolling pin and considered hurling it at her grandmother. "Mom *was* married, you know," she said, keeping her voice even. "Even if you never met him. She was *happily* married! It wasn't her fault my father was killed in an accident."

Grandmother stirred sugar into her peaches. "If she drove him to drink, it was. Just like she's driving poor Iris to drink now. Hanny has had her hand in more than one accident, I'm afraid."

Beth applied herself to her piecrusts and did not say anything for a long moment. Grandmother plunged her wooden spoon into the bowl of peaches and gave them a good stir. Then, as clearly as if he were really there, Beth heard Tom's voice in her head: "Go for it, Holmes!"

So Beth cleared her throat. "Umm, Grandmother?"

"Yes?" The old woman didn't look up from her busy hands as they peeled another peach for slicing.

"About Mom? How is she driving Aunt Iris to drink?"

"Never you mind. I'm sorry I said anything."

"No, really. I know Mom and Iris don't get along—"

"I expect your mother has been filling your head with all sorts of nasty nonsense about poor Iris, hasn't she?"

"No!"

"Hmmph. Well, they were never close, I'll say that much. Your mother was always jealous of poor Iris. Iris was such a frail girl, you know. We had to take special care of her. Make sure she enjoyed life. Her paintings were lovely—she had real talent! You may not have known your aunt was an artist, but she even won a state competition once and could have gone on to art school. But Hanny Lynn put a stop to that as well."

"But how?"

Grandmother's expression grew tight, and she closed her eyes for a moment as if in pain. "Hanny Lynn made poor Iris's life so miserable, she couldn't paint anymore! That's when she stopped eating. It's awful to watch someone you love wasting away. And then to see Hanny Lynn come back home full of beans! No wonder Iris has taken to drinking! Let me tell you, a mother's burden is a heavy one."

Beth took the bowl of peaches Grandmother handed her and carefully spooned equal amounts of fruit into the piecrust shells. She took a deep breath. "Why *did* Mom leave home, Grandmother?"

Grandmother sighed and wiped her palms on

her apron. "I'm not surprised she's never told you. It's good to know she has some sense of shame. Nothing to be proud of, leaving like that. But in a way, things were easier for us all here with her gone. It wasn't good having her here—not after what she did." Grandmother bit her lip and brushed a wispy white curl back off her forehead. The tight expression was back. For a moment Beth was afraid the old woman was going to start crying.

"But what *did* she do?" asked Beth.

Grandmother shook her head. "It's all water under the bridge. Your Grandad wouldn't like me to be talking this way."

Beth wracked her brain for the right question that would set Grandmother off again. Maybe something casually blunt would do the trick after all.

So she spoke up innocently. "Are you talking about that lodger? The one who fell down the stairs?"

Grandmother climbed off her stool and walked to Beth's side. Wordlessly, she took a filled pie pan from Beth's hands and set it on the counter by the stove. "Watch carefully now," she said. "This is how you weave the lattice."

Beth watched the plump fingers neatly slice dough into ribbons. Her question hung in the air, unanswered. Grandmother wove the last strip of dough into place on the first piecrust. "Can you do that?" she asked. "Here, try it on this next pie."

Beth reached for a strip of dough.

Grandmother sighed and walked back to her stool, sitting down heavily. "Yes," she said as if to herself. "Maybe you should be told that much, you being her daughter." She looked up at Beth, and her eyes were full of pain. "Yes, Hanny Lynn left because Clifton fell down the stairs. There's no question about that."

"But there are questions . . . ," murmured Beth, beginning to weave the long strips of dough with tense fingers. She glanced at her grandmother and saw the old woman's eyes were closed.

"We never talk about it anymore," she went on musingly. "It's history now. That poor boy. He wanted to be a writer. Never got to publish anything, though, before he was—before he died."

"That's sad."

"He fell so hard." Her voice became dreamy, and Beth felt sure her closed eyes were seeing into the past, into history. "He fell so hard that I think we all knew he was dead before we even ran down to see. Smashed his head open on the radiator. An unfortunate accident. The doctor said he never knew what happened." She ran her veined hands through her short white curls. "But I've always thought he must have known. In that time while he was falling, he knew."

"Knew who had pushed him?" Beth's voice was the merest breath of whisper.

"Knew the old jealousy had won in the end. If *she* couldn't have him, then no one ever would. Least of all her sister."

But which sister? Beth held her breath a moment, feeling chilled in the hot kitchen. She didn't want to hear anymore. Yet Tom would expect her to finish the interview, and she wouldn't forgive herself for running away at this point. She let her breath out heavily.

"You mean Aunt Iris, don't you, Grandmother? Aunt Iris was the jealous one, right?" It must be so.

Grandmother didn't seem to hear. She caressed the interlocking latticework of the pies, all set neatly on the counter awaiting the oven. She spoke as if in a dream. "Ah, my poor, dear Iris. Always lost whatever made you happy, didn't you? And that Hanny Lynn—" Here Grandmother's voice grew hard and her fingers plucked angrily at the pies, tearing one carefully woven lattice. "From the moment she was born, she was a trial to you, poor little Iris. . . ."

Beth ran from the kitchen, fighting tears.

After dinner, when the main course had been cleared, Grandmother brought in one of the peach pies. She set it in front of Grandad's place and announced that Beth had helped. Grandad gave her the thumbs-up signal. Hannah looked pleased. Aunt Iris didn't seem to hear; she just sipped her beer and closed her eyes. Tom tasted a bite and teased that the pie was just about as good as the ones he would have made if Grandmother let boys into her kitchen. Grandad responded with a laugh, but everyone else just bent over their plates, subdued.

Tom regaled the silent family with an account of his adventures that afternoon. While he was out with Romps he'd met a boy on the next block, named Mark, who had just gotten a laptop computer for his birthday and didn't know what to do with it. "Can you believe it?" asked Tom. "He's, like, a total illiterate at this point but really eager. So I said I could help him out, you know? And he invited me over tonight." He looked across the table at Hannah. "Okay, Mom?"

"Of course." She smiled. "I'm glad you've found a friend."

"I don't know, Hanny Lynn," said Grandmother with a worried frown. "Maybe we should meet this boy's parents first. We don't know those people. And kids today—"

"Now, Mama, I'm sure it's fine! You'll be back by ten, all right, Tom?"

Beth picked at her piece of pie. *Lucky Tom!* She longed for the chance to get out of the house. At home she'd call Violet and they'd hang out with her sisters, maybe go to a movie. Or she'd call Ray and they'd go out for Death By Chocolate at the Dessert Diner down the street from his apartment. Her appetite was nonexistent here, but back home—

Her thoughts were broken by the shrill ring of the telephone. Everyone started. Then Grandmother went to answer. She turned to the others with a puzzled expression on her face. "Beth? It's for you."

It must have been those thoughts of Death By Chocolate, flying across the Rockies, that made him call her at last. Darling Ray! Beth leaped up to take the receiver from her grandmother. "Hello!"

"Well, hi," said Monica's voice. "It's nice you're so glad to hear from me."

"Oh—hi. I thought you were my boyfriend calling from California. But I *am* glad to hear from you." She sat on the little stool in the corner and hunched over, aware that her family all watched from the table. The phone didn't ring all that much in this house.

"I finally got all your messages this afternoon," Monica said. "I've been out of town—back in Ohio with my mother and stepfather. They called just after I met you, I guess it was, because my little half-sister had fallen off her bike and broken her ankle and couldn't go to the summer day camp they'd planned for her—oh, it's a long story." She broke off with a laugh. "Anyway, never mind. Families are total trouble. I ended up going there to take care of Jenny while they worked. I'll tell you the gory details later. Can we get together tonight? There's a triple feature at the Waverley. Do you like science fiction?"

"Sure!" She liked anything—*anything*—that

would get her out for an evening. They arranged to meet at the Waverley, and Beth hung up with a lighter heart.

"You'll have to introduce me to your brother," Monica said as the girls stood in line for their tickets. "I broke up with my boyfriend back in Cleveland before I came to live with Dad, and I just haven't met anyone I like yet."

"Tom's nice," Beth said. "He's only fifteen, but he's tall, so he looks older. People usually think he's my *older* brother." She rolled her eyes. "The only thing *really* wrong with him is that he's a computer maniac. It's like the worst kind of maniac you could ever come across."

The girls sat in the old theater's center section in deep, padded seats and shared a large tub of buttered popcorn. Before the triple feature started they talked in low voices. Monica told Beth how she had moved from Cleveland just after Christmas to live here with her father. He owned the old-fashioned candy shop down the street from the movie theater, and they lived in an apartment upstairs. The theater smelled a bit musty but was cool and dark. A man on the stage in front of the thick royal blue curtains played dramatic music on an ornate organ. The music seemed to come from another time, as if accompanying a silent movie. As she listened to Monica's chatter, Beth felt her shoulder muscles relaxing. She slouched down in her seat. She hadn't realized her body was so tense.

The organ player took a bow and the thick curtains parted to reveal the modern movie screen. Then the films began—classic science fiction oldies, including Beth's all-time favorite, *Star Wars*. Something about the film reminded her of Aunt Iris's painting, the one she planned to work in glass. She was annoyed to have thoughts of home intruding on her night away. But the scenes from the painting kept flickering in her mind as if they, too, were scenes from a film. Was the connection simply the rockets? Or the battle for good over evil?

Later that night, Beth and Tom took Romps for his last run before bedtime. As they walked, Tom chattered on about his new friend, Mark, and the new computer. Beth told him that Monica wanted to meet him. She noticed that his step seemed bouncy again, as if some of his tension, too, had evaporated during his evening away from the house.

They returned to the house and hesitated for

a moment outside the front door. The house was quiet, the upstairs windows dark. Without saying a word, they walked over to the glider at the end of the porch and sat down. Romps jumped up and pressed his little gray body firmly between them on the seat cushion. Tom kicked the glider into motion and kept it going. The night air was still warm and heavy with the scent of jasmine. Beth scratched absently behind Romps's ears, and he wagged his stumpy tail and fell asleep.

"He snores like Grandad," commented Tom.

"Must run in the family."

"Like madness."

Beth was silent for a long moment before speaking. "Not madness, really. Unhappiness."

"Are you going to tell me, Holmes? Fill me in on what Grandmother told you. Let's have the whole story."

"You know," Beth said slowly, "you and I have been talking about uncovering secrets as if the past were just part of a story—or a game. Like Clue, you know? Aunt Iris in the Billiard Room with the Candlestick. Or, in this case, Aunt Iris on the Landing with the Big Shove. But—well, when I was talking to Grandmother I could *feel* it, you know? That what happened in the past isn't over yet—it's still real, and it's still part of their lives. Our lives, too, really, since we're here, and since we sort of belong."

"That's creepy. Like being haunted?"

"Sort of." A little melodramatic, but life sometimes was. Was that what her mother had meant when she said the house was haunted?

Tom reached over and stroked Romps's gray back. Then he cleared his throat. "Come on! What ghastly things did Grandmother tell you?"

He would have to know sooner or later, but Beth's words came slowly. "She said, well, that Mom always had it in for Aunt Iris. She said Mom would do anything, you know, to make Aunt Iris miserable. She as good as said Mom pushed old Clifton Becker down the stairs!" Beth tapped the porch floor emphatically with her toe. As the swing jerked back, sudden tears welled under her lids. Romps stirred in his sleep.

"That's totally disgusting! God, think of having your own mother believe such lies about you!" Tom's voice was tight. "Makes me sick."

Beth's foot tapped rhythmically to keep the swing in motion.

Tom peered at her in the darkness. "Grandmother was lying. Right, Beth?"

Beth hesitated. Of course her grandmother

was lying. Or else simply mistaken. Her mother would never . . . But Beth's thoughts tangled as she came up against her mother's sometimes unpredictable behavior. She knew well how impulsive and hot-headed her mother could be. Hannah liked to think of herself as a laid-back, California-mellow type, Beth knew, but there was a whole other side to her, a side Beth tried to ignore. It was the side that covered a barely contained fury, the side that had appeared in Beth's dream of her mother driving them over a cliff. And look at how weird Hannah had acted just this morning upstairs with Grandad. Beth remembered how her mother sometimes flew into a snit if a waitress was slow or if the newspaper boy missed a delivery. Her eyes would fill with a helpless rage that was inappropriate to the situation.

It seemed to Beth that Hannah's erratic nature had shown itself frequently this past year. At first she'd been all for Beth's plan to set up the stained-glass shop with Ray after high school—she'd even suggested they spend a year or so living in an artists' community in the mountains. But then she'd changed her mind and carried on about the necessity of a college education and nagged Beth to send off for applications to four-year colleges. She went on about graduate school, about Beth's becoming a lawyer or an accountant or something, making a "good name" for herself! And there had been the time last spring when Hannah had left her job, broken off with the man she'd been seeing casually—and then cried for days in her bedroom. And now she'd dragged her children cross-country.

Beth had a sudden image of her mother as an octopus, all her insecurities the tentacles reaching out to grab onto the lives of everyone else around her. Only Hannah's troubles seemed to matter now. Only *her* perspective counted. Beth took a deep breath. Was she being unfair—or could something like this have happened once before? Was it really so inconceivable that Hannah, feeling jealous of her then-beautiful older sister and in love with her sister's fiancé, had reached out that night with fury in her eyes and given him a good hard shove?

"You *don't* believe Grandmother, do you?" pressed Tom.

"Look," she said softly. "I don't *know*. All I know is that people do things they don't mean to do. People act without thinking. And people sometimes change. They grow up, they feel bad about what happened in the past, you know, or something." She felt old as she said this. Much older, suddenly, than Tom.

"So what are you saying? That Mom pushed Whatsisface down the stairs and felt sorry later?"

"I don't want to think that, really. But I can't help wondering—"

Tom leaped off the swing, nearly knocking Romps to the floor. "That stinks, Beth! It really does!"

She cuddled Romps on her lap. "Tom, listen! I'm only saying—"

"We're talking about *Mom,* Beth! God, you're as bad as Grandmother, if you can think things like that!"

"Tom—!"

But he wouldn't listen. He darted across the porch, tore open the screen door, and ran inside. Beth held Romps and jostled the swing into motion again. Where did you draw the line between blind loyalty and clear understanding? She wanted Tom to understand that she was trying to be Sherlock Holmes—as he'd suggested. To look at facts, to consider the situation with cool logic. Considering Hannah as a suspect was only logical. It didn't mean their mother had done anything. It didn't mean Beth didn't love her! It meant only that she'd realized suddenly, while in the kitchen with Grandmother and the pies, that everybody had a different memory of what happened here all those years ago, and that Hannah's own story might also be clouded by time.

First thing in the morning, Beth dragged herself outside for a run with Romps. There was still dew on the grass and bushes, but by the time she got back to the house the sun was hot and she could tell it would be yet another muggy day. When she walked up the porch steps and smelled breakfast cooking and heard Aunt Iris's quarrelsome voice in the kitchen, she felt too sick to go in. So she sat on the porch until Grandad came out, with Tom behind him trundling a wheelchair. The black look Tom shot Beth told her he hadn't forgiven her for last night. But she decided to go along on the walk with them anyway.

Grandad grumbled a bit as they set off down Spring Street together, Beth's hands holding the padded handles of the wheelchair firmly, Tom walking alongside with Romps on the leash.

"Didn't get much sleep at all last night,"

Granddad muttered. "What with the heat. Imagine you kids didn't, either. Makes the bones ache." Beth tried to ease the big wheels gently over the cracks in the sidewalk, but he grunted whenever they hit a bump. "I can walk all right on my own," he said. "Just so we don't go too far."

"Grandmother said the fresh air will do you good," said Tom soothingly.

"Nothing wrong with my lungs! It's the old legs that get shaky."

The top of Grandad's bald head gleamed in the hot morning sun. The skin was spotted and shiny—even wet-looking. "What did you put on your head, Grandad?" Beth asked, touching him with a cautious finger.

He laughed. "Sun block. Your mother's doing. Said since I'm almost recovered from the stroke, she's not about to let me get skin cancer!"

"Mom's a safety maniac these days. It's part of the new persona." Beth shoved her hair back off her already-sweaty face and stopped at the corner. "Which way?"

"Anywhere that's fast," said Grandad. "Way too hot. I need my air conditioner. Let's just go around the block once and call it a day."

"No," said Beth, thinking the last place she wanted to end up was the house again. "Remember what Grandmother said about fresh air."

"Fresh air? You call this fresh?" sputtered Grandad as a truck hurtled past them.

"I know," said Beth quickly. "Let's go over by the Waverley Theater to the candy store. That's where Monica works. She's the girl I saw the movies with last night."

"That's the shop your mother stole the candy bar from," Grandad said.

"It's still in business after all these years?" asked Tom. "Then lead on." He fingered his allowance in the pocket of his shorts.

"Hasn't changed in years," said Grandad. "Your mother went there when she was a little girl—and I went when I was a little boy. Difference was, Hanny Lynn had a few pennies to spend, and my brothers and I just pressed our noses against the window until old Mr. Clements sent us packing." He laughed. "Old guy wasn't so bad, really. If we came at the right time—Saturday evening, just around closing—he'd give us each a bag of the broken cookies and mashed jelly beans to take home."

"Where are your brothers now?" asked Tom.

"Dead, both of them. I'm next in line."

"Oh, Grandad!" Beth jostled the handles of the wheelchair.

"I'm only speaking the truth, my girl."

She pushed the wheelchair around the corner. Clements's Candy was a small shop wedged between the Waverley Theater and a bank, part of the long row of small businesses that lined Penn's Pike. Most of the stores were shabby, their windows crammed with goods, outdated mannequins with lacquered hair modeling sundresses, lots of hardware and kitchenware. One store with the words "Thrift Shoppe" painted in purple letters across the big picture window belched a musty cloud of air from an old fan as they passed.

Beth tied Romps's leash to a parking meter, then held the candy store door open while Tom maneuvered the wheelchair inside. "I'll bring you a snack," she promised the little dog.

Clements's smelled of sugar, of fresh-baked doughnuts, of age. The floors were wooden, the wide boards warmly polished. Glass-topped display cabinets held pastries and breads; bins of candies lined the wall behind the wooden counter at the back of the store. Tom headed for these bins, abandoning Grandad's chair in the middle of the floor. Beth rescued him, and they joined Tom at the far counter. She scanned the store but saw no sign of Monica.

"All right! Look at this homemade fudge!" Tom's voice sounded happier than it had in days. He pawed through his pockets for some money.

"This is the boy who is saving up for a computer?" Grandad asked Beth. "Seems willing enough to part with his cash."

"Only where chocolate is concerned," Beth said. "Tom will single-mouthedly keep Clements's in business while we're in town."

Monica walked out of a back room, her arms laden with bags of gumdrops. Her face lit up when she saw Beth, and she dumped the bags onto the counter. "Hi!"

Beth introduced Tom and Grandad to Monica.

"So this is the computer maniac," said Monica after she'd greeted Grandad and Tom. "He doesn't look so scary to me!" She glanced up at Tom, flipping her long hair back over her shoulders and setting a pair of heavy silver earrings dancing. He grinned down at her.

"It comes on slowly," said Beth, noting Tom's lingering glance at Monica's hair. "One day you find yourself trembling."

"I can believe that," she said, slanting another glance up at Tom. Then she brushed off her apron. "So, how can I help you? What'll it be? We make the chocolates ourselves."

"I haven't decided yet," Tom said. "Everything looks so good."

"If you drool on anything, you have to pay for it," said Beth, poking Tom's shoulder as he studied his choices.

"The fudge is really good," Monica said. "My dad's specialty. The doughnuts are great, too."

"Another of your dad's specialties?" asked Grandad.

"No, my own." She smiled. "But don't let me influence you. Take your time. I'll be back in a minute—there's another batch of doughnuts almost ready." She disappeared into the back room behind the counter.

"My bet is that she's Bernard Clements's girl," said Grandad. "Bernard was about your mother's age—they went to school together. Bernard's uncle ran the shop then, and Bernard always said he wanted to own the place himself one day. For a while he and Hanny Lynn dated, you know. Used to talk about how they'd get married and run the place together."

"Was Bernard's uncle the one who used to

give you and your brothers the bags of mashed jelly beans?" asked Beth.

"No, no, child. That would have been the uncle's father. This store has been in one family for about four generations. It's *the* place to buy sweets now—people like the old-fashioned look. But what they don't understand is that this is the way Clements's Candy *always* was. This isn't a look. It's just the way the place *is*."

"I like it," said Tom, still gazing at the selection. His voice was cheerful. "And I like Monica."

The dark-haired girl returned at that moment from the back room. "Made up your minds yet?"

"How about a quarter pound of jelly beans and five pieces of that chocolate stuff there." Tom pointed.

"Dad's famous chocolate mousse drops. I'll give you six for the price of five." She dropped his candy into a small paper bag.

"Hey, thanks!" He grinned at her. "That's what I call good old-fashioned service."

"The catch is that you and Beth have to promise to come back soon. Maybe we can do something all together? It's pretty dull around here. I mean, the money's good and it's fun working with Dad—but after work, there's not much to do."

"Sure!" said Tom.

"How about a mousse drop for you two?" Monica asked Beth and Grandad, offering them the candy on a small tray.

Beth grinned. "Thanks! I didn't have any breakfast."

"I'm afraid my doctor has outlawed chocolates—too much caffeine," said Grandad. "But they certainly look delicious."

"How about this, then? This is on the house." Monica handed Grandad a small bag with a fragrant doughnut inside. "Fresh from the fryer. Whole wheat and honey—just what the doctor ordered."

"You know how to do business," Grandad laughed, accepting the bag. "You Bernard Clements's girl?"

"That's right." She looked at him with new interest. "Do you know him?"

"He was my daughter's high school boyfriend—almost twenty years ago." Grandad hesitated for a moment, then peered up into Monica's face. "Maybe you can give your dad a message? Tell him that Hanny Lynn is back in town for a while. Hannah Savage—that was her name then. He'll remember her."

"Sure, I'll tell him," agreed Monica with a smile that included Beth and Tom. Then they said good-bye, promising to get together again soon, and Beth and Tom wheeled Grandad out of the cool store back into the heat of the morning. Beth untied Romps and fed him a mousse drop.

Tom pushed the chair and Beth walked next to him. He nudged her, looking pointedly down at Grandad. Interview time.

"So what was that about Monica's dad and our mom?" Beth asked in what she hoped was a casual tone.

"Nice boy," said Grandad. He sounded tired now, as if the brief outing had lasted too long. Tom noticed this and started pushing the chair faster, trying to avoid the bumps in the sidewalk.

"How long did they date?" pressed Beth.

"Don't remember. Let's see—she was in high school, of course. Seventeen, probably. I never let either of my girls date boys until they'd turned sixteen. Probably sounds strict to you." He paused. "But I was strict. With girls then you had to be." Now he sighed heavily. "Not that it mattered in the end, the way things turned out."

Beth and Tom looked at each other. Then Tom pressed for details. "So Mom was dating Bernard about the time she met that lodger guy?"

Grandad craned his head to look back at Tom and Beth. "So you got Hanny to tell you about Clifton Becker?" he asked in surprise. "What did she say?"

Beth spoke softly. "She said he was wonderful and that she was in love with him."

Grandad snorted. "Did she mention, perhaps, that he was also Iris's fiancé?"

"Of course," said Tom. "And she told us how jealous Aunt Iris was when she found out that Clifton Becker loved Mom instead."

Grandad was silent for a long time. He lifted his hands from the chair sides in a helpless gesture, then let them drop again. Beth motioned for Tom to stop pushing, and she walked around to the front of Grandad's chair. She knelt in front of him.

"Grandad, Mom told us she had to leave home because everyone thought she had pushed Clifton Becker down the stairs."

"But we know it can't be true!" Tom added

in a staunch voice. He came around to the front of Grandad's chair and crouched next to Beth. "Mom isn't like that!"

In the moment of silence that followed Beth imagined how they would look to a passerby: a tableau in the middle of the sidewalk on a hot summer's day. An old man in his wheelchair with his two grandchildren kneeling before him as if for a benediction. Who would guess they were talking about murder?

When Grandad finally spoke, his voice was more than tired—it was shaking. "Knew this would come up again sooner or later. Wanted more than anything for Hanny Lynn to come home again—but I knew this would come up. I never wanted to believe she would do something like that—never. Not my Hanny Lynn."

"Oh, thank you!" Beth stared up into Grandad's eyes; her own suddenly tear-filled ones shone with the relief she felt. "Oh, Grandad, you believe she's innocent! You know she didn't do it!"

His weary voice was gentle, and he closed his eyes, one hand reaching out to touch Beth's hair. "Beth, girl, I don't know anything for sure. But I never could believe it of her. Iris swears she saw Hanny Lynn push him—and Hanny Lynn swears she didn't, says that Iris had more reason . . . . And who knows? Your grandmother believes what Iris says, though it has nearly killed her all these years. Sometimes I wonder if that's the main reason I believe Hanny Lynn. Just to keep a balance in the family."

"That *can't* be why!" objected Tom. "You must know Mom is innocent! Grandmother didn't see Mom push Clifton, did she? She believes Aunt Iris without any real proof at all!"

"Maybe so, maybe so, my boy. Your grandmother has always championed Iris—I often wonder if Iris would have had a happier life if she hadn't been so coddled. Hanny Lynn was born, you know, the same year Iris had polio. I think all the attention Hanny deserved as a new baby went to Iris instead, and poor little Hanny Lynn never got her fair share. Not from her mother, anyway. I guess I've tried to make up for that in my own way, favoring Hanny over Iris at times. . . ." He sighed and opened his eyes. "Ah, but who really knows why we do what we do? Our family has always been divided. Lots of families have little problems like that. But the business with Clifton Becker cracked us right smack down the middle—never mind it all happened twenty years ago."

Beth took one of his thin, age-spotted hands in hers. "But, Grandad, maybe the crack can be fixed up? Sort of soldered back together?"

He shook his head and withdrew his hand. "It's not like a stained-glass window, girl. Things have gone on like this for too long. You two kids shouldn't be worrying about it. It has nothing to do with you—and there's nothing you can fix by stirring things up."

"But she's our mother," said Tom in a low voice. And Beth found herself nodding.

"We're family—all of us," she said, surprising herself. "And it's hard to live in a house so full of tension. Even for a summer."

Grandad rubbed his eyes, suddenly querulous. "I'm tired. It's too hot out here."

Beth and Tom rose to their feet without another word. Tom resumed pushing the chair, and no one spoke as they continued along the route home, bumping gently up and down curbs. But as they turned the corner onto Spring Street, Grandad's rumbling broke the silence.

"Let's just get it straight, for the record. I didn't see Iris push Clifton. And I didn't see Hanny Lynn do it, either. But it's Iris who has the violent streak in her. We didn't see it much when she was young—only sometimes in her paintings. She didn't drink then, but you've seen her now. And when she gets going, I wouldn't be surprised to find her standing over my bed with a knife in her hand. Would she have had it in her to push the man she loved—if she felt he'd betrayed her? Maybe so. Maybe so."

They had reached the house. Aunt Iris poked her head out the porch door as they came up the driveway. She held the door open for them as Beth guided Grandad up the steps and Tom carried the wheelchair.

"Did you enjoy your walk?" she asked brightly into their silence.

Hannah drove Beth to the glass shop to buy more glass later that week. On the drive, she asked two or three times if Beth was all right—she'd noticed how little Beth was eating. But, as on the night she'd gone to the movies with Monica, Beth felt almost entirely recovered—renewed—once she was out of the house. "I'm fine," she'd told her mother.

But as the days went on, working down in the basement was the only thing keeping Beth sane. The window was going to be big—it had to be if Beth were to etch in any of the details from the original painting. She had sketched the painting into the version she would use for her window pattern, then began tracing the pattern shapes onto the pieces of glass and numbering them with a felt-tipped marker. She ran her glass cutter lightly along the lines and broke the different shapes free with her rubber-tipped pliers. Then she set up the grinder and donned her goggles. She had to smooth the edges of each piece, one by one, before arranging them like puzzle pieces on the paper pattern.

There were four islands stabbing up through a stormy sea, under a heaven dotted with rockets and stars. Beth wished she knew what was in Aunt Iris's head when she came up with this painting. But of course she wouldn't ask her. Her aunt was paranoid enough already; she would be furious if she knew that Beth had snooped among her canvases.

The other day Beth had been out in the backyard with Romps when Aunt Iris came out to empty the kitchen trash into the big garbage bin behind the garage. A woman from the house next door walked over to the garden fence separating the two houses and said hello. She was young, with faded blonde hair and a friendly face. "The flowers are lovely this summer, aren't they? But the heat! It's just awful!"

Aunt Iris hadn't answered. She'd kept her eyes down and hurried back to the house, clutching the kitchen trash bin. Beth had smiled at the neighbor woman, embarrassed, and tried to cover for her aunt's odd behavior. "We're visiting from Northern California. I never knew the true meaning of the word 'muggy' before!" Then she followed her aunt into the house.

Thinking about Aunt Iris was detrimental to her work, thought Beth, as she moved the shapes of glass around. She had pressed too hard and broken a point off one of the star shapes. Now she would need to cut another.

She ran her glass cutter firmly over a new pane of yellow glass, using her pliers to break the piece along the lines she had traced. When the triangles were ground smooth, she assembled a star, and she fitted it into her puzzle, glancing over at the Notfilc painting, which she kept propped against the back wall. As usual, the brilliant warmth of the oil painting cheered her. She couldn't think of anyone she'd less want to be than Aunt Iris, who had had an amazing talent and just let it get lost. But maybe there was something to her aunt's warped psychology, after all: You feel guilty, so you want to punish yourself. You stop doing what you love to do, what you're best at doing. Right?

Still no letter from Ray. Beth sat out on the swing again, her pad of scented paper on her lap. How long had it been? A new sadness weighted her shoulders as she realized he seemed much farther away than the three thousand miles that physically separated them.

She sucked on the end of her pen a moment, picturing his hair, his smile, the turn of his wrists as he worked. Then she began to write.

Dear Ray,

Hi! How's life in cool, temperate California? Remind me never to move to this oven of a state. The heat is totally awful. You wouldn't believe it!

Things are still weird here, family-wise, but at least I've met someone and gone out to a movie. Are you jealous? Don't worry—it's a girl named Monica! She's as sweet as the candy shop where she works—and Tom seems to be head-over-heels already! I hope I see her often. It's great getting out of the house.

I'm still waiting to hear from the guy I'm *head-over-heels about. Please write soon, my darling.*

Love,
Beth

When she finished writing, she read over the bright, breezy letter, frowning. It said nothing about what was really going on, nothing about how she really felt; and she knew it. But maybe the light approach would keep him interested. Maybe he'd answer this time.

When the phone rang after breakfast the following morning, Beth rushed to answer. Though she hoped it would be Ray, she knew by now it was more likely to be Monica. The voice in her ear, however, introduced its owner as Bernard Clements, and he was asking for Hannah. Beth hung around the phone while her mother spoke to him, voice excited, tense face momentarily at ease. When Hannah finally hung up, she turned to Beth.

"Nosy!"

"I thought it was going to be Monica. What did he want?"

"To see me again. To meet all of us, actually—and to take us into Philly today for a tour of the historic district." Hannah's eyes were happy. "God, it's been such a long time! I haven't seen him since I was seventeen. We dated for a while, but then . . ." Her voice trailed off, but Beth could fill in the missing half of the sentence.

"But then you fell in love with Clifton Becker, right?"

"And to think he has a daughter your age! I can't believe it." Her laugh sounded young. "So, do you want to come with us? He's invited everyone."

"Of course I'm coming," said Beth. Any reason to leave the house was a ray of sunlight in the dark, grim summer. She went upstairs to put on a pale green sundress and was ready in twenty minutes, complete with camera and guidebook.

Grandad certainly couldn't make the trip into Philadelphia, and Grandmother announced she would stay home with him and Romps. "You'd have to get a wheelchair for me, too, after twenty minutes in this heat," she said. "Besides, this is my baking day."

Hannah was in such a buoyant mood, she even asked her sister to come along. Beth and Tom were relieved when Aunt Iris shook her head and snapped, "Forget it, Hanny Lynn. Definitely not! You know how it is for me."

Beth didn't know at all how it was for her aunt, but decided she didn't really want to know. As Beth, Tom, and Hannah waited for Bernard and Monica to arrive, Aunt Iris passed them to climb the stairs awkwardly, carrying a bottle of beer. Beth grimaced and whispered to Tom. "Beer for breakfast!"

"She'll be drunk before we get into town," he predicted. "What did that Clifton Becker ever see in her in the first place? No wonder he liked Mom better!"

"Sometimes I can't help feeling sorry for her," whispered Beth, following him out to the porch. "You should get her to show you the photo she has of when she was engaged to Clifton. She was gorgeous. You'd never recognize her."

"Hmm," was all he said, and then the Clementses' car pulled into the driveway. Tom ran down the porch steps to say hello, and Beth was just about to follow when Aunt Iris's hoarse voice through the screen door called her back.

"Elisabeth?" Aunt Iris stood inside on the stairway.

"What is it?" Beth opened the screen door and looked in.

"Have a good time." Aunt Iris leaned over the banister, trying to peer out onto the porch without being seen herself. Her gray hair lay in damp wisps against her forehead, and her lips looked chapped. Beth longed suddenly to rub some cream onto them, to comb that straggly hair back into a neat wave. She felt filled with pity for the figure that was her strange aunt and yet was, unbelievably, the same person who had painted the vibrant Notfilc picture.

Impulsively, she smiled up at her aunt. "Wouldn't you like to come with us after all? I'm sure there's room. I'd really like you to come." Maybe Aunt Iris would improve if they could get her away from the scene of her tragedy. Maybe she'd be totally different away from the house.

But Aunt Iris drew back in alarm, her thin fingers tight on the banister. "Oh, no!"

"We can walk around together," pressed Beth. "I've never seen the Liberty Bell, Aunt Iris! How long has it been since you've seen it?"

Aunt Iris began backing up the stairs, her eyes glittering. Could it be tears that made her eyes so bright?

"Please come," Beth urged one more time.

"I'll stay with you the whole time. We'll be together!"

Then the tears Beth thought she'd seen in Aunt Iris's eyes were gone, and so was the quavering voice. "No!" shouted Aunt Iris. "I wouldn't be caught dead out in public with that snake of a sister of mine. I warn you, Elisabeth—watch out for your mother. You can't be too careful, you know!"

Why had she ever thought for a minute that Aunt Iris wanted to come with them? Why had she imagined she'd seen pain in her eyes—when clearly there was only malice? Beth pressed her lips together and turned to go.

"You watch out! Just watch out that Hanny Lynn doesn't—doesn't *do* anything. You know. Shove Bernard under a bus or something."

Beth drew in a shocked breath, then blew it out angrily. "Thanks for the warning." She turned on her heel and bolted out onto the porch, then down into the driveway. It was all just fine to feel sorry for Aunt Iris with her limp and her ruined wedding plans and her lost talent, but really. Beth's face was flushed as she joined her mother, Tom, and Monica and met Bernard Clements.

Monica's father shook her hand vigorously, pumping it many times before letting go. "I'm Bernard," he said. "Wonderful to meet you! Ready to go?" He opened the car door. "I call the front seat with beautiful Hanny Lynn! You infants get the backseat. Life's tough, huh? But Hanny and I have a lot of catching up to do."

Bernard was tall and slender, with dark, unruly hair tumbling over his forehead into his eyes. Beth watched the way he walked to the driver's side of the car, liking the loose-limbed gait, the almost clownlike shamble. She looked at Monica, who raised her eyebrows as if to say: "Parents! What can you do?" And Beth was surprised, because she thought Bernard seemed nicely funny, not embarrassingly funny.

"Where's your mother? Didn't she want to come?" Tom asked Monica.

"My parents are divorced. I was born here in Philly, but I grew up with my mom in Ohio—then I moved back here last semester to live with my dad." She fingered an ornate, dangly earring. "What about you guys? Are your parents divorced, too?"

Tom climbed over Beth into the backseat, wedging her firmly against the window as he settled himself between her and Monica. "No. Our dad died in a car crash when we were really little."

"Oh, that's a shame," Monica said. After a moment she continued. "I hardly know anyone who has a simple, straightforward, old-fashioned nuclear family anymore. You know—mom and dad and two kids. House in the suburbs, two cars, a dog. Dad works, mom stays home with the kids and makes apple pies. Everybody happy."

Beth shrugged. "I wonder if that kind of family ever really existed. Everybody happy, I mean. Sometimes things look happy on the outside, but they're a mess inside." Then she wondered exactly what she meant by that.

Up in the front seat Hannah and Bernard had their heads together, laughing about something, as the car sped onto the highway. Bernard drove fast, too fast, Beth thought. But at least he didn't have a Lite Rock tape playing. They barreled along to Mozart. They whizzed across the Schuylkill River and soon turned off at the exit marked "Historic District."

"Look to your left as we go by this little street," Bernard called back to them. "This is

Elfreth's Alley—a preserved colonial street. You should see it at Christmas, when the whole lane is decorated and the people give house tours of their eighteenth-century homes. Fantastic!"

Monica, Beth noted, had to lean onto Tom's lap in order to see out the window. She noted, too, that Tom did not mind in the least.

They parked in a garage near the visitors' center and walked the short distance to that modern building. Inside they were given maps of the walking tours and directed up the long ramp that led to the theater. There they sat down on hard benches just as the lights were dimming for the documentary film *Independence!*

Beth tried to concentrate. Thomas Jefferson was writing the Declaration of Independence. On Beth's left side, Tom was leaning against Monica's arm. Beth reached out and pinched him. "Cut it out, Valentino," she hissed. "Remember: computers are your first love."

"What's a computer?" he whispered back.

On Beth's right side, Hannah was leaning against Bernard Clements, and he had his arm around her shoulders. Was anyone watching the educational film? It seemed she sat alone, a single island in a sea of suddenly amorous couples. A wave of longing for Ray splashed up on her shores.

After the film Beth trailed behind the two couples as they walked out into the heat and crossed the street to Carpenters' Hall, site of the first meeting of Congress. Bernard and Hannah climbed the steps and entered Carpenters' Hall without a backward glance. Monica laughed. "What do you make of this new development?"

"Which development?" Beth held the door open for the other two.

Tom grabbed her arm. "Holmes! Aren't your eyes open? This is high drama!"

"I'm surrounded by high drama," said Beth. "But if you're talking about Mom and Bernard, I've noticed. Mom was nearly on Bernard's lap during that patriotic film."

"What film?" asked Tom innocently.

" 'That among these rights are Life, Liberty, and the Pursuit of Happiness,' " intoned Monica. "I think that's Pursuit of Happiness we're witnessing."

Tom laughed. "Part of the American experience—history in the making. Right before our very eyes!"

It was nice that Tom could laugh; he had

been so miserable lately. Beth just wished she could feel like laughing, too. She walked on into the high-ceilinged room. She followed her mother and Bernard, peering into the glass-topped display tables of colonial memorabilia and documents.

Then Tom was at her shoulder again. "Holmes, here's our next step—plain as day," he whispered. "We ask Bernard about Mom when they were dating and about what happened with Clifton."

"I think Bernard is busy just now, Mac."

"I didn't mean now. We'll talk to him some other time when we can get him alone."

"Yeah, but he's not going to know whether she pushed Clifton Becker or not. He wasn't there that night."

"But he knew Mom really well! He'll know she couldn't have done it."

"He won't have any proof. But I suppose he'll be a good character witness."

"You make it sound as if this is a trial," he objected.

Beth glanced at Hannah and Bernard. They were standing at the door talking, totally engrossed in each other. Bernard had a big silly grin on his face as he bent attentively over

Hannah, who was laughing up at him. Beth couldn't remember seeing her mother look so carefree and, yes, young in ages. "Okay, not a trial. An inquiry," she said.

They moved on to the Liberty Bell in its pavilion, then stopped for lunch. Beth feasted on a mammoth cheesesteak sandwich dripping with juice, a salad, and a slice of cherry cheesecake for dessert and found all thought of Spring Street receding as she chatted with Tom and Monica. Hannah and Bernard giggled together at the next table over a shared sandwich, then hurried off to wander around the little shops in the Bourse, arms linked.

"Amazing, aren't they," said Beth, peering down over the balcony by their table. She had an aerial view of Bernard's and Hannah's heads, bent close. "Maybe they'll fall in love and get married, and Mom will give up her plan for college."

"Or maybe they'll get married and she'll go to college anyway," said Tom.

"Or maybe—no, *probably* Dad will take her to see our apartment and she'll be so turned off by the mess that she'll run all the way back to California and never see him again," said Monica. "Even more than a wife, Dad needs a housekeeper. Someone trained to deal with chaos."

Beth was intrigued. Her room was usually a mess, so she could sympathize with Bernard. "I identify with chaos!"

Monica raised her eyebrows. "I doubt you know the meaning of the word, Beth. Wait till you see our apartment!"

Beth wanted to hear more, but Tom suggested they buy a few more slices of cheesecake and go find Hannah and Bernard. He wanted to move on to see the site of Benjamin Franklin's house.

While they were walking along, Bernard ran to the corner of Market Street and bought each of them a huge, thick hot pretzel slathered with mustard. "Eat up," he said, handing one to Beth. "It's a Philly specialty. You can't come here and not eat one. Against the law." His big laugh boomed out, and Beth found herself grinning back at him. He was a nice man, even though he did embarrass his daughter and live in chaos. Hannah was glowing today, and the tense set to her shoulders had disappeared. Had they been this crazy about each other twenty years ago? Beth watched Hannah lean close and lick some mustard from Bernard's pretzel. He kissed her nose.

Beth walked on ahead of them. She'd never seen her mother so relaxed with a man in all the years she'd been dating. Relaxed and carefree—although it seemed to Beth the air around them was charged the way she sometimes felt the atmosphere around her and Ray was charged. Ray scoffed at her when she started talking about atmosphere, but still . . . It was there. Call it chemistry. And chemistry was working in a big way with Hannah and Bernard today. Had the air tingled around them this way twenty years ago? If so, how had Hannah ever been able to break up their relationship? Beth glanced back and saw Bernard's arm close around her mother as they walked. She was confiding something behind her hand, her eyes alight with the mischief Beth knew meant a major punchline was on the way.

That Clifton Becker must have been something *really* special, that was all she could say.

July

❦❦❦❦❦❦❦ Clifton had the porch to himself that Saturday afternoon in mid-July. Iris and Mrs. Savage (who now urged him to call her "Mama") had taken the trolley into the city to order the flowers for the church. Then they were going to meet Iris's old high school friend, Louise, and take her to lunch before going to Bensen's Bridal Boutique for another fitting of the bridal gown. Clifton forgot why this was necessary—something to do with having the side seams taken in or let out. It didn't matter; it was just one more of the little details women liked to fuss over when they planned a wedding. He was happy to sit back and let them go to it; he wanted only to be married to lovely Iris, living comfortably—first in a little apartment near the Main Line, then eventually out in the country somewhere. All the planning that went into *becoming* married he would just as soon stay out of.

There had been some sort of stink this morning just before Mrs. Savage and Iris left. Mr. Savage had taken the car out of town on business a few days before, and so Mrs. Savage and Iris had to walk the mile to the trolley. Hanny Lynn was supposed to go with them because she was another of the bridesmaids. But Hanny had vanished. Iris and her mother were furious, and they waited until they could not possibly wait another minute and still catch the trolley. So they set off up the street, calling every few steps for Hanny Lynn, as if they expected she might materialize out of thin air or pop out from hiding in the bushes. They turned the corner, their calls fading, and Clifton settled himself contentedly on the glider swing with a collection of Isaac Asimov stories.

He read science fiction avidly whenever he had a break at work, or on weekends, as on this Saturday. He thought a writer ought to keep up with what was being written in the genre. Then he would try very hard, while typing late at night, to find new solutions to old dilemmas and new twists for tried-and-true plots. Clifton had no doubt that he was a good writer—in fact, he wouldn't be surprised if one day he were classified as a *great* writer, right up there alongside Isaac Asimov himself. But the going was often slow and, lately, with all the planning and upheaval of the coming wedding, he found himself simply too tired at night to do anything more than tumble into the high old bed in his bedroom.

After two hours of nonstop reading he closed the book. He leaned back on the cushion and closed his eyes, kicking the glider into motion, tempted to head up to his room for a nap before Iris returned. The family used to refer to his room as "the Lodge," since they had rented it out often to lodgers in the past. Now that he had been with them nearly a year, the room had come to be known as "Clifton's Lodge." And he approved the name, liked having a room called for him. He imagined how, when he was famous, tour groups would make regular stops at the Savage home on Spring Street. Mrs. Savage—or perhaps there would be a guide from the Clifton Becker Fan Club and Guild specially hired for the purpose—would show the people up the narrow, uncarpeted stairs, warning everyone to be careful not to slip on the polished wood. Up onto the tiny landing, then up to the hallway and straight ahead into "Clifton's Lodge." There would be a brass nameplate on the door. "Yes," she would tell them. "It's hard to believe that this humble bedroom in our own little home is where young Clifton Becker wrote his first masterpiece." The crowd would murmur, awed beyond all human control.

This pleasant daydream was interrupted by voices on the sidewalk in front of the house. The porch was screened by the tall, heavily scented boxwood hedge, and so Clifton could not see the speakers, but he easily recognized the voices of Hanny Lynn and the boy she dated. What was that kid's name? His uncle ran Clements's Candy, the store where Iris bought her favorite red licorice sticks. Hanny and the boy went to school together. Had gone, he corrected himself idly. Hadn't the boy just graduated, with Hanny still having another year to go? Something like that.

From the sound of things, they were arguing. Clifton sat up straight in order to hear better and stopped the sway of the swing with his toe. Not that he condoned eavesdropping—but good dialogue might inspire him in his work. Here he was, after all, minding his own business, and there they were, deep into their fight. What should he do? Call to them so they knew he was here—and interrupt? Go quietly into the house so they would never know he had been there at all? Clifton remained in the glider, leaning forward slightly with his feet firmly on the floor to prevent the creak of the glider from giving his presence away. He held his book of short stories open on his lap.

The boy's voice rose. The angrier he got, the more his voice threatened to squeak. Clifton smiled, remembering his own struggles years before with a voice that hadn't deepened right on schedule. It had been a source of embarrassment to him, as it no doubt was to Hanny Lynn's boyfriend. He recognized the boy's cough—it had been his own way of trying to tame the unmanageable squeak in the middle of conversation. "Hanny Lynn! I don't see how you can do this to me!" (Cough, cough.) "To us! We love each other. You know we do!"

Her voice was lower, perfectly clear and firm. "Look, I'm sorry. I know we like each other a lot. I *do* care about you, Bernie! But—not enough, I guess."

"Not enough for *what,* damn it? It's not like I'm asking you to marry me or anything!" (Cough.)

Hanny Lynn sounded exasperated. "Oh, it's no use. I knew you wouldn't understand. We're just not right for each other, Bernie. I need someone—older."

"I *am* older than you!"

"More mature, I mean. You're too—well, young."

"Give me a break!" The squeak was out and there was no calling it back. Bernie didn't even bother to cough but rushed on in desperation. "Come on, you sound like something out of one of those stupid romance books you've always got your nose in. How old do you want me to be, for God's sake? You're only just seventeen yourself!"

There was that exasperated sigh again. "Oh, Bernie. Let's just forget it. I mean what I'm saying. You're a very nice—boy. You're like a little boy! But I need a man." She paused. Clifton could imagine Bernie struggling to control his rage at being called a little boy. Hanny's voice continued softly, but not so softly Clifton couldn't hear: "I need a man—and, in fact, I have one. I think you should know."

They were both silent now. Clifton strained his ears. Then Bernie coughed and cleared his throat, and his voice was deep again. "So you've been seeing someone else?"

"That's right."

Clifton raised an eyebrow. But, then, Hanny Lynn was not known for sticking to the truth.

"For how long?"

"Just about a year."

"A *year!*" The squeak was back. "I can't believe you, Hanny Lynn! Who is it? Who the hell is he?"

"Never mind! I'm sorry, Bernie, because we've been friends since kindergarten, and I hope we can still be friends. But that's all we can ever be." She took a deep breath. "I'll never forget you."

"Spare me the teen romance theatrics." He spat the words.

"Oh, Bernie—"

But he was walking away, and Clifton could see him now as he passed the house and continued down the street. Bernie had a funny sort of walk, a shambling gait that, especially now that he was agitated, seemed almost clownlike—or like the awkward lope of a young giraffe. Clifton felt a fleeting spasm of sympathy for the tall, dark-haired boy. It hadn't been so long ago that he himself had been dumped by a girl. Thank God it hadn't taken him too long to recover from Abby. Thank God he had found his wonderful Iris! Bernie would find someone else, too. That's the way these things worked.

Hanny Lynn ran lightly up the steps onto the porch, then stopped short, staring at him. "Oh!"

"Oh, there you are," Clifton said, one hand raised to turn the page of his book. She looked flustered, fingering the strap of her summer camisole. She reminded him of a skittish colt, long-legged in her hot pants and sandals, her mane of light brown hair hanging down her back. He tried to look casual. "Your mother and Iris were really mad when you didn't show up in time to go with them."

"Oh—" She sank into a wicker rocking chair near his glider. "I forgot all about that. I had—something important to do."

"Good. I hope they think it was important, too, when you make your excuses." He smiled at her, distantly, he hoped, and buried his nose in his book. She sat there a while, silent, staring at the bushes. Then she reached over and tapped him on the knee.

Her voice rang with suspicion. "How long have you been out here?"

Should he tell her? Oh, why not? Maybe she needed a shoulder to cry on. And after all, soon he would be her brother-in-law. It wouldn't hurt to have a little talk with her, maybe make her feel better. It wasn't exactly that he had ignored her until now, but he really couldn't help lavishing all his attention on Iris. Understandable, of course, but maybe it was time now to become more brotherly. (Was now the time to become more sonlike as well? Maybe he really *would* have to go on that camping trip with Mr. Savage.) Being part of a family meant taking on some responsibility. This he firmly believed. And he was ready for it.

He smiled at Hanny Lynn. "I've been out here long enough to hear you giving some young man the brush-off. Poor kid! I know how he felt."

"You—you do?"

"But don't worry too much. He'll get over it. I did."

"I hope it doesn't take him too long," she said, biting her lip, for a second looking vulnerable. "I really do like him. We've known each other practically forever! But I had to break up—we're just not right for each other."

Clifton nodded. "That's a perfectly good reason in my book. There's no virtue in wasting your time with someone who isn't right for you."

She glanced at him from beneath long lashes. "Do you really think so? I mean, well—I need to know you think I did the right thing. It's important to me."

He was flattered his opinion mattered to her. "Sure you did the right thing, if you'd rather spend your time with someone else." He smiled. "You just have to follow your heart." Didn't he sound big-brotherly? That was pretty good advice for anyone.

"I like Bernie a lot," she said softly. "But following your heart is never easy. Still, in the end, I know it is what I must do." She swept her smooth brown hair off her shoulders and tilted her head, regarding him steadily. Something about the way she looked at him made him uncomfortably aware that something else was going to happen.

And he was right. The next moment she flung herself out of her chair and onto the glider next to him. She wrapped her arms around his neck and pressed her head against his shoulder. "Oh, Clifton, darling Clifton! I'm so glad you think I did the right thing! Next to you, Bernie is a child. He's much too young for me. You're—oh, you're mature, you're strong, you know about love. You know what it's like to love someone hopelessly—and then find out that there's a chance after all!"

My God! Clifton pressed himself back into the cushions. What was she talking about? A chance for what?

Hanny Lynn shook her hair back and gazed up at him from his lap. "My love, my darling. I've followed my heart, just as you told me to. I've taken the first step in breaking off that silly, childish relationship with Bernie Clements, and now it's up to you. If we're going to be together, well, you know what you have to do."

"What—?" He couldn't think. What in the world was going on?

"Call off the wedding!"

"Hanny!" Clifton shoved her off his lap and she slid to the floor. He stood up. "Hold on just a minute here!" His mind was whirling. She was saying that *he* was the older man she loved? That *he* was the reason she'd broken up with Bernie? But that was utterly absurd! She was just a girl—just Iris's kid sister.

"Wait a minute, Hanny Lynn. Hold on." He tried to raise her to her feet, but she stayed on the floor, her hands over her eyes. He knelt on the porch floor at her side and tentatively touched her thin, bare shoulder.

"This is all news to me, Hanny. I like you a lot. I think you're a nice girl. Young woman. But—"

"You don't know how I've longed for you," she whispered. "The first minute I saw you, I fell in love. You're like a god or something—I love everything about you. Your curly hair. Your body—"

"Hanny Lynn!"

"Every time I see you with Iris, well, my heart shrivels up just a little bit more. I've longed for you to touch me. And now, at last . . ." Her voice trailed off.

"Now at last what?" he asked wildly. "What do you mean?" He tried again to raise her to her feet, and this time she let him. They stood facing each other in front of the glider, her head tipped up. He was shaken by the pure light of desire he saw in her eyes. The air around them was fragrant with jasmine. Did Hanny and Iris share the same shampoo? Was it the scent of the jasmine growing at the side of the house? Or had Hanny Lynn been dipping into the perfume he'd given Iris for Christmas? He wouldn't put anything past her. He shook his head as she moved closer and put her arms around him.

"*You* know," she said. "You know you know. I've thanked God every time I've seen you look at me over Iris's shoulder when you held her, and she never knew your heart was with me. I thank God for every wink you've given me—every time you've let me know there is something for me to live for. That there is a chance. That there's hope!"

"Oh, Hanny Lynn, no. You've got it wrong." This was amazing. But he had to let her down gently. "I really do love Iris, and I want to marry her."

She smiled up at him, her mouth gentle. "I know you feel sorry for her—we all do. She's been coddled all her life because of her limp. It's natural you would want to take care of her. But there's no reason to go through with this, Clifton. You can't marry someone just because you feel sorry for her. You need to marry for love!"

How could she be serious? He didn't feel sorry for Iris at all. She was a strong, brave, talented woman, and he wanted more than anything to spend his life with her. Hanny's theatrics must be some bizarre practical joke she'd cooked up for a lark. Bernie was right: she had been reading too many teen romances. But maybe Bernie was in on it, too! He remembered now he'd once heard that Bernie was a great one for practical jokes. How to respond to something so ludicrous? That he didn't love Iris—that he loved, instead, this long-legged, stringy-haired little girl not even out of high school? Absurd! His mind told him how ridiculous the whole situation was even as his arms went up to hold her against him as she clung, face upturned, ready to be kissed.

How long they stood there he couldn't have said, but after a while he sat down on the glider again and it seemed somehow natural—or if not natural, then inevitable—that she would cuddle beside him, curled up with her head on his lap. He stroked her hair, not saying a word. She looked up at him, wide eyes brimming with joy.

Then a lovely, bright, flutelike voice, his own Iris's voice, reached his ears. She and her mother were walking up to the house, screened by the cover of bushes. In a split second Clifton thrust Hanny Lynn off his lap and leaped to his feet. Even before Iris and Mrs. Savage reached the top of the porch steps, Clifton was at Iris's side, helping her up the steps, reaching for her packages, holding her close. He felt his heart racing as if he had just narrowly escaped from some very great danger.

And what of Hanny Lynn? He darted a glance over at her where she stood, cornered now by her irate mother, who demanded to know why she hadn't been ready to leave when they were. Her look was contrite, but he knew that was purely for her mother's benefit. As he ushered Iris ahead of him through the screen door into the dimness of the house, he looked back once. And he met Hanny Lynn's wide blue gaze and her sexy, blatant wink.

4

*ear Ray,*

I've been feeling pretty low. The tension around here is so draining—worse, even, than the horrible heat. We spent a day in the historic district, which was a relief, but now I keep thinking about history—not about America's history, but how families are connected to each other by bloodlines that stretch backward in a chain through time. How weird it is that we're all links on a long chain, like it or not. And I don't *like it. This family of mine seems so complicated. It makes me wish for the legendary happy family—you know, parents who love each other, two kids, a dog, a house in the country with a picket fence. . . .*

Beth stopped writing. This wasn't the right tone. Ray wouldn't want to hear about her family problems. "You've got to go with the flow, sweetheart," she could imagine him saying. He'd drape one muscled arm across her shoulders in one of those spine-tingling hugs and lead her back to the worktable. He'd put a glass cutter in her hand. "You're an artist," he'd say, as he'd often said before. "And you're good. But you've got to concentrate. Don't let anybody get you down. Keep smiling."

But Beth didn't feel like smiling. She dropped her pad of notepaper, then kicked off against the grass and sent the old swing soaring. She pumped hard, wishing she could just fly off the swing and over the house, away from everyone inside. She'd fly back to California, find a house with a white picket fence and a perfect family, and move in with them.

It was funny to think she more or less had had that sort of family when her father was alive, even though the house they lived in was shared. Her father and mother looked happy in the pictures she had of them. There was a great photo of them standing in the chicken pen with their arms around each other. Her father carried Tom in a baby pack, and Beth was in the foreground, about two years old and a bit out of focus, laughing and throwing chicken feed. She liked that picture. They all looked so nice. The fence around the chicken pen was regular wire mesh, but if it were white picket, the legend would be almost perfect. Two kids. A house not really in the country—but when the mist came down on the Berkeley hills, civilization seemed miles away. Only the dog was missing in that picture. They didn't have Romps then.

Beth pumped the swing higher. Romps lay in the flower bed in the side yard, sleeping. He was old now, and Tom had changed from a cute thing in the baby pack into a dewy-eyed thing in love with Monica. Old Computer Brain—Beth still couldn't believe it. It was not that she had anything against love. But it did seem remarkably inappropriate that both her mother and her brother seemed to be falling in love while living with a family almost *destroyed* by love. Ray would say it was ironic. Beth let the swing slow, then scuffed her bare feet in the grass to stop. Damn that Clifton Becker! Everything was his fault.

When Beth and Tom entered the candy store later that afternoon, they found Monica struggling with an armload of boxes. "Hi!" she greeted them, depositing her armload onto the glass-topped counter. "Wouldn't want to buy a couple pounds of Gummi Bears, by any chance? Fresh shipment."

"How about one of your homemade doughnuts?" asked Tom. "I'm only going to buy the things touched by your own hands."

Beth rolled her eyes, but Monica laughed. "Oh, good. Then maybe you'll buy a couple of my pots, too."

"You sell pot?" he bantered. "Sorry, lady, but I make it a point not to dabble in drugs. I don't want my grandmother to think she's right about California boys!"

"I'm a potter," she told him, laughing. "I'll show you sometime. But they don't come cheap."

"Nothing about you is cheap," Tom said in his deepest voice. "I find you extremely valuable."

"You're a potter?" Beth asked before Tom could burst into a love song or something. "I'd love to see what you do."

"Beth's an artist, too," said Tom. "But the family genius stops there. I did, however, win a coloring contest at Pizza Plaza when I was eight."

"True talent!" Monica grinned at him, then ripped open the boxes of Gummi Bears and dumped the loose candy into the big bin. She dropped a metal scoop in on top of them and shut the lid. "What kind of artist are you?" she asked Beth. "Do you paint?"

"No. I work with stained glass. I'm going to open a shop with my boyfriend when I finish school next year."

"Wow! Can I see your stuff? Maybe we can get together soon and show off for each other!" She handed Beth and Tom each a doughnut. "Here. On the house."

"You're not going to make any money if you keep giving us freebies," Tom chided her.

"My dad would kill me if I charged Hannah Savage's kids one cent!" she said. "He told me last night that as far as he's concerned, the sun rises and sets in your mom's eyes. I wish I had a boyfriend who said things like that to me!"

I have, thought Beth, remembering Ray's thin face and intense gaze as he'd hugged her and said she was the best teenage glass artist he'd ever seen. She waited indulgently as Tom dropped to one knee on the wooden floor and declared with passion that the sun rose and set in Monica's baby browns.

The shop door opened and a pack of little kids rushed in. "The movie starts in three minutes!" one called to Monica. "We need stuff to eat in there! Quick!"

She smiled at Beth and Tom, then shrugged. "Duty calls, I guess. Can we get together later?"

Tom nodded eagerly. "Sure! I'll call you before dinner and we'll set something up."

Beth remained silent, unsure whether he was planning a date or something that would include her.

"We wanted to talk to your dad for a few minutes," Tom told Monica. "Is he home?"

She had turned to the group of little kids but looked back now, curious. "He's upstairs. Looking for the bills he hasn't paid, or something. But why?"

Tom shrugged lightly. "We just wanted to talk to him."

"About Mom," added Beth.

Monica looked at them quizzically. "Want to know whether he'll be able to provide for your mother in the manner to which she's become accustomed?"

Tom glanced at Beth.

"Come on!" a little boy begged Monica. "Now it starts in two minutes!"

Monica shook back her dark hair. "That's what disapproving parents in books always ask the callow youth who comes to court their innocent daughter."

"Don't worry," said Beth. "We're not Mom's parents, and we don't mind at all if she dates your dad! We just want to ask him what Mom was like in high school."

"There's only one more minute!" shrieked a little girl.

Monica shrugged and waved a graceful hand at a door marked "Private" just inside the storeroom. "Through there and up the stairs. But don't blame me if you get lost in the rubble."

At the top of the narrow flight of stairs was a closed door. Tom rapped softly. Bernard's booming voice welcomed them: "Abandon all hope, ye who enter here!" They pushed the door open and stepped into the Clementses' living room.

Beth immediately saw that when Monica had said "chaos" she had not meant mere disarray. Beth stared at the incredible mess before her and thought perhaps this room was the very definition of "chaos."

"Well, hello!" cried Bernard from his seat at

a desk by the window. "Come on in and sit down!"

At first glance Beth thought the curtains were drawn, but then she realized the light was obscured by the piles of unfolded laundry on the bookcases under one large window and by towering stacks of old newspapers on a radiator under the other. Bernard jumped up from his desk. "Just step over everything," he said cheerfully, and Beth and Tom waded toward him, past bundles of mail on low tables, stray socks, a broken alarm clock, a phone off the hook—Beth stared at it a moment before realizing it wasn't even plugged into an outlet.

Two cats twined themselves around and through the room's wreckage. There were lots of things for them to rub up against before they reached Beth's legs: droopy potted palms in wooden tubs, a floor lamp leaning to one side, several boxes of books. When the cats reached Beth, she knelt down to pat their heads and they purred in welcome.

"Great to see you!" Bernard shoved some stray papers off the couch. He didn't seem to care that they fluttered onto the floor. "What a nice reason to take a break. There's nothing worse than paying monthly bills, unless it's doing yearly taxes. You know what good old Ben Franklin said, don't you? 'Nothing is certain in life except death and taxes.' Or something like that."

"We don't want to interrupt," Beth said politely. "We just wanted to ask you a few things about Mom."

"No one I'd rather talk about!" Bernard moved a pile of library books off the couch, sidestepping quickly as the books tumbled onto the floor. "Why don't I get us something cold to drink? Soda? Lemonade? I might even be able to offer you some ice—if there is ice. Monica keeps after me, but I always forget to refill the trays." He grinned cheerfully.

Beth and Tom said they'd have lemonade. They settled back on the couch to wait for him to return. "Mom should see this place," whispered Tom. "She'd never call me a slob again!"

Bernard returned with their drinks and a paper plate of cookies. He set the refreshments in front of them on a box, then pulled a cushion off the couch. He settled himself comfortably on the floor with the cushion at his back, stretched out his long legs, and took a sip of lemonade. "Ahh, this is the life. Now, what can I tell you two about lovely Hanny Lynn?"

Tom and Beth looked at each other. Beth spoke first. "We heard that you and Mom dated in high school. We just wondered—well, you know. What she was like at that age?"

He raised his brows. "Writing her biography, are you?"

"We're just nosy." Tom grinned.

"It's more than that," Beth admitted. "She's never told us much of anything about her past, and now here we are—sort of surrounded by it. We're interested."

"The woman with a past," murmured Bernard. "It's usually best not to ask people about their pasts. Especially women. That's what I've learned." Then he winked at them. "Just a joke! So, seriously, what can I tell you? We dated only about a year—informally. Her parents were pretty strict, so we didn't really go out much. Sat out on her porch a lot. And we were together as much as we could be at school. I graduated a year before her. But we were friends for years before that—since she was in kindergarten. I've always known her. The candy store kid always gets to know everybody, one way or another."

"Were you her first boyfriend?" asked Beth.

Bernard smiled at her. "I think so. Hasn't she told you about the beginning of our romance?" When Beth and Tom shook their heads, he sighed. "Funny, that was. And funny in a different way that she never told you about it. It's one of my favorite stories. I'm sure I've bored Monica with it a dozen times. Picture this: two kids—I was seventeen and she was sixteen. I'd been madly in love with her for a few years and finally asked her during study hall whether she'd go see a movie with me. She looked a bit surprised; I think it was because we'd always been just friends as far as she was concerned. But she hadn't ever been out on a real date, and so she begged her dad and he finally said we could go—this was only after we promised we'd come straight home after the movie. He assumed we'd go to the Waverley. After all, it's right here. But I borrowed my uncle's car—my dad was a salesman and always on the road, so my mom and I lived here over the shop with my dad's brother. Mom helped him run the business, and I helped after school and on weekends. Anyway, I convinced him to let me take his old Chevy, and Hanny and I spun down Penn's Pike doing eighty. Idiotic, of course—what a show-off! I blew a tire after we'd gone only about a mile, down by the doughnut place. And since I didn't want to have to call Uncle Stan, we changed it right there in the parking lot. I was totally inept about such things—still am, actually, though I drive a little slower now."

Not much, thought Beth, but remained silent, smiling at him encouragingly. So far he hadn't told them anything pertinent to Clifton Becker's death, but she thought if they were clever, she and Tom could work his reminiscences around to that time.

Bernard's big laugh boomed out. "So there was poor Hanny Lynn in her lacy, first-date sundress, down there under the car with the spare and the jack, while I stood by and spoke encouragingly. I had no idea how to change a tire! But Hanny Lynn—she was capable. Both her parents were no-nonsense types. You know, firm believers in getting things done, keeping things fixed, knowing how to repair what needed mending." He glanced around his living room. "I'm afraid I've never been one for repair work—not even basic maintenance."

"So Mom fixed the tire," Tom prodded him. "Then what? Did you see the movie?"

"Never made it to the movie. It had already

started. Hanny and I just bought a big bag of doughnuts and drove to the park."

"Did your uncle ever find out about the tire?" asked Beth.

"Eventually—the next time *he* blew a tire. I'd forgotten to replace the spare. And then—man, was I in trouble. But that had nothing to do with Hanny Lynn. Uncle Stan didn't have his flat for about another year—and by then Hanny had—" He broke off.

Aha, thought Beth. "What had she done?" she pressed.

Bernard flexed his big, bony hands. "Ah, she'd ditched me by then. That Hanny Lynn. I never could figure her out."

"What, she just broke up with you and never even said why?"

"Oh, she gave a reason all right, but I didn't buy it. Didn't then and don't now." He looked pensively at the piles of laundry by the windows. "We'd been together about a year. Then suddenly she said she had been seeing someone else, an older man. That was ridiculous, of course. An out-and-out lie. I would have known about it if she'd been dating some other guy. We spent so much time together. When she wasn't out with me, she was at home—her dad saw to that!"

Aha. Didn't he see what he was saying? But Beth didn't want to be the one to break it to Bernard at this late date that there *had,* in fact, been someone else. An older man. And right in the same house with Hanny Lynn all the time.

There was a long pause, then Tom cleared his throat. "So you think she was just making it up?"

"Oh, absolutely. She made it up to spare my feelings. It was all Hanny Lynn could manage to get permission to see *me* as often as she did. She'd never have been allowed out on dates with some older guy." Bernard sighed. "It's just that your mom was a kind-hearted girl. She'd rather leave me feeling jealous than hurt me with the fact that she found me boring, or funny-looking, or obnoxious. I'm sure I was all three. Probably still am." He made an attempt to smile again and said brightly, "But time heals all wounds, right? Didn't Ben Franklin say that? He might have."

Beth finished her lemonade and set the glass on the floor. She wanted to phrase her question with care, didn't want to hurt Bernard any more than Hannah already had. But she needed some details. "Um, did you ever ask Mom, you know, to describe this older man? Had she been seeing him for a long time?"

He shook his head. "Look, the breakup happened very quickly. I'd phoned to ask if she wanted to go for a walk—see, sometimes we'd just walk for hours, talking. She wasn't allowed to entertain at her house much, and we had no room here. She said she was supposed to go shopping with her mother and Iris, or something, but I convinced her I needed her more than they did. So she came and was really quiet the whole time we were walking. I jabbered on about God-knows-what, and then she told me. Let me tell you—it was the shock of my life. In my mind we were already married with three kids." He smiled ruefully. "You two and Monica, I guess!" He ruffled his big hands through his already-mussed hair.

"I didn't give up easily, though! I persisted, made a pest of myself. But whenever I came over, she was always home. She kept refusing to see me, but she was there in the house all right—not out with any old 'Tall, Dark, and Handsome.' She wouldn't come to the door and just told her mother to say she was busy. So eventually—well, even with a head as hard as mine, it sinks in after a while." His voice trailed off.

Beth felt sorry for him; he looked so sad—just like old Romps when she showed him the box of dog treats was empty. She tried to imagine how she'd feel if Ray suddenly got sick of the age difference between them and opted for an older woman. She pushed the thought hastily away. Their case was totally different.

"That's a sad story," she murmured.

"Strange to think it would have been comforting, in the end, if she really had fallen in love with someone else, isn't it?" Bernard smiled again, the sad eyes gone. "As much as he hates it, it's easier for a boy to think he's being ditched for some worldly, mature man than to think his girl just couldn't stand the sight of him anymore. That she'd prefer to stay home alone rather than be with him. But look, enough of all this old stuff. What's it got to do with now? Are you wondering whether I'm going to try to start things up again with your mom? I can tell you right now, the answer is yes!"

"Oh, we don't mind at all," Beth said quickly. But she worried for a second he would be hurt again. Surely the new Hannah would not let a man from the past she'd run away from stand in the way of her plans for college and her new life as a "together" person.

Tom cleared his throat. "I guess we were mostly interested in this older man."

"There was no older man. I told you—it was all in her head. Made up to soften the blow for me, you know? Hanny Lynn was always a sweet one at heart."

Beth felt sorry for him again. "But maybe—" she began. "Maybe there really was somebody! I mean, maybe she loved you but was just sort of *infatuated* with this older guy." Tom shot her a warning glance, but she ignored him. They had to work Clifton Becker's name into this conversation somehow. It was supposed to be an interview, after all. "Maybe Mom was in love with that guy who was going to marry Aunt Iris!"

But Bernard was chuckling. "No, no, Beth, that's just plain ridiculous. I'm sorry, but that fiancé—Clifford something—he was wild about your Aunt Iris. Never any doubt about that. He and Iris would come to the shop often for a soda or a snack after a movie. I remember seeing them. And, of course, before Hanny Lynn chucked me out on my ear, I was over on their porch a lot, and Iris and that guy were out there, too. You only had to see them together. You could see in their eyes how much they loved each other. It was a real shock when he died. All I could think when I first heard the news was how shattered Iris would be. They looked like such a perfect couple. In fact, I used to spin a lot of fantasies after seeing them together—daydreams of how in a few years Hanny and I would be planning a wedding just like theirs. . . . No, kids, never think for a minute that Clifford was Mr. Mystery Man. It's true he was older—but I'd be surprised if he even noticed Hanny Lynn was living in the same house!"

"You know how he died, of course," said Beth.

"Fell down the stairs, poor guy." Bernard shook his head. "That was a real tragedy, and Iris has never gotten over it, I hear."

"Aunt Iris accused Mom of pushing Clifton Becker down the stairs—of wanting to kill him!" Tom burst out. "Did you know that?"

If Tom had been trying for shock value, his revelation didn't succeed. Far from looking shocked, Bernard merely looked sad. "Yes, I'd heard that one. But it doesn't surprise me. Iris and Hanny Lynn never did get along. It figures that Iris would try to blame her unhappiness on someone else, and why not on Hanny? Poor

Hanny! That old pattern was set up when they were both little kids. I always thought their mother encouraged the gulf between the girls."

"But why would Grandmother want to do that?" asked Beth.

"Most mothers try hard to make their kids get along, right? But your grandmother seemed to have a different mentality. I always thought of it as 'Divide and Conquer.' You know—get the girls fighting, play one against the other, and thereby keep control of both. And boy, let me tell you, strict as your grandfather was about dating, your grandmother was the control sergeant around that house. It was her way—or no way!" He stopped suddenly, looking uncomfortable. "I'm sorry, kids. I shouldn't talk about your grandmother like this. It's just that she often seemed to be standing in the way when Hanny Lynn and I wanted some time together. Hanny couldn't go sit on the porch until she'd eaten dinner, done her homework, washed the dishes, watered the plants, sorted the laundry—anything, it seemed to me, to keep her from me!" He turned up his palms and looked sheepish. "Or maybe I'm remembering wrong."

"Never mind," said Beth. "We asked you and

you told us what you think. I've noticed it, too—Grandmother likes to be in control. You haven't insulted us or anything."

Tom had been sitting quietly, his head bent over his lemonade glass. Now, abruptly, he set his glass down on a pile of newspapers and stood up.

"Thanks for talking to us. We've got to get home now." He started for the door.

Beth rose to her feet. What was with him?

"We should get together for a meal soon," said Bernard, accompanying them to the door. "Get the families together." Beth agreed that would be fun and suggested that he and Monica plan to come for dinner the following Sunday. She'd clear it with Hannah when she got home. Having other people besides family in the house on Spring Street would come as a breath of fresh air.

Tom had his hand on her arm a little too tightly—a warning?—and was saying good-bye to Bernard in an unnatural, strained voice. Beth waved to Bernard as she and Tom descended the steep steps to the shop.

Monica was busy serving a young mother with two small boys demanding chocolate and gumdrops. Beth expected Tom would want to linger a moment, but his hand was still tight on her arm, steering her toward the door.

In the street she pulled out of his grip. "No need to break my arm!"

He looked about to burst. "Beth! Did you hear that?"

"What?"

"Oh, Beth—now we know who did it!"

Beth's eyes widened. "Who? What do you mean?"

"Weren't you listening? It was Grandmother! I'm sure of it! Not Mom at all!"

"I think you're having a heatstroke."

He practically dragged her down the sidewalk, away from the candy shop, and stopped by the bench at a bus stop. He sat and pulled her down next to him.

"Listen to me. This really could be it. He said Grandmother is a controlling person. You heard it yourself, right? And she loves Aunt Iris more than anything. Right? She wanted Aunt Iris to marry Clifton. And so she must have been totally furious when she found out that Clifton really loved Mom. Furious enough to kill him for hurting her beloved Iris!"

Beth considered this. "You could be right." Tom wanted so badly for Hannah to be innocent, he was ready to grasp at any straw. Still, what he said *was* possible. Grandmother had been on the landing that night. It *could* have happened that way.

She looked at Tom as they walked. His face was grim, but she felt the air lightening around him. He was happy to think Grandmother was guilty, and his sense of relief at this new possibility was tangible. It solved a lot of questions. It really did make sense. In fact, the more she thought about it, the more it seemed to Beth that Grandmother must have pushed Clifton—just as Tom suspected. Grandmother had a hard look around the eyes, after all. The hard look of a guilty woman.

Beth lay across her bed that same afternoon and wrote another letter to Ray. The house was hot and quiet. The fan on the radiator whirred on high. Outside she heard the spurt of the hose as Hannah watered the flowers in the yard. Grandad was taking his afternoon nap. Grandmother was down in the kitchen watching her soap opera.

Dear Ray,

It used to be just Aunt Iris, but now Grandmother gives me the creeps, too. I've come upstairs to escape because I can feel her everywhere else in the house. Wherever she is, I know she's thinking about Tom and me and Mom, and I don't get good vibes. I bet she wishes we'd never come. She's got Tom out on the porch topping and tailing the green beans for dinner now—even though she says she doesn't like males in the kitchen. Apparently they can do kitchen work just fine in other places. Tom wanted me to sit out there and help him—but I have to admit Tom's getting on my nerves now, too. He's always going on about Monica and how great she is and how wretched that we live in California, three thousand miles away from her. They've taken Romps on a million walks together these past few days—and left me sitting with a book on the porch. Okay, you get the feeling I'm in a bad mood? Well, you got it.

So—no help with the beans. What a mean sister! Maybe my sense of humor is shrinking away like the rest of me. It's mammoth meal upon mammoth meal around here, and yet I'm losing weight because whenever I sit at the table with Grandmother and Aunt Iris my stomach just tightens up. I come up to my lumpy bed in the world-famous Lodge for a little privacy, but even writing long letters to you can't shake me out of this mood. Maybe the fact that you're not such a great correspondent has something to do with it. And what's with the answering machine? You used to change the message every few days—and yet every time I call, you've got the same recording. I think you could at least give me a call. I mean, really, Ray. And I know you don't like to write, but I was hoping for at least a postcard or two—if only to keep me sane!

She read over what she'd written and flung down the pen. She knew she shouldn't send this one, either. He'd read it and groan and say she was obviously still in the melodramatic teen years when atmosphere hangs heavy. She hated it when he said things like that.

She lay back and studied the crack in the ceiling over the bed. It seemed to change. Once it had looked like a giant winged insect. Then it had rather looked like Ray's profile. But now the chin seemed rounder. And the crack that defined the ear seemed to have stretched up into the head, fanning out into a map of little fissures, like fault lines. She thought now it was Clifton Becker with his smashed-out brains, come to haunt her.

At dinner Beth watched Grandmother shovel great forkfuls of green beans into her mouth and dab the melted butter off her chin with her napkin. Then she glanced over at Aunt Iris and saw her hide her beans under the pile of mashed potatoes Grandad had ladled onto her plate. Beth pushed her own beans around in circles.

She looked up at her mother, and Hannah smiled across the table. "It was a good idea you had, Beth, to invite Bernard and Monica for dinner." Hannah turned to her mother. "You think so, too, don't you, Mama? Your Sunday meal is always so good, it'll be nice to share it with company."

"We haven't had people here for years," murmured Grandmother. "But the Clementses are good people. It should be fine."

"Sure it'll be fine," agreed Grandad. "About time we opened the house and shook out the dust."

"You had no right to invite them, Elisabeth!" cried Aunt Iris, throwing down her napkin and struggling up from her chair. Beth saw her aunt's frail body was trembling, and she felt a stab of pity that anyone should be so afraid of guests.

"I'm sorry. I really didn't mean to upset you, Aunt Iris," Beth said earnestly. "Maybe I should tell them not to come, after all." She glanced to her mother for help.

But Hannah was staring helplessly at her salad.

Help came from Grandad instead, who banged his fist on the tabletop. "Come on, Iris! It's only a dinner!"

"Don't yell at her, Henry!" chided Grandmother. "You know what she's suffered."

"Maybe we could go out to a restaurant for dinner, instead," pressed Beth. She must have been crazy to imagine even for a moment that having people to dinner here would ever work out.

"Nonsense!" said Grandad.

"Iris, darling, it'll be a very nice dinner party. You'll see." Grandmother spoke encouragingly. Aunt Iris backed away from the table, her hands pressed against her stomach. She ran into the kitchen. Though the sound of water running into the sink was very loud, everyone could hear her retching.

Beth felt just about as sick and pushed her dinner plate away.

Later in the evening Grandmother and Grandad sat in the living room with Hannah, watching TV. Tom took Romps for such a long walk Beth knew he had gone to visit Monica. Beth sat by herself out on the porch swing. She was thinking about the scene at dinner. It hadn't been just meanness that made Aunt Iris say she didn't want company. Aunt Iris really *had* looked as if she were suffering—it wasn't just melodrama that made her clutch her stomach like that. And now Beth felt responsible. They should just forget the whole thing. She would go in now and tell her aunt not to worry anymore. It wasn't worth getting sick about. This was Aunt Iris's house, too, after all—and if she didn't want company, she shouldn't have to have company.

Beth walked into the house and headed for the kitchen, full of resolve. But she stopped short just inside the doorway as Aunt Iris spun sharply from the sink, where she had been pouring herself a drink.

"So!" hissed Aunt Iris, her pale eyebrows drawn together in a taut frown. "Spying on me, were you?"

Beth's conciliatory words were suspended by surprise.

"Of course not," she said after a second. "I was just coming in to talk to you."

Aunt Iris reached out a bony, surprisingly strong hand and grabbed Beth by the shoulder. "You think I don't know, don't you? Little spy!"

"Know what?" Beth tried to back out the door.

"Coming here to snoop around! Coming here to gloat? I'm telling you—"

"You're drunk," muttered Beth, and she pushed Aunt Iris's hand off her shoulder.

"Don't think I don't know what you're up to!" screamed Aunt Iris, following her into the living room, her drink sloshing over the rim of her glass.

"Iris!" Hannah jumped up from the couch. "What is going on?"

"You!" growled Aunt Iris. "You think I don't know what you want? Get out of my way!"

Now Beth's grandparents were on their feet. Grandad pressed the pause button and the film on the VCR stopped in mid–car chase. "What's all the ruckus?" asked Grandad. "You'll wake the dead, carrying on like this."

Aunt Iris began to laugh, a high, unpleasant sound. "Oh, oh! That's rich!"

Hannah turned to her father. "Better go upstairs, Daddy. Iris is drunk." Beth could see her mother fighting to keep her temper under control. Hannah's fists were clenched in the folds of her plaid cotton sundress.

But Grandad walked shakily across the living room toward Aunt Iris. He looked pale and tired. "Oh, Iris. Why are you doing this to yourself?"

"I'm not doing anything! You'd do better to ask Hanny Lynn what *she* has done to us all!" Aunt Iris broke into wild laughter.

Grandmother crossed the room to Iris, holding out her hands. "Come on, Iris, baby. Put down the drink. Here, give it to me, darling."

Tom and Romps ran up onto the porch just then. Tom peered into the house from the screen door for a long moment before opening it and stepping inside. Romps barked sharply at Aunt Iris, who clutched the glass to her chest, still laughing wildly.

Grandmother fluttered her hands helplessly. "Iris, calm down, baby. Come on, honey! My poor, sweet, Iris!"

Beth edged over to Tom, and they stood together at the foot of the stairs.

Suddenly Aunt Iris drew her arm back and hurled her glass straight at her sister. Hannah ducked and the glass crashed against the radiator and shattered.

"Bitch!" screamed Aunt Iris.

Grandmother started to cry in high, fluttery gasps: "Oh, no! Oh, no!"

Grandad attempted to restrain Aunt Iris, and Tom hurried over to help him. Beth pressed herself against the banister, unable to move.

Hannah stared at the broken glass, then walked slowly to her sister. Fury flashed in her eyes. "Iris," she began in a soft, determinedly calm voice, "it's just all the drink. If you stop, you'll calm down and see—"

Aunt Iris's hand whipped out and slapped her sister's face. "Shut up, Hanny Lynn! Lying, sneaking, gloating whore!"

Hannah covered her face with both hands and sank to her knees on the carpet.

Tom dropped Grandad's arm so fast the old man nearly fell back onto the couch. He whirled across the room to Aunt Iris. "Don't you hit my mother, Aunt Iris! How dare you!" His face was a mottled red beneath his mop of orange hair. Aunt Iris raised her arm again, but now Beth's paralysis disappeared and she flew to Tom's side, pulling him out of their aunt's reach.

"Upstairs!" she cried, and dragged him toward the stairway as Aunt Iris hurled abuse after them.

Grandmother wrapped Aunt Iris in her arms, crooning. Hannah bent over Grandad, who had lowered himself onto the couch and was breathing heavily.

Beth pulled Tom into her bedroom. "Oh, Tom! She was going to hit you!" Her whole body was trembling. "She hit Mom!"

Tom sank onto the bed. He was also shaking. "If I stayed down there, I'd be hitting a few people myself!"

Beth collapsed onto the bed next to him and drew a ragged breath Her voice broke. "If she hurts Mom—"

Tom stood up. "I'm going back down there."

"No, wait a sec. Listen!"

From downstairs they could hear Grandmother's soothing voice still trying to calm Aunt Iris. "It's all right, Iris, love. It's okay now, baby."

"It will never be okay!" cried Aunt Iris. "How

can you let her in this house again, Mama, after what she did? Bringing her kids back here to gloat!"

Grandmother's answer was another soft murmur.

Beth gritted her teeth. "I hate her!"

"I'm going down," said Tom.

Beth lay back and closed her eyes. Enormous fatigue folded itself over her like a quilt. The hubbub from downstairs receded and she felt a sudden, desperate desire to fall asleep. The air in the room was hot and close. The heaviness, though, seemed to come less from the humidity and more from the unsolved mystery of Clifton Becker. For a moment Beth thought she heard the beat of the old Rolling Stones song pulse across the hall. No satisfaction—how appropriate! She thought she heard the clatter of a typewriter, even imagined the little jingle of the warning bell when the carriage reached the end of a line on the page.

She wasn't sure whether she had actually slept or not when she felt a soft hand on her forehead and saw her mother sitting next to her on the bed.

"Are you okay, Bethie?"

"She hit you!" Beth sat up. Downstairs the

voices were muted, but Beth could tell her grandparents and Tom were still dealing with Aunt Iris.

"I'm okay. She didn't know what she was doing."

"She did! I hate her."

"No, don't. Don't, Beth. She can't help it."

"How can you defend her? You heard the vile things she said to you!"

Then a loud crash resounded up the stairs. Aunt Iris's cracked voice started shrieking as Beth heard Tom's footsteps racing up the stairs. "Don't you go running to your mother until you hear what I have to say, boy! Listen to me! Can't you bear the truth?"

In another instant, Tom was in the room with them. "Lock the door!" he said wildly.

But Aunt Iris's voice didn't come any nearer. Apparently she was standing at the foot of the stairs, but they had no trouble hearing. "Hanny Lynn? It's time someone told your precious children the truth about their mother! Told them how you schemed to get him! Told them how you wanted him! I know the truth, and they should, too! But Hannah Lynn, there's justice in this world after all, isn't there? Even you couldn't have him in the end, could you?" Then there was more hysterical laughter, and Grandmother's frantic, soothing murmur.

Hannah set her lips. "I'm sorry, you guys."

"Oh, Mom, let's go home." Tom's voice was nearly a sob.

"I can't. Not yet."

"*Please,* Mom," pleaded Beth.

"No." Hannah dragged her fingers through her hair. "We can't go back yet. I've come back to deal with this, and I have to stay. I know now it's the only way I'll be able to move on. To survive. I've got to be able to stand on my own feet."

Now there was silence from downstairs, and then footsteps on the landing. Grandmother's gentle voice: "Come on, Henry. I've got you. Let's go to bed now."

Hannah reached over and stroked Tom's tangled hair. "It isn't just Aunt Iris who is torn apart, you guys. Our whole family is in pieces of one kind or another." She squeezed Beth's shoulder. "We have to face facts."

Facts? If they only knew the facts, there would be no mystery. How Clifton Becker died would be just one more sad story. But there weren't any facts! For an instant Beth envisioned a shattered piece of colored glass, broken fragments impossibly scattered. Could the fragments of her own family be reassembled somehow if the mystery of Clifton Becker's death were solved? Her lips tightened. She'd read too many detective novels this summer; that was her trouble. An artist wouldn't even try to fix a shattered pane but would start over with a strong, whole piece.

Then there were dragging footfalls on the stairs and Beth knew that Aunt Iris was making her way up to her room. When she heard her aunt's door click firmly shut, Beth realized she had been holding her breath. She let it out in a sharp burst.

"The coast is clear, I guess," sighed Hannah. "I'd better go see how Mama and Daddy are."

Tom went out onto his sunporch without another word. He closed the connecting door softly behind him. Beth lay back on the bed. She could see a few stars dotting the sky through the screened window. Her ears strained against the silence for the sounds of more bitter chaos but heard nothing. The light from the back porch below her window sent a yellow glow up onto the ceiling, the perfect soft yellow of pearlized glass. Beth closed her eyes and tried to sleep, falling almost immediately into the calming fantasy she had told Grandad about the last time she'd talked to him by his bed.

Is was a good fantasy and soothing—something all the more wonderful because it didn't have to remain a fantasy. It was a dream that could come true.

She and Ray opened their shop and became well-known teachers and artists. They got married and had a baby or two. Eventually they expanded their business to Europe and went there to live. Beth was experimenting with new methods of glasswork. One day, while they were living in Italy or somewhere, she stumbled upon the secret process by which the ancient glass artists had made the deep colors in the medieval glass. The fantasy grew a little weak here because Beth couldn't think how anyone could figure out the secret to the beautiful old colors. Those colors were something no modern artist had been able to duplicate, though many had tried. Still, somehow she managed to unlock history! Her discovery catapulted her to international fame. Her work was sought after by everyone, and her windows hung in churches and museums and homes around the world—all because she alone had succeeded where all others before her had failed, in getting the past to yield its secrets. Grandad had smiled at her tale and wished her well. If anyone could do it, he'd said, she would be the one.

She turned her head on the pillow restlessly. Tonight the fantasy lacked its usual luster. All of Aunt Iris's angry words seemed to reverberate in the still, hot house, and it was possible only in fantasies, Beth now suspected, to make the past reveal the truth.

In the morning Beth lay in bed for a long time, trying not to think about Aunt Iris and the miserable scene the night before. She stared up at the crack on the ceiling. She was quite sure now that Clifton Becker had had a profile just like that. When she heard Romps whining outside the door, she hopped up to let him in, then returned to bed, patting the mattress next to her for him to jump up. The old dog had trouble since the bed was so high, so Beth had to haul him up. He settled next to her, panting slightly. The fan whirred in the window but did little to stir the heavy air. Beth longed for the mild summer of Northern California and the morning mist from the bay.

Then the door opened softly. "Good morning," murmured her mother, coming in to sit on the edge of Beth's bed.

"Hi."

"I just wanted to see how you and Tom were. You know. After last night." She stroked Beth's hair. "You look lonely, lying here wide-awake "

"I'm just hot."

"Hot and lonely. Don't think I don't know it. And I'm sorry, honey, really I am."

"I'm so sure." She just wanted to lie there with Romps. In peace. Was that impossible, too? "If you were really sorry, you'd pack up and take us back home."

Hannah shook her head. "Look, why don't you work some more on your new window? When will you let us see it?"

"I'll work on it later."

"It's such a wonderful hobby for you," said Hannah.

"It's not a hobby, Mom! It's my life's work." Beth's voice was bitter. "You used to say I had real talent! And you were all for my opening a shop with Ray when I finish school. But now my work is just a hobby. Probably you don't even like Ray anymore, right?" She felt her temper flare but was aware somewhere deep inside that her real anger was at Aunt Iris, not her mother.

"Of course I like Ray," Hannah said mildly. "Though he *is* really a bit old for you."

"Oh, great. You didn't think that when we first went out."

"I'm not going to meddle in your love life, Beth! But I've just been thinking about a lot of things. Being back here puts things in a different perspective, I'm afraid. Makes me remember living here and loving Clifton. . . . He was just as much older than me as Ray is older than you. Ten years."

"So he was too old for you?"

"Probably. But I didn't know it then." She hesitated. "When you're young and in love for the first time, it's hard to see clearly."

"Look, I'm not in the same situation at all."

"Not exactly," Hannah agreed. "And I hope you end up much happier than I did." She glanced around the room, and her voice grew dreamy. "Still, I *was* happy when I was in this room. I've always loved this room."

"The Lodge," said Beth with a scowl. She stared up at the ceiling. "See that crack, Mom?"

But Hannah wasn't listening. She was staring

around the room as if enraptured by it. "I used to come in here," she murmured. "I'd go through his things when he was at work. I just wanted to be near his things, touch them. It was almost like being with him in person. They had this smell to them; all his things did. A wonderful, Cliftony smell."

This was getting embarrassing. Beth traced circles on the sheet with her finger, listening.

"I'd pick up the papers on his desk and run my hands over them—he had held them in *his* hands! Oh, I was lost then. I'd come in when no one was around and look at his clothes in the dresser drawers, crumple them against my face, try to imagine what it would be like to be Clifton. Or to be held by him. Later I knew about *that!* And I'd lie across the hall at night in my room and hear him typing. Everyone else would fall asleep, but I'd be there listening, feeling close to him." Hannah dropped her head into her hands.

"Oh, Mom!"

"I loved him more than I've ever loved anyone, Beth! It's something I'm still not over. Even now, sitting here in this room, he's drifting all over the place. I can feel it. And I get this incredible urge. The pull to—"

"To what?" asked Beth as Hannah jumped down off the bed.

"To snoop! To hold something of his! Oh, Beth, I just wish—" Then she fell silent. Beth watched while her mother moved restlessly around the room. "I don't know."

Beth didn't know, either. She couldn't believe the way her mother was acting. Talk about drifting . . . Finally, because Hannah just stood at the dresser staring at herself in the mirror, Beth cleared her throat. "Well, you're lucky he never caught you snooping."

Hannah laughed shakily. "I wish he had. We enjoyed our confrontations." She turned away from the dresser, and her face seemed pale despite her tan. "We were in here together that night—" She closed her eyes. "That was when they found out how much we loved each other. I thought your grandmother was going to kill me."

"Bernard sort of mentioned she was that type," mused Beth.

Hannah's eyes flew open. "What type? What do you mean?" Her gaze was sharp. All the dreaminess of the moment before dissolved.

"Oh, I mean—well, he did! Tom and I saw him the other day at the shop, and we asked him if he thought Aunt Iris had pushed Clifton and he said no, but then he said how Grandmother likes to control people, and then Tom thought maybe Grandmother pushed Clifton herself because she was so mad she couldn't control him. . . ." Her voice dwindled, sounding unconvinced.

Hannah frowned. "I don't like that, Beth. I don't like it at all. You are not to go gossiping about family matters to outsiders! All families have problems, and the problems are to be kept private. You're talking about my mother! Please try to remember that you're part of this family! You're not some detective out to solve a crime! What about family loyalty?"

"Well, what about it, Mom?" Beth clenched her fingers in Romps's soft fur. "Loyalty and devotion aren't really familiar concepts in this house, are they? But okay! I won't talk about anything with anybody. I'll just sit tight and wait till we can get out of here!"

"Fine." Hannah crossed her arms over her chest. She turned and left the room.

Beth stood staring after her for a moment, then flopped back down onto her bed. Family loyalty! She'd start laughing in that hysterical Aunt Iris voice if her mother said anything else about family loyalty. She might start laughing wildly anyway, just from the strain of this horrible mystery that went nowhere. She was actually considering letting out an experimental chuckle when the phone began to ring downstairs.

It would be Mark calling for Tom, predicted Beth, gazing up at the crack on the ceiling. They were working on some thrilling new computer program.

But Grandmother's voice called up the stairs: "Elisabeth? Bernie Clements's girl is on the phone wanting to talk to you!"

She ran down the stairs to the dining room and picked up the receiver from the phone on the little wooden stand in the corner. Tom sat at the breakfast table with a plate of scrapple. Grandmother was finishing a cup of coffee. There was no sign of Aunt Iris.

"Hello!" she said.

"Hi, Beth," said Monica's cheerful voice. "Hope I didn't wake you up or anything. But I was wondering whether you—and Tom, I hope—would come with me to the art museum downtown. They're having a summer exhibit of local artists and some of my pots are in it."

"Wow! You're really in a museum? A real museum?"

"A real live museum!" giggled Monica. "Really and truly. I can hardly believe it myself. It's because I won the city award for high school pottery last semester. So the stuff I made in my art class gets a place of honor."

"I'd love to come. When should we leave?"

"How about now? We can get lunch in the city."

"No problem!" Beth felt lighter suddenly. If ever she needed to get away from Spring Street, it was now. Just knowing an escape was at hand made the heavy atmosphere of the house seem to lift. The tense moment with her mother just now might have happened ages ago. And she was suddenly quite hungry—for the first time, it seemed, in weeks. She'd devour a cheesesteak sandwich and a big, salty Philadelphia pretzel slathered with mustard.

"Great! I'll see if I can get Dad's car. Otherwise we can take the bus." Monica hesitated. "And Beth? Can you let me talk to Tom?"

"Oh. Sure. He's stuffing himself with breakfast, but I'll try to convince him to come talk to you." She motioned for Tom to come to the phone. "Well, you're in luck," she said into the receiver. "He's on his way, though it's a hard thing you're asking of him. A boy needs his food, you know—"

Tom grabbed the phone with a growl, and she ran back upstairs to get ready.

Monica was a much better driver than her dad, Beth noted with relief as they drove down Penn's Pike toward the highway. She was glad Tom hadn't been able to come with them after all; he had already made plans with his computer buddy, Mark.

"Am I a computer widow already?" Monica had joked when she arrived to pick Beth up and found Tom waiting on the porch, a stack of computer magazines on his lap.

"I really would rather be with you," he told her earnestly. "It's just that I promised Mark I'd teach him HyperCard—"

"Say no more," Monica protested, holding up her hand. "I could never hope to compete with HyperCard!"

"Oh, I don't know about that," he said, getting up to hug her good-bye. "She doesn't know a thing about making pots."

Beth had felt a pang as she watched them. They'd fallen into their new relationship so easily. Maybe there would be a letter from Ray today.

Now the two girls drove along the highway toward the Philadelphia Museum of Art. Beth leaned her head back and turned her face to the warm breeze rushing in from the window. The wind on her face blew the last of the Spring Street cobwebs from her mind. Even the memories of last night's scene with Aunt Iris and this morning's argument with her mother faded.

Monica asked Beth about her glasswork. Beth told her about the plans for a shop with Ray.

"Sounds great," Monica said, signaling to exit. She changed lanes carefully and piloted the car down the exit ramp. "I sometimes think I'd like to own a shop, too—or a gallery. But it's too soon for me to make plans for the far-off future. I'm trying to concentrate on my applications to different art schools now. There's this one in New York City that's supposed to be fantastic. But there are also two great programs I'd kill to get into—one's in Portugal and the other's in Paris."

"Europe!" Beth had only ever considered

travel in Europe as part of the fantasy in which she ferreted out the secret of the ancient glass colors. "That seems so far away."

"Not to me. Maybe it seems farther from California than from the East Coast. I can't wait to go! Only problem is—my French is lousy and my Portuguese is nonexistent!" She laughed. "There's always the Philadelphia Institute, if Europe doesn't work out. And it's a good school—but I want to travel. You know—see the world and all that. Don't you?"

"Well, I guess it would be fun. I mean—" Beth scanned the street for a parking place as Monica slowed the car. "Ray works full-time at the shop during the days and holds classes there at night, so he probably wouldn't be able to go to Europe."

"So go without him. Live somewhere a year or two to study stained glass—I bet there are lots of great schools. And then set up shop with him when you get back."

Beth caught herself frowning. "You sound like my mom! She's been after me about going to college for months."

"There's a place!" cried Monica, and she applied herself to the task of parallel parking.

The art museum stood at the end of a long

avenue of trees. A statue of George Washington flanked by two moose and two buffalo marked the wide steps up to the imposing entrance. As the girls began walking along the avenue, Monica touched Beth's arm. "Well, I don't know about college, but it would be fun if you'd at least think about art school," she said. "None of my friends are into art. Maybe you and I would end up at the same place."

"I think my mom wants me to be an accountant or something," Beth said dourly. "She used to think my art was the greatest thing in the world, but suddenly she got on this self-improvement kick and applied for college herself. Now my art is just a 'hobby.' "

"That's bad," said Monica.

"Yeah."

They climbed the steps and entered the museum. At the information desk in the vast hall Monica asked for a map and consulted it to find the location of her pottery exhibit. The vast corridors echoed as they walked along. "Here it is, I think," Monica said, and led the way into a smaller, high-ceilinged room lined with glass cases.

The room was hushed. A guard nodded at them from her post near the wall. Several visitors were leaning over the cases. Monica hugged herself. "I've got the shivers!" she whispered to Beth. "I can't believe they're looking at my own stuff!"

"Artists probably always feel that way," Beth whispered back. "When they're making a piece of work they're usually not thinking about when it will hang in a museum. They're just into the work itself." At least that's how she felt when she was hard at work on a stained-glass window.

She started walking toward the back wall. "Come on."

But Monica hung back. "I want to look around by myself, I think. You go ahead." She walked over to the side wall where the exhibit began and picked up a pamphlet of information about the artists.

Beth headed straight for the case that had MONICA CLEMENTS on a sign on the wall behind it. She leaned over the case and caught her breath.

Inside the case were eight delicate pieces—more like sculpture than utilitarian pots. There was a teapot with a deep rose glaze, a vase with shadowy, translucent stripes in green and gray, a bowl large enough to hold a watermelon. There were two unusual pieces about two feet tall that arched gracefully toward the ceiling and looked more like statues of human figures than pots. Then there were three fat, colorful pots set apart from the others and labeled Hiding-Place Pots. Beth peered at them.

"Those are my favorites," said Monica at Beth's side.

"They're all gorgeous!" Beth turned to Monica, admiration shining in her face. "God, it's so exciting! I can't believe you made these—they look totally professional."

"Thanks! I'm kind of stunned myself. They look a lot better here than they did in the case outside the gym at school." She laughed. "Last time I saw these pots they were wrapped in newspaper in a big Gummi Bear packing box! The people who set up the exhibit knew what they were doing."

"Oh, don't be so modest," said Beth. "Your pottery is awesome. But what does it mean about hiding places?"

"I'll show you." Monica leaned on the case. "Look—see the cracks along the base of that first one?"

"Excuse me, girls. Please don't lean on the cases." The guard was at their side, frowning.

"Sorry!" Monica jumped back.

"But they're her own pots!" protested Beth. "She's Monica Clements! In the flesh!" She pointed to Monica's name on the sign.

The guard's frown deepened. "The rules are the rules," she said. "Don't touch the cases." She walked back to her post, still watching them.

"She didn't believe me!" said Beth.

"Oh, it doesn't matter," said Monica.

"They should have hung your photo up next to your name."

"She'd still go on about not leaning on the glass, I bet." Monica shrugged. "Maybe I'll make a mug of her face. And exhibit it—that'll teach her!"

Beth laughed and turned back to the cases, careful this time not to lean on the glass. "So, go on and tell me about the hiding-place pots."

Monica pointed out the cracks along the base of the first pot. "See that? The base unscrews. Inside there's another pot and then another and another. Four pots in one. And on this one"—she indicated the second, blue pot—"there's a little trapdoor on a spring. When you push on the base of the pot, the door opens. The third pot's handle twists off—see the little crack? Inside there's a hollow where you could conceal a rolled-up message."

"They're amazing! How did you get the idea?"

"I was reading about how in olden times spies would carry snuff boxes or tobacco pouches or even makeup containers that had false bottoms or secret compartments. They'd hide poison in there, so if they were ever captured, they could commit suicide rather than give away their information."

"Pretty cool," said Beth. She walked on to examine the other cases of pots but found none she liked as well as Monica's. "I love your stuff. It's better than the rest."

"Thanks!" said Monica. "Tom was telling me how good *your* stuff is."

"He was? That's nice of him. I didn't think he ever noticed what I do."

"Oh, God, yes. He admires you like anything. You know—you're the Big Sister!"

"Well—" Beth shrugged. She admired Tom, too, but hadn't ever admitted it to anybody. "I'll show you a window I'm working on when you and your dad come to dinner on Sunday."

"I can't wait to come. Tom's been telling me a lot about your family."

"I'm surprised you still want to come, in that case." Beth felt a quick flutter of panic at the thought of the upcoming party. Would it be a total disaster? She wondered what Tom had told Monica. Did she know about Clifton Becker? Did she know how horrible Aunt Iris could be? For a second Beth felt like telling Monica all about the scene last night. She really needed someone to talk to about it. Letters to Violet and Ray weren't good enough. She couldn't really talk to Tom. He was too defensive about their mother's role in everything that had happened at the house on Spring Street twenty years ago. But why ruin her day away from the house by bringing the story up now?

"So you're working on a window now—during your vacation?"

"It's the only way to stay sane around there," Beth said and forced a smile. "I left most of my supplies and tools at home, but I did bring the basics, and I sort of set up a studio down in the basement."

She and Monica wandered around the other rooms of the big museum until their stomachs were rumbling with hunger. "I need a cheesesteak," Beth whispered at last.

"Let's go!" agreed Monica. The two girls left the museum and walked several blocks until they found a café.

• • •

Over lunch the conversation moved from pottery to stained glass and back again, then became even more personal. Beth told Monica more about their life in Berkeley and all that had led to their living on Spring Street for the summer but didn't, in the end, touch on the unhappiness she'd found there. Monica would see for herself, if the party turned sour. She talked about Violet, Jasmine, and Rose—the triplets named for flowers—and more about Ray and their plans that her mother now opposed.

Monica was sympathetic. "I wish you wanted to apply to art schools with me, but you really have to go ahead with what you want," she said. "My mom was upset when I told her I wanted to live with Dad for my last year and a half of high school. But she knew I needed to get away, and she knew Dad could give me a job in the shop to earn money for art school."

"I never really thought about art school," admitted Beth. "When I met Ray it was love at first sight, you know? I took a class at the glass shop and he was the teacher. Then he helped me get a job there, helping him and Jane Simmons, the owner. Ray's got this plan all worked out—about the shop. He's been out of school for years, working and teaching—he's exhibited his windows a few times in San Francisco, too!"

"But the plan for the shop was really his," said Monica. "Right?"

"Well, at the beginning, I guess," said Beth. "But it's what I want to do, too! I mean, why spend years in school? I want to be an artist—and I don't think books can teach me that."

"No. You have to have the talent in the first place," agreed Monica. She took a big bite of her cheesesteak sandwich and wiped the juice from her chin. "But you'd probably learn a lot from studying other people's techniques—at least, that's a lot of my own reason for wanting to go to school. Really learn the craft. There are some fantastic people out there making pots, and I want to meet them. You can make a lot of contacts at art school—find out how to be in exhibits and stuff."

Beth sipped her Coke. "Hmmm."

"And you end up with a degree, you know, which is no small thing if the worst happens and your work doesn't sell. I figure I can try to teach art in schools, then. At least I'll be qualified. And I'd still have summers off for my own work."

"Hmmm," Beth said again. "I'll have to think

about it. But Mom has her heart set on my being a lawyer."

Monica laughed. "You said accountant earlier!"

"Something respectable, anyway."

"*My* mom will be so relieved to have me away in Europe, she'll back any career choice I make!"

"I thought you said your mom didn't want you to move out."

"No, she just didn't want me to move in *with Dad.* That's really hard for her. They had a pretty messy divorce, actually. And I spent a lot of time shuffling back and forth between them before they agreed I'd be better off in one place. So I ended up with Mom—and Mom carried on as if she'd won a contest." Monica threw back her long hair and made a face. Then she reached for her purse on the back of her chair. "Here, look at this." She pulled out her wallet and withdrew a photograph. "This is my mom and her husband. And their kids. My half-sisters."

Beth peered at the snapshot of a thin, dark-haired woman who looked very much like Monica. The woman stood next to a heavyset man with a beard. Each adult held a little girl with messy hair.

"Jenny and Jean are four and five now. They're good kids. I miss them, even though I love being away. I had to do a whole lot of babysitting after school when I lived with them. I never had time to be by myself or to make my pots. That's a lot of the reason I came back here to live. I really needed a change."

"Families are weird," Beth said as Monica tucked the photograph back into her wallet. "And mine is especially weird. But you'll see for yourself on Sunday." She put the last bite of cheesesteak sandwich in her mouth and chewed hard, trying to ignore the sinking feeling that assailed her again at the thought of Sunday's party. She felt better hearing about Monica's family problems. It made her realize that her own life was not the only one full of troublesome people. Probably Monica's family had secrets, too.

"Maybe you can arrange a special show of weirdness at dinner Sunday," joked Monica. "Or does it just have to happen naturally on its own?"

Beth almost told her about how Aunt Iris went on the rampage the night before, but remembered her mother's warning about keeping family business private. She bit back her response and forced a smile.

They stood up and walked to the front counter to pay for their meal. Before they left, Beth went back and left a tip on their table. A blast of heat and humidity hit them as they left the air-conditioned café and started the walk back to the car.

As they drove along the highway toward the Penn's Pike exit, Beth closed her eyes and let the warm air from the window rush over her face again. She thought about the glass case of Monica's prizewinning pottery, objects of such beauty and delicacy that had come from the heart and hands of this girl sitting in the driver's seat next to her. It didn't matter that Monica's home life had been troubled. Her artwork was able to thrive despite outside turmoil. Beth thought of her own family and all the tensions of the house on Spring Street. She mustn't let them stop her from her work. She longed suddenly to be down in the cool basement, hidden from Aunt Iris and the rest of the family. She could almost feel the weight of a glass cutter in her hand, hear the whirr of the grinder. Her fingers tingled with the itch to be at work, fitting shapes and thicknesses of glass together like pieces of a puzzle, rendering bursts of color into pictures.

At home in Berkeley they had people over to visit all the time. Hannah's men friends came for dinner or to chat with Beth and Tom before taking their mother out dancing. Hannah's women friends would stop by whenever they felt like it, just to talk over mugs of herbal tea. Tom always had his computer cronies in his room after school, all of them going into raptures over their programs and disks and HyperCard menus. And, of course, Violet and Beth were almost always together whenever Beth was not working in the glass shop. Sometimes all the triplets came over. Entertaining at home was never a problem. It just wasn't a big deal.

It almost seemed as if Beth had suggested they all take off their clothes and cavort naked around the Liberty Bell, the way Aunt Iris continued to carry on about the dinner party. Beth was surprised Grandmother and Grandad were handling the idea so well. Grandad kept smiling, as if he thought the whole plan rather amusing. Grandmother actually seemed pleased and went over and over the menu she planned with Hannah, who said she was glad Beth was feeling enough at home here now that she wanted to invite friends over. Beth didn't tell her mother it was precisely because she felt so *horrible* here that she'd invited Monica and Bernard.

"I still don't like it," fumed Aunt Iris at five-thirty on Sunday evening. "I don't like it at all." She gripped the wooden railing tightly as she wavered on the stairs. "I'm just not up to company. Mama? Are you listening?"

Grandmother called from the kitchen, her voice patient. "Yes, I hear you, dear. I've been in the kitchen all day preparing the meal for tonight, and I'm not through yet. Come down if you want to talk."

Aunt Iris moved slowly toward the kitchen and caught sight of Beth seated on the kitchen stool just inside the door and frowned. "Elisabeth! You're responsible for this!"

Beth was shelling fresh peas into a large glass bowl. She didn't answer.

"Please don't keep fussing, Iris, darling." Grandmother's voice was low. "It will be good for you to see some neighbors again. You must remember Bernard from when he was a boy."

"I've told you and told you, Mama! I don't want to see people! I don't want people coming here!"

"Listen, Iris. Please. I try to make things easier for you. I understand it's hard. You know I don't agree with much that Hanny says or does, but I'm with her on this. If she and the children want to invite friends here, they should be able to. I'm tired of being a recluse." She sighed. "It's taken Hanny's coming back to show me that."

"You'll regret this," muttered Aunt Iris.

"Oh, Iris!"

Beth slit open the last pod and flicked the peas out. Then she set the glass bowl on the wooden sideboard that held Grandmother's tablecloths and linen napkins and slipped out of the kitchen. She found Tom in the living room. "Aunt Iris is still furious!"

"Too bad," he said with satisfaction. "Life comes to Spring Street after all."

Twenty years after Death came, thought Beth, but kept her mouth shut. She still had to get ready—at least take a quick shower to cool off. Tom looked better than she'd ever seen him, casually dressed in neon green shorts and an oversize black T-shirt dotted with constellations. His dark red hair was shiny and freshly washed, and his eyes sparkled with anticipation of seeing Monica again.

Beth left him in the living room and dashed up for her shower, reflecting that his crush on Monica made him look older. She put on a boldly colored sundress with green and blue stripes that brightened her eyes and highlighted her flaming hair. Ray had first kissed her when she was wearing this dress—the first time he drove her home after their evening workshop. Maybe it would bring her luck tonight. She wound her hair back into a thick ponytail, fastening it in place with a green band that matched the dress. Then she went downstairs to wait with Tom in the living room for the first guests the house on Spring Street had seen in two decades.

Grandmother sat on the couch with them, wearing a thickly brocaded black dress with a heavy brooch pinned at the breast. She had applied powder and rouge to her soft, lined skin. Beth thought she looked ghastly—or was it ghostly?—but at least Grandmother was happy Monica and Bernard were coming. Grandad was in the rocking chair by the window, rubbing his hands together, then smoothing them over the top of his bald head, as if neatening the hair that once had been there. He hadn't dressed up in anything fancy but wore his usual loose brown trousers and a short-sleeved shirt.

Hannah sat in the armchair, hidden behind the entertainment section of the Sunday paper. Romps lay at her feet. Beth felt relieved that her mother, at least, looked relaxed. But then Beth noticed how tightly Hannah's hands clenched the edges of the newspaper she was reading, wrinkling the pages. She looked young and pretty, though, in a backless blue sundress and sandals, her hair swept up in a neat French braid. Little tendrils escaped, brushing softly against her forehead and the nape of her neck.

Hannah and Grandmother had been cleaning all day in preparation for this dinner party. The coffee table and end tables shone with lemon polish, and little glass dishes had been resurrected from some deep storage and filled with small hard candies, then centered carefully on each table. Grandad had ventured outside at Grandmother's insistence, walking shakily with shears in hand, to cut some roses off the bushes in the side yard. These blooms, artfully arranged by Beth in a crystal vase, now graced the center of the dining-room table. As Beth sat waiting, she could feel the tense atmosphere of the house wafting in puffs all around them like a giant cloud.

How were they going to have a good time with everything so formal and everyone so nervous? The clink of ice in a glass told them all that Aunt Iris was drinking in the kitchen. Grandad sighed heavily.

"Shouldn't she be sober tonight, Clara? Can't you say something to her?"

"Oh, Henry, it's just been her way of coping since Hanny's come back. You know that." Grandmother folded her hands on her black brocade lap.

Grandad snorted. "I'd say she hasn't coped with anything for twenty years."

The doorbell rang then, and Beth jumped up to answer it, grateful that their conversation—and, she hoped, Aunt Iris's drinking—would have to stop.

"Come on in!" she said to Bernard and Monica as she held the door wide. Grandmother was right there, holding out her hand to shake theirs, a tremulous smile on her face. Hannah stood behind her mother with a bright, welcoming expression Beth recognized. The wide eyes and confident grin meant Hannah was nervous but determined not to show it. Grandad tried to struggle to his feet, but Bernard hurried over to him, hand outstretched.

"No, please don't get up." Bernard shook hands, and Grandad sank back onto the couch.

"We came as soon as we could, as soon as we closed up the shop for the day," Monica told Grandmother, handing her a bouquet of mixed summer flowers. "It's so nice of you to invite us."

"I'm afraid we don't get out nearly as much as I'd like to," said Bernard.

"These are lovely, dear," said Grandmother, accepting the flowers and sniffing them. Beth couldn't help but wonder how long it had been since anyone had brought Grandmother flowers. She was afraid she knew the answer. At least twenty years.

"Let's get them in water. Beth? Can you work your magic with these?"

"Sure." She took the flowers and headed toward the kitchen.

Grandmother wiped her hands on her black dress. "Well, now!" she said brightly. "Dinner will be ready in about fifteen minutes. What can I get you to drink before we eat?"

Beth had to grin as she slipped through the

kitchen door. Grandmother didn't sound rusty at all.

Aunt Iris turned hastily from the sink.

"They're here, Aunt Iris. Why don't you go on in and say hello?"

"Are you patronizing me, young lady?" Aunt Iris tipped a tumbler full of clear liquid—but not water, Beth would bet—to her mouth. "They aren't *my* guests."

Beth felt wings of worry flutter in her stomach. Her aunt hadn't dressed for the company, and she looked like a scarecrow in an old print housedress. "Please. Grandmother has worked so hard to make things nice. She really wants the party to go well. If you hide out in here all night, you'll ruin everything!"

"You fresh little brat! You should get a slap across the face for that!" Aunt Iris banged her glass onto the counter and advanced on Beth. "I'll ruin your evening if I don't come out and make nice-nice? I? Well, what about *my* evening? What about my whole *life?*"

"Ssshhh! They'll hear you!"

"Let them!" Her voice rose to a shriek. "My whole life has been ruined—and you want me to come out and play hostess to Hanny Lynn's little boyfriend?"

"He's not her boyfriend!" hissed Beth. "Please, Aunt Iris, keep your voice down. They'll hear—"

"Who could help but hear everything?" Hannah stood in the doorway behind Beth and rested her hands on her daughter's shoulders. "Beth? Give me the flowers. I'll get them some water." Her voice trembled.

"Mom—"

"Please, Beth. I need you to set the table. And tell Grandmother I'll bring the drinks in a minute." Hannah gave Beth a little push toward the dining room. Then she shut the kitchen door behind her.

Beth stood in the dining room staring at the table, which had been fully set hours before. Grandmother had taken her best silver and crystal out that morning and instructed Beth and Tom how to polish it. Tom tried to get out of the work by reminding her about men's work and women's work, but Grandmother said there wasn't enough time to argue. Company was coming and everything needed to be perfect. And she'd handed him the polishing cloth.

Now Beth could hear her mother's and Aunt Iris's voices rising in the kitchen. She longed to grab Tom and Monica and Bernard and run down the street to the candy shop, away from the storm that was brewing. So what if the Clementses' apartment was a mess? Their homely clutter was nothing next to the chaos in this neat-as-a-pin house!

But she steeled herself and marched back into the living room. Grandad was telling Bernard about the candy shop as he remembered it from his youth, and Monica was telling Grandmother and Tom about her pottery exhibit at the museum. Everyone was politely pretending not to hear the angry voices from the kitchen.

"Think you can get away with everything, do you?" shrieked Aunt Iris from the kitchen.

Beth touched Grandmother's shoulder. "Mom will bring the drinks in a minute." And no sooner had she spoken than Hannah entered the room with the beverages on a tray. Her head was held high, but two bright spots of color flared on her cheeks. The smile on her lips did not reach her eyes. She handed Monica a glass of lemonade and Bernard a daiquiri. His fingers brushed hers as he took the drink.

"Iris okay now?" Bernard asked softly, never dreaming, Beth realized, that he was breaking a house rule: Never inquire; always pretend you think everything is okay even when it's clear nothing is okay.

Hannah stared at his fingers against hers, then moved back, tears welling in her eyes. Beth closed her own eyes, half in sympathy, half in mortification. What kind of dinner party was this, anyway?

"Nothing is okay!" Hannah's whisper broke on a sob, and the glasses still on her tray slipped as her hands trembled. Now Beth's mother had broken a rule, too: Never admit anything is wrong.

Tom lunged off the couch to the rescue as the glasses slid to one side, but was too late. The drinks spilled onto the rug.

"Oh, goodness gracious!" cried Grandmother, jumping from the couch and running for a towel. "Hanny Lynn, be careful!"

Hannah was leaning against Bernard now, and his arms were around her. His big hands awkwardly stroked her hair and patted her back as she sobbed openly.

Grandad looked on with concern from the rocking chair. His brow furrowed. "I say, Hanny Lynn, girl."

Beth sank onto the couch with Tom and Monica, silent. She didn't dare look at anyone. She didn't know what to do next.

"Oh, Bernie!" Hannah was crying in earnest now. "To answer your question—no! Iris *isn't* okay. *Nothing* is okay. Nothing is ever okay here!" She turned wildly to her father. "I can't stand it! Poor, poor little Iris! Her boyfriend dies and so the whole world owes her something? Well, not me, let me tell you. Not me!"

Hannah's shrill voice brought Grandmother running back into the room, the towel pressed to her lips. "You hush, Hanny Lynn! You just hush up right now and start wiping up those spilled drinks. Poor Iris is in the kitchen in tears—I'll not have any more of it! What kind of dinner party is this, the way you're carrying on?"

Hannah dropped to her knees and pressed the towel against the dark stain on the rug. "I can't help carrying on," she sobbed. Bernard knelt next to her, one big hand on her shoulder.

"I wonder if—" he began. "Ah, I think that maybe it would be best if Monica and I went—"

But his words were cut off as Aunt Iris appeared in the doorway, brandishing a sharp kitchen knife high above her head. "I've had it!" she screamed. "I know what you all think of me! Maybe you'll like me better when I'm dead!"

And then everyone was up and rushing toward her. Beth jumped up high, trying to reach her aunt's arm, hoping to pin it down. Bernard, Monica, Tom, Hannah, Grandmother, and Grandad—for even Grandad had made it out of his chair when she screamed—all had the same idea. Outstretched hands tried to reach Aunt Iris, but it was Bernard who grabbed the knife and toppled her to the floor, where she lay moaning: "You've stabbed me, you've stabbed me!"

Bernard dropped the knife, aghast. He bent down close to Aunt Iris, who lay in a heap. "Iris? Oh, my God! Iris?"

Everyone else leaned over them in panic. For a long moment it seemed Aunt Iris was beyond answering, and Beth felt cold fingers of dread clenching and unclenching her stomach. But then, still moaning softly, Aunt Iris sat up and held out her left hand. Blood seeped from a small cut on her palm. "I'm bleeding," she said in a small voice. "Will you get me a cloth, please, Mama?"

Beth sank onto the couch and closed her eyes. Talk about melodrama.

Grandmother hurried to help stop the bleeding, little cries of "my darling girl, oh, my poor Iris" trailing after her as she wrapped her arms around her daughter and led her from the living room. Grandad accompanied them both to the kitchen.

Hannah clung to Bernard, but this time it was he who looked about to burst into tears. "Did I do that to her, Hanny? Did I stab her?"

"Of course not! You were just trying to get the knife away from her." Hannah hugged him tightly. "You were doing what we were all doing. But you were the one who got it away. Thank God!"

Bernard shook his head, "I had no idea she was so unhappy. I can't believe it."

Beth frowned. "If she really wanted to kill herself, why not just do it back in the kitchen where no one would stop her?"

"Beth!"

"Mom, I just mean I don't think she really wanted to die. She wanted someone to stop her."

"You mean it was a bid for attention?" asked Bernard. "You could be right."

"It's the horrible thing about Clifton," Hannah said tearfully. "It's torn this whole family apart."

Grandmother and Grandad came back into the living room with Aunt Iris between them. Her hand was now bandaged, and she looked pale. They settled her on the couch solicitously. Monica handed her a small pillow to rest the injured hand upon.

"Well, we can be thankful it was only a small wound," said Grandmother. "And that my knives are spotless. I think Iris will be just fine."

"Unless she does a more thorough job on herself the next time she has a few drinks," said Grandad sourly. He looked over at Aunt Iris. "Come on, then, Iris. Let's hear about it. It's been weeks since we've heard you talk without a drink in your hand. Somebody make her some coffee. Strong as you can get it. I want to hear what that was all about."

"Henry! Give her a chance to settle down. The poor girl's had a shock!" Grandmother patted Aunt Iris's arm. "Maybe you should just go up and lie down."

"Not so much a shock as the one she gave us—threatening to stab herself to death right in front of everyone." Grandad pointed a long finger at his elder daughter. "No, Iris Anne. You need to talk to us, and yes—in front of these neighbors, too. You owe Bernard sincere thanks—and you owe everyone an apology. I can't believe a child of mine would ever stoop to such theatrics!"

Beth watched this exchange between her grandparents as if a tennis match were being played in front of her. First one, then the other, with Aunt Iris as the ball—batted to and fro. Beth moved off the couch to sit on the floor with Tom and Monica. The three of them leaned against the radiator under the windows, out of the way, silent, watching. The thought flitted through Beth's mind that "theatrics" was the right word. It really was a drama this time. Not melodrama. And not a tennis match. A play—complete with audience and actors, and Clifton Becker offstage in the wings. Or was he the scriptwriter?

"Henry!" Grandmother's voice trembled.

Everyone was surprised when Aunt Iris spoke. "No, Mama. He's right. And I am sorry." Tears slid down her sunken cheeks as she turned to Bernard, now in the armchair with Hannah standing by the side. "Bernie, I'm sorry. Thank you for pulling the knife away. Of course I don't want to die. I didn't really want to kill myself—I just—" She stopped and wiped the tears from her face with her uninjured hand.

"It's all right," Bernard said. His voice was deep and kind. "We understand."

But Hannah moved forward. "No, we don't! We don't understand anything. Iris, what's with you? Why do you hate us so much?"

"You're a fine one to ask that!" Aunt Iris's icy tone was back.

"Me? Listen, Iris, as far as I can see, you're the one to blame for all our unhappiness."

"I like that!" Iris stood and faced Hannah. "People who live in glass houses shouldn't throw stones, Hanny Lynn! Haven't you ever heard that before? How dare you blame me for anything, when it was you who—"

"Please! That's enough!" interrupted Grandad. "It's very tedious. You two sound like broken records—records stuck twenty years ago, still playing the same old song. I know I don't want to hear it again—and I bet that goes for everyone in this room."

Bernard raised his hand, almost, thought Beth, as if asking permission from the teacher to speak. Grandad nodded at him. Hannah and Aunt Iris were glaring at each other, and Bernard spoke into their taut silence.

"Actually, I think some of us *would* like to

hear it—that 'same old song,' as you said. Certainly we all seem to be involved."

Then he looked over at the three young people sitting against the radiator. "Well, maybe not you kids. But everyone else remembers that summer twenty years ago when Hanny Lynn broke up with me and left home. The summer when Iris's fiancé fell down the stairs and died."

"Was pushed," said Aunt Iris succinctly. "He was pushed."

"You bet he was!" Hannah's voice spat venom. Beth cringed against Tom.

"And we know who did it, don't we?" shouted Aunt Iris.

"You bet we do!"

"Stop it! Stop it!" Grandmother jumped to her feet, tears streaming down her wrinkled cheeks. "Oh, just stop it, both of you. This is all over and done with! Can't you just forget about it?"

"Forget that Hanny Lynn pushed my sweet Clifton?" Aunt Iris burst into tears. "Oh no, Mama. Never."

But Hannah was crying, too. "It wasn't me! It *wasn't*, Iris! You did it yourself, you know you did! You did it to get revenge!"

Bernard's voice was dry as he pulled Hannah back to the chair where he sat. "You see? It isn't a stuck record, exactly. It's two records playing together, each drowning the other one out."

"Come on, Dad," said Monica in a low voice from her place on the floor. "I think we really should go now. This isn't any of our business."

Bernard ignored her and pulled Hannah into his arms, right in front of everybody. She looked down at the floor. "Listen to me, Hanny." His voice was hard—out of character with his usual easygoing manner. "Stop crying. Iris, you, too. Let's try to straighten everything out. Not bottle it all up again. Okay? Tonight. Right now."

Grandad snorted. "A sensible suggestion if I ever heard one, my boy. You go right ahead and straighten us all out. Please be my guest."

Bernard *was* being arrogant, thought Beth. But who cared? There were no rules for how dinner guests should act when fake suicide attempts and family fights erupted right in front of them, were there? At this point all she wanted to do was sit so quietly no one would notice she was there. Her stomach was tight, and she knew eating dinner was an impossibility—not that anyone even seemed to remember the reason for their get-together, anyway. She dragged Romps into her lap, then pressed herself back against the radiator with Tom and Monica. Her eyes were riveted on Bernard. She felt she was sitting in the audience at a play—a drama begun long ago.

It's a play about people accusing each other, back and forth, forever throwing words like sticks and stones, thought Beth wildly. She remembered Aunt Iris's words. A family living in a glass house, dangerously hurling rocks at each other. Meaning to wound. At that moment it seemed quite possible that the whole house would shatter around their heads.

Aunt Iris glared at Bernard. "All right, Bernie Clements. You always were a nosy kid. I'll set the story straight." Beth saw her thin hands trembling.

"I loved Clifton. And he loved me more than anyone else ever has or will—don't smirk, Hanny Lynn! He did. And we were going to get married at the beginning of September, just after his birthday. He told me not to get him a present. He said I was all the present he ever needed." Aunt Iris was in tears again, but she dabbed them away with one finger and continued, her voice low and intense. Everyone in the room was quiet, listening, even Hannah.

"He never gave me reason to doubt his love for me—except once." She drew a deep breath. "And that was the night he died. I couldn't sleep, I was so excited about the wedding plans. I was lying awake, and it was very late. Everyone in the house had gone to bed. Or so I thought." She closed her eyes and sank onto the floor. She leaned her head against the edge of the coffee table, and for a moment Beth thought she wouldn't speak again. Still, everyone waited, mesmerized by her soft voice and the tale she was unfolding. Finally she sat up and opened her eyes.

"Clifton was typing. I could hear him. He often worked late on the book he was writing. The heroine in it was named Siri—get it? 'Iris' spelled backward. She was a beautiful princess from another world, with long red curls like mine, and she didn't limp at all. She didn't even have to walk—she could fly everywhere she wanted to go. I lay there listening to the clack-clack of his keys and wanted to be with him, but I knew he needed privacy to work. I was content, really, just knowing he was there next door."

Her voice grew hard. "But someone else didn't care about interrupting him. He'd stopped typing for a few minutes—I knew he was plotting out the next chapter—and I heard his door opening. No knock, just the creak it always made. I heard the murmur of voices, and I knew it was Hanny Lynn in there pestering him."

A sharp intake of breath from Hannah made Beth drag her eyes off Aunt Iris to where her mother now sat with Bernard. He had his arm around her shoulders and pressed them as a warning to remain silent. Hannah nodded stiffly, and Aunt Iris continued.

"Yes, it was Hanny. I waited for her to come out. She should have known he needed peace and quiet to work." Again Aunt Iris was quiet, and when she resumed her voice was even softer and lower than before. Beth leaned away from the radiator and strained to hear.

"But Hanny Lynn didn't come out. So I thought enough was enough, and I got out of bed to go tell her to get out and leave him to work."

This time the silence was so long that Beth feared her aunt would not finish the story at all. But Bernard spoke up, prompting her: "So you went into the room. And what did you find?"

"Whore!" Aunt Iris turned venomously on Hannah. "Trying to turn him from me, even thinking you could succeed! Really, it was a laugh. It was so pathetic, it really was. I shouldn't have been so upset—I know that now. He'd told me just that day after dinner how you were a nuisance. He thought you were the biggest laugh since God-knows-when. He cared nothing for you! But—seeing the two of you like that in bed—well, it shook me up. I started yelling—"

"As you do so well," spat Hannah.

"—yelling at her to get out," finished Aunt Iris, looking at the others. Her face was flushed now, beaded with sweat. "Yelling so loudly that Mama and Daddy woke up and came running. Remember? Mama was furious with Hanny and Daddy was furious with Clifton for letting her into his room in the first place."

"That's the first accurate thing you've said so far," Hannah broke in angrily. "Stop poking me, Bernie! It's my turn to talk now, if we're going to keep on playing Truth or Consequences."

"Try to keep it civil," he muttered. He sounded curt with Hannah now, and Beth wondered whether he was angry or sad to hear that she had been with Clifton after all, that there had, in fact, been an older man all the time.

Hannah stood up and appealed to her parents. "You both were angry—understandably so. But Iris is wrong; Clifton did love me. He told me he loved me! He'd been attracted to me for a long time. By August he'd given me very good reason to believe he intended to break off your engagement. It wasn't that he didn't like you, Iris," she amended, glancing at her sister. "It was just that, in the end, I was more his type. You really were like that alien princess. Lovely, perfect. Icy."

Almost perfect, thought Beth, remembering Aunt Iris's limp. But no one said anything, not even Aunt Iris. And Hannah kept talking.

"I was someone he could really be himself with. He told me that I made him come alive. And he always welcomed me into his room. He let me read some of his book and help him with it. We kept our feelings quiet. We thought you'd be hurt if you knew how we felt. But that's why I had to break up with you, Bernie." She glanced at his clouded face. "It wasn't honest to keep on seeing you, knowing that Clifton and I were soon going away together. We were going to get married as soon as I graduated. So, yes! That night I went to his room. He was glad to see me, damn it!"

"You're inventing this, Hanny Lynn," cried Aunt Iris. "You had a schoolgirl crush—we could all see that. But the big romance was just in your head!"

"You're forgetting what you saw with your own eyes, Iris! Did I invent his arms around me? Did I invent those kisses?"

"Look, wait a minute," Bernard broke in. He glanced over at Grandmother and Grandad on the couch. "Could we have someone else's story about what happened that night?"

Grandad was looking ill, Beth thought. The excitement and tension were too much for him. What if he had another stroke? Grandmother fingered the brooch on her black brocade dress and spoke haltingly.

"Well, we came running when we heard the girls yelling. And when we saw Hanny in the bed—well, you can imagine. What a betrayal of her sister—that was what I thought, and what I still do think! And as for that young man, well, we'd been thinking of him as a son, but just then I didn't want him in my house anymore. Would I want a man like that marrying my little Iris?"

"So she sent him packing," said Grandad in a gravelly voice. " 'Get out of here and don't come back!' she told him, and I agreed—but not so much on Iris's account. No, I was looking at Hanny Lynn huddling there in the hall in her nightgown, and I thought, Christ, the girl's only in high school! How dare he mess with my little girl? Still, when I think back, we didn't give the lad much of a chance to talk. And as for Hanny Lynn—" His gaze rested on his younger daughter for a second, eyes suddenly blank. "As for her, she was crying for him not to leave her, saying he'd promised to stay with her. Iris was howling that her sister was a liar and that Clifton was a traitor—she wanted him to leave that night, though I suspect she planned for them to talk the whole thing over in the light of day. You know these lovers' tiffs. Usually something can be worked out."

"But it was a little more than a tiff," Beth murmured to Tom. "And they never had a chance to talk things over in the light of day."

"I just wanted that young man out of my house after such disgraceful behavior," exclaimed Grandmother. "Under my roof! And as for Hanny Lynn—she may have been a high school girl, but she knew how to get what she wanted. I didn't have too much sympathy for her. But my poor baby, my innocent Iris! How she suffered that night."

Aunt Iris began crying. "Oh, God! When Clifton was packing his things he was saying he loved me and that I shouldn't worry, that we'd talk it all out—and then Hanny started hanging on him, wailing that it was time to tell the world that *she* was the one he loved, garbage like that. And then, oh, Mama was shoving him out of the room and Daddy was handing him his bag and even I was saying, 'Get out of here, how could you do such a thing!' "

Hannah took up the story then, without missing a beat. "And then we were all there at the top of the stairs, and poor Clifton was pleading with Mama and Iris to let him explain. But Daddy shoved the bag in his hand, and Mama and Iris were pushing him toward the steps, and I was reaching out, crying for him to stay with me, not to leave me with *them*—"

"And then you screamed that you'd *never* let me have him," hissed Aunt Iris.

Hannah towered over her sister, who still sat

on the floor by the coffee table. "And you screamed that he would never have anything to do with me again if *you* could help it!"

"And then you *PUSHED* him!" screamed Aunt Iris.

"YOU did, you must have! You've been blaming me all these years, but I swear I never—oh, Iris! You did it yourself!"

Aunt Iris leaped to her feet, shoving Hannah back with both arms. Hannah fought, raising her hands to pull Aunt Iris's wispy gray hair. Beth and Tom jumped up, too, and tried to pull them apart—but then Grandad struggled up from his seat and cut through all the commotion with a single word that left the walls ringing:

"Wrong!"

Everyone stopped and stared at him. He still looked sick, Beth thought, with his face glowing as if with fever. But when he spoke, his voice was calm. "This is where you're all wrong," he said. "So sit down. Give yourselves a break."

Everyone sat down. The atmosphere in the room was overpoweringly tense. Beth's stomach ached fiercely.

Grandad rubbed his hands over his bald head. "You're both wrong. This happened so long ago, you're not even sure of your stories, let alone your facts. But you do have a lot of the details right about those last minutes at the top of the stairs. I remember, too. And I may be older than anyone here, but my memory is the clearest on this. It has reason to be." He looked around the room at all of them listening and moved his hands as if painting a picture in the air for them to see.

"Think of it. Try to remember. We were all there. It's a small space. We were crowding him on the landing as he was starting down. Hands were reaching out all over the place—your mother shaking her fists in righteous anger. Iris pointing for the door, giving him what for. Hanny Lynn trying to grab him back, screaming that if he left her now she'd never forgive him. And then there was me. Standing there, too. Holding out his suitcase. Remember?"

And indeed, Beth seemed to remember that moment; she could see it all so clearly. She nodded. When she glanced at the others, they were all nodding, too.

Grandad's voice changed, grew gentle. He looked at his two daughters sitting before him on the floor and reached out his hands to them. They rose and stood next to him, not looking at each other.

"What happened in that next moment has torn us up for twenty years. And yet you two have got it all wrong." Grandad reached out and stroked Hannah's tear-stained cheek, then did the same to Iris's. "Iris, Hanny Lynn did not push Clifton. She was trying as hard as she could to make him stay with her. And Hanny—Hanny, honey. Iris truly loved Clifton and would never have hurt him, not even to keep you from having him." Grandad sighed a sigh so deep, it seemed to come from the past, whistling along to the present from all those long years back. "No, girls."

"Then who—?" Beth's own voice startled her. It sounded terrified.

"I did it," said Grandad simply.

The silence was absolute. Then Iris whispered, "No! Daddy—no, you couldn't have!"

"I didn't mean to, but I did it," Grandad said, reaching out again to touch her face. "I threw that suitcase into his hand—oh, yes, I was as angry as anyone that night. I shoved it at him and then—and it *was* right then, right at that second, that he fell backward. I've spent years denying it to myself, letting you both imagine. . . . But it was my hands that pushed him, girls. Not yours. Not ever yours. Mine."

Hannah was shaking her head. Beth found she was shaking hers, too.

But Grandad's voice continued, still surprisingly calm. "Oh, yes, I did, Hanny. I've been denying it to myself for so long, I've almost managed to convince myself. Sometimes I pretend it never happened at all—but it did. And I could have saved this family years and years of suffering if I'd owned up right when it happened."

"They might not hate each other so much today," said Grandmother, staring at her husband.

"That's right," he said. Grandad and Grandmother seemed to be holding a discussion with their eyes that Beth could not translate.

"Not hate!" cried Hannah. "I don't *hate* anybody! I just thought Iris—"

"But she didn't," repeated Grandad. "I did. It's my guilt. Not yours." He rubbed his bald head. "What a coward I've been. What an old fool." He sagged suddenly and groped for a chair.

"Oh, Daddy," said Iris weakly. She ran a hand across her eyes, then knelt by his chair. "Oh, Daddy, I'm sure you didn't mean to! It was just—"

"It *was,*" added Hannah, moving to his side. "It had to have been an accident."

The room was dead silent for the space of a heartbeat, then both Hannah and Aunt Iris were in his arms—and they were both crying. Grandmother walked slowly to them and placed one hand on Grandad's shoulder, one on Hannah's. They parted to make room for her, and the four of them huddled together in the corner of the living room, joined in one huge, long-overdue hug.

Bernard sat back, his face puzzled. Monica started crying. Tom saw his chance and wrapped his arms around her.

But Beth couldn't tear her eyes from the figures of Hannah and Aunt Iris and Grandmother and Grandad in the corner. She was staring especially hard at Grandad—that lanky, bald old man with the red-fuzzed arms who she would swear was as honest as the day is long. She couldn't grasp what he had said. *He did it?* she thought. *That old man pushed Clifton Becker crashing down the stairs and kept quiet about it all these years?*

And while she was trying to make sense of it, she saw him looking over at her even as she looked at him. And—could it really be?—he dropped her a slow, broad wink.

August

❦ ❦ ❦ ❦ ❦ ❦ ❦ The planet Notfilc was preparing for war. The evil overlords of the dark world Redrum had abducted the Notfilckian princess, beautiful Siri, and were preparing to sacrifice her to their violent slime-god, Timov.

Clifton gnawed on the end of his plastic blue pen. Although he used the typewriter to write his novel, he needed the pen for thinking. He was chewing thoughtfully now, trying to bite off the tip of the blue cap. Should he describe the details of the torture that awaited the princess before her rescuers found her in the island prison—for of course they would come!—or just leave the torture to the readers' imaginations and get on with the big rescue that was, after all, to be the climax of the entire novel. He bit off the small ball of plastic and spat it onto the floor.

Then he laid the pen down on the desk and leaned back in his chair with a mighty sigh. It wasn't working tonight. He had too many other things on his mind just now, and the plight of the lovely Siri could not blot out the fact of the lovely Iris just next door. Nor the fact of her little sister—that Hanny Lynn! He could strangle that girl.

But he knew he'd kiss her again first. First the kiss, because she kept insisting on demonstrating her kisses, and then the strangle, because he was utterly sick now of her whole fantasy world. How dare she? This was the question that plagued him now. So she wasn't content with her skinny schoolboy, Bernie. Okay. So she wanted some Big Romance in her life—preferably, because all teenage girls seemed to want this, with an older man. Fine! Go for it, Hanny! But he wasn't her man. It just wasn't fair that she should keep throwing herself at him, writing him into her script for the Big Romance.

Clifton smiled to himself, liking his imagery. Was he great with words, or what? *Forget it, old Hanny Lynn!* He was starring, co-starring, actually, in another drama. He shook his head and stood up, pushing back the desk chair with a scrape. No more typing tonight. Poor Princess Siri would have to lie on that island in agony until he could find time for her tomorrow night after work.

He left the sunporch and returned to the bedroom, then undressed and lay down on his bed in his underwear. It was beastly hot. Every few minutes a breeze puffed the lace curtain at the window across the room, but even the air was hot. And he was sticky! The August humidity was even worse than the August heat. He wanted a cold shower but knew the rattle and spray of the water would wake Iris's parents. He closed his eyes and imagined someplace cool—maybe Vermont in autumn. He hoped Iris would like to move somewhere like that with him. Small-town life—that's what he wanted. A quiet place to write, a backdrop of mountains outside his garret window. A couple of cute kids and a dog . . . He shifted on the bed, cursing the lumpy mattress.

He let his mind drift in the heat. Lazily he reached up one arm and switched off the bedside lamp, then turned on his side. Sleep was washing over him, but as it did he heard the soft pad of feet outside in the hall. His eyes flew open. *Iris!* Then, instantly, another thought hit him: *Or Hanny . . .*

"Oh, no," he moaned, burrowing his head deep into the feather pillow. He had really and truly had enough. Ever since that time on the front porch last month, Hanny Lynn had been a trial. She sidled up to him whenever they happened to be alone even for a second, wrapping her thin brown arms around him tightly, lifting her face to his, murmuring, "Kiss me, my love. . . ." He always pushed her away sharply, saying, Cut it out; don't be ridiculous. And once when she'd taunted, "You know very well you're just trying to deny to yourself that you're longing for me," he had sent her on her way with a sharp, little-girl spank to her blue-jeaned bottom, making her yelp. With embarrassment, he hoped.

And there had been the notes on his pillow. God, he was paying good money for the room even now that he was nearly a family member himself—you'd think there'd be a lock for the door. But no. While he was away at the zoo she would come in and read through his manuscript, pencil love notes in the margins. And she'd leave lines from Beatles songs on tiny scraps of paper in his shirt pockets and on his pillow—notes begging him not to hide his love away, notes crying out for help—she needed somebody, but not just anybody. The most recent note claimed that she loved him eight days a week. The little pest didn't even compose original lyrics.

Clifton groaned. But maybe it was Iris! She would sometimes slip in after the rest of the family had gone to bed, and they'd cuddle until she was nearly asleep, then he'd urge her back to bed in her own room. They were sticking to the rules, especially here in her parents' house. He couldn't wait till they had their own place.

His doorknob turned with a tiny click. He slipped under the sheet, drawing it up to his neck as the door opened.

"Darling? I need to talk to you."

Hanny Lynn. Clifton kept his eyes closed and tried to relax, tried to look as though he were deeply asleep. He could feel her standing at his side now.

"Clifton? How can you be asleep? You were working only fifteen minutes ago. I heard you typing!"

He made his breath deep and regular.

"Did you finish that torture scene? I was going to keep trying to convince you that the princess should be me, not Iris, but when I read what you had in store for her, I realized it had to be Iris after all. Clifton? Come on!" She grabbed his shoulder and shook.

He snored gently and turned slowly onto his other side. Maybe she'd go away. He simply wasn't up to a repeat of the other night when she'd come to him, just like this, and sat at his side for nearly an hour weeping out her longing for him. He had really felt sorry for the kid—you could see she'd thrown herself totally into her dream; the fantasy was real life to her, no script to a romance novel. And she was a nice girl, really, he had to admit. She had looked sweet—she was adorable—sitting there in her lacy cotton nightgown, imploring him to love her the way she loved him—grasping his hands, staring into his eyes as if hoping to hypnotize him. He was flattered!

And when he had taken her hands and told her for the millionth time that she was a darling girl, an exquisite child, but really too young and not the woman for him anyway, since he really and truly did love Iris, she had collapsed against him, sobbing her heart out.

And somehow he had been holding her and kissing her, first just on her forehead, then her cheeks, then her soft mouth—and she was kissing him back hungrily. It had been ages before he could get her out of his bed and out of his room. It had been a terrible mistake. He had been weak. Nothing like that must happen again tonight.

She shook him now. "Listen, you faker. I *know* you're not sleeping. And I can prove it!" And in that instant he felt her fingers on one eyelid and remembered too late that he should have rolled his eyes back into his head. Instead he stared at her. He pushed her hand away and sat up. She was wearing the same soft cotton nightgown. The scooped neckline was trimmed with lace.

"What are you trying to do? Blind me? What kind of thing is this for a guy to wake up to?"

"Ssshhh!" She giggled, settling herself on the bed next to him. "You know very well you weren't asleep. You look different when you're really asleep."

"Oh, no. Don't tell me—"

"Of course I do. I come in and watch you nearly every night."

"You crazy kid! You mean you stay awake just to come in and watch me sleep?" He marveled at this kind of devotion. He found it pleased him, even though, God knows, he didn't want it.

"Oh, no. I usually fall asleep right away. But I set my alarm for around three or four and come in then."

"You amaze me."

"Oh, Clifton, do I really? Oh, darling!"

"Look, give me a break. I like you a whole lot, Hanny. But you're getting on my nerves. Now go to bed. Go directly to bed."

"Do not pass GO? Do not collect two hundred dollars?"

"Precisely." He sighed and rubbed his eyes. "Look, I really am tired. The book didn't come along well tonight, and I need some sleep."

"Have you thought of where you can put me in it, Clifton?"

"I've already told you. Hannah isn't a good name for my book because you can't spell it backward. Right?"

"Well, how about *Hanny* backward?"

"You try to pronounce it." He lay back on his pillow. "Come on now. Out."

She fingered his sheet, watching him. "Promise me you'll dedicate the book to me. Promise!"

"I can't promise that, Hanny. But don't worry, I'll make sure you're there in spirit. I'll have you in as one of the nasty overlords."

She poked him in the ribs. "But they're all slimy! Come on, Clifton!"

"Go to bed, Slimy Overlord."

She poked him again, harder, then lifted the sheet and slid in next to him. "Okay. Here I am, in bed as you ordered."

This was going to be hard, damn it. He sat up again, knees sharp humps under the sheet, and stared down at her. She grinned up at him saucily, her long hair loose and dark against his white pillowcase. One bare shoulder peeked out from the top of the sheet covering her. His eyes lingered at the scoop of lace, then fastened intently on her throat, on the pulse beating wildly there. He met her eyes, and his were angry.

"Hanny Lynn. Get out of here. Now."

She stared up at him, stubborn, lips pressed together. The pulse pounded above her collarbone.

"Hanny—please!"

"I'm staying! You know you want me to stay. I can tell! And I could tell the other night when you—"

"Ssshhh! That's enough!"

Their voices were harsh whispers slashing through the dim room. "You kissed me! You held me and kissed me, and I could tell that you have fallen in love with me."

"No I haven't! It isn't true!"

"And you want to marry me! We'll get married as soon as I graduate!"

"No we won't!"

"You know you love me. Okay, you won't say the words, but I don't need to hear them. All I needed was that kiss—all those kisses—the other night. They're worth more than a zillion words!"

"I love Iris," he hissed at her. "Why can't you get that through your thick head?"

"Say that you love *me!*"

Oh, damn, now she was crying. Why did this sort of thing have to happen to him? What was he supposed to do with her? He raised his hand, intending to push her over the side of the bed onto the floor and out of his room, but found instead that his hand was somehow capable of betraying him, just as his lips had betrayed him the other night. His fingers stroked her cheek, wiped the tears from under her eyes with the flat of his thumb. He ran his fingers through her long hair, traced her lips with one finger.

She was silent, lying very still, her eyes on him steadily.

Yes, she was lovable. And desirable. He bent over to kiss her, and her arms moved up to hold him. And he did love her—yes, he *did.* But not as much as he loved Iris. Even through the passion she had aroused in him now, he knew that. But how could he make her understand without hurting her? He knew he had to try.

He whispered into her ear, one hand cradling her to him, the other still stroking her hair. "Yes, little Hanny Lynn. I do. I do love you, but not the way you think. I love you as a—" But he pulled back in alarm as the bedroom door flew open and Iris limped in, her bright hair flowing over her shoulders like a burst of flame, and her eyes ablaze.

He hardly knew the order of what happened next. There was Iris in the doorway, one hand frozen on the knob. There were he and Hanny Lynn, springing apart. He leaped out of bed, still only in his underwear, holding his arms out to Iris, saying he could explain it all. She screamed at him, called him names he didn't think she even knew. Screamed at Hanny Lynn: "You little whore!" And Hanny screamed back:

"You don't know anything! We love each other! He loves me, Iris. *Me*, not you!"

There were footsteps running down the hallway and Clifton made a dash for his clothes, managing—almost—to zip a pair of shorts as Mr. and Mrs. Savage burst into the room behind Iris.

They were livid. Mrs. Savage ripped Hanny Lynn from the bed and slapped her; Mr. Savage, hands on hips, bellowed for an explanation. And there went Hanny again, fouling everything up with her garbled version of reality: "We love each other! Ask him, if you don't believe me!"

Aha—at last he'd have a chance to explain. "No!" he shouted, intending to keep calm and failing. "Hanny doesn't understand. Iris!" He turned to her, but she shrugged away and went to stand by the window. "Iris, you know I love you. You know that! We're getting married, for God's sake! I can explain everything—"

But then he saw Hanny Lynn's shocked face, and she didn't seem a child anymore but a woman. And one he had wounded.

"You said you loved me, Clifton Becker." Her voice was hard, though almost inaudible. The others fell into a sudden hush and her words dropped like icicles into the hot room, their points sharp and dangerous. "Only two minutes ago. We were holding each other in that bed and you said—and I quote!—'Hanny, I do. I do love you.' Can you deny that?" What she saw in his eyes made her wild with anger, and she leaped toward him, betrayed and screaming: "You bastard! You can't deny you said it!"

"Look, can't we discuss this reasonably? I did—okay, I did say that. But you didn't let me finish." He kept his voice calm, hoping to calm the others who were, he sensed, wound tightly just ready to spring at him. *Clifton Among the Savages*, he thought. It would make a good title when he got around to writing all this down. "I didn't have a chance to finish."

Mr. Savage struck his fist heavily on the oak dresser, rattling the big mirror. "This is appalling," he roared. "I won't have this kind of stuff going on in my house! We all thought you were honorable, young man. And look at this! What have you been doing here? Playing one girl off the other? I won't have that kind of game in my house, no sir! I'll thank you to get right out of here. You are no longer welcome."

"Oh, Daddy!" That was Iris, but Mrs. Savage shushed her, pulling her out into the hall.

"Let him go tonight, Iris, baby. Daddy's right. You and he can try to work things out later."

Hanny Lynn broke away from them all and tore into her room, howling at the top of her lungs. "Someone should slap her," Clifton said angrily. "She's getting hysterical." He pulled his small overnight case out of the closet, itching to slap her himself. Actually he felt like beating up the whole lot of them, savages that they were. Single-handedly.

He threw the case on the bed and started gathering his clothes.

"If anyone gets slapped around here, it ought to be you," yelled Mrs. Savage from out in the hall. "Carrying on like this behind my back. Behind Iris's back! You ought to be ashamed. I want you out of here!"

"Oh, Mama! Oh, Clifton!" wailed Iris, pressing tearfully into the room around her mother. Clifton shoved his underclothes and socks and a bottle of shampoo haphazardly into his case. "Clifton, how could you?"

"Let's meet for lunch sometime and I'll tell you the whole story," he said coolly, going out to the sunporch and grabbing the pages of his manuscript off the desk. Iris turned away, tears streaming down her cheeks.

At last he was packed—not all his things, of course, but enough for a few days until everyone calmed down and they could discuss this rationally. While he'd been packing he'd been thinking that this really might be just one of those storms in a teacup you heard people talk about. Give everyone a day or two—maybe even a week—and they'd be ready to listen to him. And then he'd hold Iris and make her understand how Hanny Lynn had been tormenting him. She would have to understand that! She, better than anyone, knew how Hanny Lynn was. And he'd talk to Hanny, too. Firmly and sternly. The whole Older Brother bit. Yes, he cared about her. Yes, he'd said he loved her—but hadn't been able to finish because Iris stormed in right at that second. *But—read my lips, Hanny Lynn!—I am going to marry Iris. Not you! I love you only* as a sister! *Get it? You're a nice kid, okay. And in the moonlight in my bed you look lovely. But none of that means I'm going to throw Iris over for you, you little twit.*

He felt better just making these plans. Then Mr. Savage was there at his elbow. "You'd better not come back to the house for a while," he said. "We've all had quite enough of you and your games."

"I wish you would give me a chance to explain, sir," Clifton said.

"Oh, you'll get it. But I wouldn't be surprised if the damage you've done is irreparable. You don't mess around with people's love, my boy."

Clifton moved out into the hall. There was just no talking to these folks tonight.

When she heard him in the hall, Hanny Lynn came tearing out of her room and threw herself against him. "Don't go!"

He shrugged her off, only to be assaulted by Iris. "I wish you were dead, you—you—," hissed Iris.

"Just go!" shouted Mrs. Savage.

"Iris! Believe me. We'll talk about this soon, when we've calmed down—"

"You do not love Iris! You *DON'T!* You just feel sorry for her!" Hanny Lynn clung to him again, even as Iris reached out to slap her.

Then Mrs. Savage was pushing him toward the stairs. "You have money for a hotel, don't you? Then go! We have had quite enough for one night."

Mr. Savage shoved the overnight bag into his hand, and at the same time both girls surged forward, Hanny howling: "Take me with you! I'll kill you if you leave me with them!" and Iris gagging on her fury: "You'll never have him! I'll see to that!"

Clifton almost laughed as he stepped back hastily away from all of them, laughed at the way they were fighting over him as if for some prized toy.

But then his laugh caught in his throat as his ankle twisted under him and he slipped and felt himself falling backward, falling down the entire flight of shiny wooden steps. *What a stupid thing to do!* he was thinking wildly, and then at the last, as his head shattered on the iron radiator at the foot of the stairs: *It's true what they say—you really do see stars.*

5

At the dinner table Beth tried to find safe topics of conversation. She asked Bernard about the candy store's history. She asked Monica for information about art schools in Europe. As her guest talked, Beth could almost see their words filling the room like smoke. From where she sat, everyone began to look like figures worked in the sooty dark glass she was using for shadows in her window downstairs. Beth kept her eyes on Grandad. She stared at him across the table, trying to make her eyes as penetrating as possible. Trying to read his mind. Grandad never once looked her way. But he *had* winked, hadn't he?

Everyone declined second helpings. Bernard announced to everyone's relief that Monica and he wouldn't be able to stay for coffee but must be going. Good-byes were said quickly, and then the family was alone. Nobody said anything for a few minutes, then Grandad said he was tired and would go straight up to bed.

"We're all tired out," Grandmother murmured. "Please—let's just leave things till morning." It was a sign, Beth thought, of how upset Grandmother was: she was willing to leave the dirty china to soak overnight in the kitchen sink. Tom followed Grandmother and Grandad up the stairs.

Without conferring about it, Hannah and Aunt Iris stayed together in the kitchen to tackle the washing up. The silence as they worked was broken only by the clink of silverware, the trickle of rinse water, the clang of a pot lid being put away in the cupboard near the stove. Beth stood for a moment watching from the doorway. She sensed that, despite the silence, some of the tension between her mother and Aunt Iris was gone now. It had something to do with the way they held their bodies. Aunt Iris seemed to move with less rigidity. And when she handed Hannah the deviled-egg platter, their fingers touched briefly.

Beth slipped down into the basement, closing

the door softly behind her. Unlike the others, she didn't feel tired at all. Instead she felt energized, almost edgy. It was, after all, not yet nine o'clock. If the dinner party had gone as planned, they'd all be upstairs drinking tea or coffee and eating Grandmother's peach pie with vanilla ice cream. She and Tom and Monica would have left the adults to carry on while they came down here to view Beth's new window.

She pulled the protecting sheet off the window now. It was nearly finished. She had only one last section to solder. She spread newspaper on Grandad's work bench and centered the window carefully. She plugged in the soldering iron and set out the clamps and the coil of solder. Then she perched on her stool and wrapped the last few shapes of glass in copper foil. She moved the pieces slowly into place, almost hypnotized by their colors and textures. Beth let the tangles of the evening recede from memory, losing herself in the pleasure of her work. An hour or so later she heard Aunt Iris and her mother leave the kitchen to go up to bed. No one came down into the basement, and no one called her name.

Beth felt the house around her as she worked. It was full of sleeping troubled people, but down here in her work space she felt a little core of energy, like light, pulsing as she worked. She wanted—no, *needed*—to finish the window tonight. She couldn't say why. But she stayed downstairs until two o'clock in the morning etching the last details onto the glass canvas, and the time passed as if in an instant.

It was only when she finally stood back to look at her creation propped against the wall next to Aunt Iris's Notfilc painting that exhaustion rushed over her like a wave. She felt too tired now to exult in the completion of her project. She cleaned up mechanically, washing the grinder, separating the different colored leftovers into piles, and sealing them in envelopes for future use. She swept the floor, plodded up the stairs to the kitchen and then into the living room and up the steep, narrow flight to the bedrooms.

Beth's head was pounding when she woke up. Her left wrist was cramped and painful, as if she'd slept on it bent back the wrong way. She shook her arm and pressed on her temples, then shielded her eyes against the morning light streaming through the window.

Tom opened the door from his sunporch and tiptoed quietly across her room to the door.

"I'm awake," Beth said, keeping her voice low.

He walked over to stand by her bed. "I've been awake in there for ages, thinking about last night."

"Don't remind me. I have a splitting headache."

His face was bright with excitement, but he kept his voice a whisper. "So, what do you think? Isn't it weird? All these years Mom and Aunt Iris have been enemies—and it was Grandad all the time! Here we were, suspecting Aunt Iris and Grandmother—*you* even thought it might be Mom!—and we never even considered Grandad!"

"But that's just it!" Beth struggled out of the mattress's valley and sat up. "Think about it, Tom! We never suspected Grandad for a good reason. He's the calmest, gentlest, most reasonable man I've ever met! Who could really believe he pushed Clifton Becker down the stairs and never told anyone?"

"*I* never would have guessed, that's for sure. God, he must have felt so guilty all these years!"

"But that's just what I mean. I can't believe Grandad wouldn't have owned up to what he'd done when it happened."

Tom sank onto the edge of the bed. "But he was trying to pretend it hadn't happened. He couldn't face it. You heard what he said last night."

"Yeah." Beth leaned her head against the headboard. "I heard what he said. But I saw him wink after he said it."

"What?"

She threw off the sheet and swung her legs over the side of the bed. She groaned as pain stabbed her temples.

"He *winked?* You must have imagined it. . . ."

"Well, I didn't."

"Why would he wink? That doesn't make sense."

She shrugged and moved past him, out of the room and down the hall to the bathroom. The hallway was quiet, and all the bedroom doors were closed. She splashed cold water on her face and pulled on some clothes from the laundry bin.

When Beth emerged into the hall again, Tom was gone. She stood on the landing, gazing down at the iron radiator. Then she slowly went downstairs, massaging her wrist, and let herself out onto the front porch. Romps began woofing in the backyard, and she ran to untie his leash. She looked up at the bulk of the house from her place by Romps's elm tree in the yard, and the house seemed peaceful. Now that Grandad had confessed, there was no more mystery—right? They could all let Clifton Becker rest in peace.

But Beth couldn't stand the quiet house and the sense of peace on this hot August morning. It all seemed so wrong. She clapped her hands for Romps, who was rooting in the rose bed. "Come on, boy!"

And she took off running down the street with the little gray schnauzer at her heels. She ran and ran, down block after block, veering away from Penn's Pike and the candy shop.

Maybe it was just the runner's high she'd always heard about but never experienced, but as she ran, she began to feel lighter. Her head thudded at first, right along with her pounding heart, and her wrist ached with every jolt along the pavement. But as her legs kept up their sturdy pumping, her head cleared. The strain of all the weeks in the tense house seemed to flow right out of her as she flew on, and when she circled back down Spring Street, her body felt loose and her wrist didn't hurt anymore. She sank onto the grass in the front yard, burying her face against Romps's heaving side. Then she lay back and stared up at the sky. The leaves of the trees and the clouds above seemed part of a giant stained-glass window, through which she watched Grandad wink and wink and wink.

She lay there a long time, thinking. Then finally, resolved, she hurried into the house. From the kitchen came the smell of bacon and scrapple and freshly brewed coffee, and her stomach rumbled with the first real hunger pangs she'd felt in weeks. She heard Tom's and Hannah's voices, then laughter. Laughter? In *this* house?

She climbed straight up to the front bedroom and tapped lightly on the door.

"Yes?" Grandad called.

"Open up. It's the police." She stepped into the air-conditioned room. "Come out with your hands up."

He was lying in bed, arms folded behind his head, the picture of contented repose. His smile lit his entire face. "Good morning, Beth!"

"Oh, Grandad." She pulled up the bedside chair. "You are the biggest liar in the history of the world."

He raised his bushy eyebrows. "What—me?"

"You!" She sat down with a thump, shaking her head at him. "I can't believe it."

"Maybe so, maybe so," he conceded. "But what's the proof, officer? A man's innocent until proven guilty in this country. It's what the founding fathers quite kindly arranged."

Beth sat staring at him for a long moment, then she put her hand on his wrinkled arm. "Grandad, listen. You didn't push Clifton Becker."

"I said I did and so I did."

"I know you didn't!"

"You can't know that, Beth. There are some things that can't be known."

"Please, Grandad! Tell me why you said you pushed him."

"Look, I'm old, Beth." He crossed his long legs under the sheet. "I've learned a lot in my time. I've learned that people have their own little views of the world, and they try to fit things into their own narrow scopes of vision." His mouth pursed bitterly. "And if something doesn't really fit—they often twist it until it does."

"But you're the one who's twisting things. You *know* someone else pushed him. You know it—so why take the blame yourself?"

"I know nothing of the sort." Grandad frowned at her. "You're not thinking clearly. You want to blame someone because you've been told that someone pushed him. Right?"

Beth looked puzzled. "I guess."

He leaned forward. "Then listen carefully, my girl. Hanny told you Iris must have done it. And Iris told you Hanny Lynn certainly did it. And Grandmother hasn't wanted to believe either of them did it, but because she has always favored Iris, she has tended to believe Iris. And I have tended to think Iris sometimes can't tell an egg from her elbow, and I've seen her in her rages, so I've half-believed Hanny was right. But what if we're all wrong? What if *no one* pushed him?"

"You mean, what if he just fell—by himself?"

"Right—tripped over his own big feet and fell while all of us were shouting at him. It was a nasty scene on that landing, Beth, but I can tell you my mind was certainly not on murder. And if mine wasn't, perhaps no one else's was, either."

Beth's thoughts were racing along with his, trying to keep up. "But if it was an accident and he just fell by himself, how come there were accusations of murder in the first place?"

"Because of the problems between Iris and

Hanny Lynn!" He lowered his voice, and she leaned closer to the bed. "Because of the jealousy, maybe even hatred. I'm not saying either girl accused the other just to be vindictive; I'm saying that things were so bad between the sisters that each one truly *believed* she had seen the other stick out her arm and push him—" He broke off and kicked away the sheet. He was sweating, despite the air conditioner. "That's the saddest thing for me, Beth. That each girl believed the other capable of murder—and *wanted* to believe. Makes me feel we've failed as parents somewhere along the line." He rubbed his forehead.

"Then just last night it came to me that the only way this family might be saved would be if each girl stopped seeing the other as a possible killer. I've thought for years that the whole thing could have been a horrible accident, but when I brought up the idea, just after the poor lad fell, everyone pushed it away. You see, they were all too angry about the circumstances of his death." His eyes held hers, intent. "Don't you get it? They needed to think someone pushed him."

Beth stood up and walked to the window. She looked down at the boxwood hedge, at

Romps still lying in the grass. "I don't see why you don't just tell everyone you saw him fall. That you know *absolutely* it was an accident."

"No one will believe me. Even after all this time, they still need to blame someone. It's better this way."

"No it isn't! I'm not going to sit back quietly and let people say you're a murderer!"

"Well, it *could* have happened as I said it did. Maybe my hands *were* the last he felt before he fell, after all. We just can't know."

Her words burst out loud and sharp over the hum of the air conditioner. "It isn't *right!*"

"Come here, Beth."

She walked back to his bed, rebellion making her eyes sting. She would tell everyone! She would announce Grandad's lie at the breakfast table!

He put out one arm to pull her closer, and his voice was very low. "You listen, and you keep quiet. I don't want this to leave this room. I hope I can trust you."

She didn't like the sound of this at all.

"Now, you listen hard," he whispered. "I haven't been the greatest father, I know that. But if I *had* seen the whole thing really was an accident, there is no way I would have kept quiet." His voice rose. "What man in his right mind would stand by for twenty years and let his daughters accuse each other of murder when he knew there had been no murder? I can't think what kind of man would do that—can you?"

She couldn't.

"So let them think I'm a weak old man who was too cowardly to face his own guilt all these years. If they can believe that, they can believe the whole thing is finally over now that I've confessed. You saw how quick they both were last night to forgive me!"

He rubbed his head. "I think a lot of the angry accusations came about because each one worried secretly that she had been the one to touch him last. . . . Believing I pushed him relieves each girl of that burden of guilt as well. I think it's about time the hating stopped around here."

Beth traced a pattern on his white sheet with her finger. "It makes you into a martyr," she whispered. "Why do you have to do it?"

Grandad snorted. "Martyr! Don't be ridiculous! I should have thought to do this years ago." He shook his head. "I'm a selfish old man, Beth."

"Grandad, that's not true! God, what a thing to say."

"I insist you never tell anyone about this talk we've had. Promise me, Beth."

She shook her head stubbornly. "I don't want people believing a lie about you."

He patted her hand. "We all believe lies. We just don't know how many lies we believe."

She pulled her hand away. "Murder is a serious crime, you know! People can't just go around confessing to murder!"

He cleared his throat, and she thought for a moment the cough overlaid a chuckle. "I promise I'll never confess to another one—how about that? And it wouldn't be murder, anyway. Manslaughter, at the most."

"Well, people can't go around lightly confessing to manslaughter, either." Her voice remained stubborn. When he reached for her hand again, she twined her fingers together in her lap. "You think you're safe from the police because we're your family. But what about this—I bet you never thought about what might happen if Bernard or Monica tells the police what you said last night!"

"Justice must be done, eh?"

"You can't mean to say you don't even care!"

"I'm not going to live forever, my girl. I want to leave my family something worth having when I go."

Beth didn't like this kind of sacrifice, didn't understand it. She resolved to beg Bernard and Monica not to turn Grandad in to the police.

Footsteps in the hall made Grandad sink quickly back into his pillows, and Beth jumped up and stood by the chair. Tom opened the door. "Good morning! I'm here to help you down to breakfast, Grandad."

"Breakfast, is it? Well, you go along now, Beth. I'll just stay here and rest up for lunch." He smiled. "Those stairs are sometimes too much of a challenge."

"It's a special breakfast," Tom told them. "Everybody's waiting. I have orders to bring you down, Grandad." He grinned. "Even if I have to sling you over my shoulder."

"Spoken like the gentleman that he is," muttered Grandad, getting out of bed.

Beth followed them down with a frown on her face. At the entrance to the dining room, the frown changed to a look of amazement. The table was set with the best china again and groaned under the weight of the platters of scrapple and bacon and fried potatoes, the baskets of muffins and fresh fruit, and the uneaten peach pies from last night's dinner. Frosty pitchers of orange juice and milk stood in the center, next to a large bouquet of zinnias from the garden. But most astonishing of all was the sight of both Bernard and Monica sitting there, hands folded neatly atop the table, waiting for them.

"About time," said Bernard, checking his watch. "We're starving!"

"But what are you two doing here?" cried Beth.

"A fine way to greet our guests," scolded Aunt Iris, entering from the kitchen bearing a plate of fluffy scrambled eggs. But she smiled at Beth. "The usual greeting is 'Good morning. How nice to see you.' "

Her voice was light, but her eyes held a flicker of uncertainty as they probed Beth's face. It was, Beth thought, as if Aunt Iris were trying to act in a friendly manner, but wasn't quite sure she knew how anymore.

Beth sat down next to Monica. "Of course it's nice to see you," she said. "I just didn't expect—"

"Nor did I," said Grandad, as Tom helped him to his chair. "This is a surprise indeed."

Grandmother carried in a stack of hot buttered toast and set it on the table. Hannah came in with two jars of jam. "I think we're ready now," she said to Aunt Iris, and the sisters started passing the platters of food. Beth noticed how they both stood near Grandad as he filled his plate, urging large helpings on him and filling his juice glass.

"Yes," said Grandmother, as if she were continuing a conversation already going on, "the girls and I got to thinking what a shame it was that no one really seemed in very high spirits for our little party last night. So we thought we'd try again with breakfast." She took her seat opposite Grandad. "Hanny Lynn got on the phone to Bernie, and Iris and I started cooking, and here we all are."

"And, of course, Monica and I were delighted to come," said Bernard. He wiped egg off his mouth with a linen napkin. "I could never turn down a home-cooked Pennsylvania Dutch breakfast!"

"The muffins are delicious," Monica added.

"Iris made them," Hannah said quickly. "She's always been a wonderful cook."

Aunt Iris smiled shyly and glanced around the table to see how people were responding to this praise. Beth noticed her aunt was actually eating one of the muffins herself. "But just taste the scrapple," Aunt Iris urged Monica. "Hanny Lynn's the only person I've ever known who can fry it to perfection. It sticks to the pan for everyone else. Imagine that—after all these years away from Pennsylvania Dutch country, Hanny's back home frying up our scrapple again!" And Aunt Iris heaped a few slices on her own plate and passed the platter to Monica.

Beth met Tom's eyes across the table. He was beaming. Grandad and Grandmother were grinning at each other like maniacs, too. Beth tasted her scrapple, then put down her fork. Wasn't this the best time for her announcement about Grandad's big lie?

Yet the table talk was so happy and friendly, she didn't want to spoil it. Hannah and Aunt Iris kept complimenting each other about the food until it seemed to Beth their sweet words powdered the table like sugar. The scene was almost surreal. She expected her family to burst into song and dance over their meal at any moment—just like actors in an old musical. Anything seemed possible. She actually wondered for a second if Grandad's bogus confession had really been a magic spell.

When she glanced at him again, he was looking right at her. And he winked. Was the joke on her?

Monica nudged her knee under the table and nodded toward Beth's plate. Beth picked up her fork obediently and dug into the mound of scrambled eggs. Were they all going to pretend nothing had happened? Could so many years of anger and accusation disappear so quickly? What would happen now if, ever so casually, Beth were to mention Clifton Becker's name?

Grandad would kill her, that's what would happen. And so would Hannah and Aunt Iris and Grandmother. Tom, too. Everyone seemed content to accept Grandad's gift—without even knowing it *was* a gift.

After the huge breakfast, Beth helped clear the table. Grandmother and Hannah and Aunt Iris were in the kitchen, fussing cheerfully about who would wash and who would dry. "You girls go chat with our guests," urged Grandmother. "This is my kitchen!"

"Now, Mama," said Hannah, "they're your guests, too. Go on in and rest your feet. You, too, Iris."

But Aunt Iris chimed in: "Oh, but Hanny

Lynn, you and Bernie must have so much catching up to do after all these years. I'm happy to wash up."

It was truly nauseating. "Look, you guys, I'd *love* to do the dishes," Beth announced, pulling the dish towel out of her mother's hands.

"Why, Elisabeth, how nice of you!" cried Aunt Iris.

"Sweet of you to offer," added Grandmother.

Only Hannah heard the ironic tone and glanced at her rather reprovingly, but then she smiled, too. "Thanks, Beth honey." And the three of them left the room together.

Beth stretched her face into a huge, mocking smile and grinned after them, then at the dirty dishes piled on the counters. She forced the smile even wider and beamed into the sink, turning the hot water on hard. She filled the pans and left them on the stove to soak, then attacked the silverware, her face relaxing once more. *What a bunch of lunatics.* She listened in astonishment to the hum of bright chatter from the living room, wondering how a single lie could transform so many people.

"Pretty amazing, isn't it?" asked a deep voice behind her, and she whirled around to find Bernard lounging against the refrigerator with a cup of coffee in his hand. Had he read her mind?

"You mean the merry maniacs?"

He nodded toward the living room. "Quite a party this morning. Much nicer than the theatrics of last night, don't you think?" He pulled a tea towel off a hook on the side of the refrigerator and began drying the cutlery as she laid it on the drainboard.

"Well, thank God at least *you* admit it was an act," Beth said slowly. "I wondered if I was the only one who noticed."

"Oh, I think on some level everyone knows what happened. But your grandfather's story has made everything all right again—at least he's got everyone talking without snarling. First time in twenty years! I'd say that's quite an accomplishment."

"So—you know the confession was a lie?" Relief flooded Beth's face.

"Let's just say I understand what he was trying to do."

"Oh, I'm so glad you know! I was afraid you might turn Grandad in to the police."

"What for?"

"For murder! I mean, for manslaughter. I mean, if you'd believed his story."

"Oh, Beth." Bernard touched her shoulder and she turned from the sink. "The police couldn't arrest an old man on the strength of that story alone. There'd have to be witnesses. There's got to be evidence of a crime."

"I was getting so worried—" Her eyes filled with tears.

Bernard patted her awkwardly on the shoulder. "His version of the truth has made it possible for this family to start healing. You all owe him a lot." He picked up a serving spoon and polished it vigorously.

"But doesn't the *real* truth count for anything?" wailed Beth.

"Certainly it counts. Of course we should all seek the truth. But sometimes the truth simply can't be known—as in the case here, with this Clifton fellow. And in this case, I'd say it's what you *perceive* to be the truth that counts. In cases like this you have to make your own reality. For twenty years there's been one reality. Now your grandad's story—his 'lie,' as you insist on calling it—has simply made another reality possible. A better one, I think you'll agree."

"Bernard—are you going to tell my mom?"

"No way! I bet this is what Hanny has needed for years. She can finally stop blaming her sister—and she can stop worrying secretly that maybe she pushed the guy herself!"

"That's just what Grandad said," murmured Beth.

"Smart man, your grandad."

Beth shrugged. Was this what Grandad had been trying to explain to her upstairs? She remembered the brainteaser he'd shown her. What was true and what was false, and did it matter? She felt confused. She finished washing the dishes in silence. Bernard dried the last fork, then balled up the dish towel and tossed it onto the counter. He hugged her shoulders briefly.

"Think about it, Beth." And then he went back to the family in the living room.

She shook out the wet towel and hung it neatly back on its hook.

Beth thought about what Bernard and Grandad had said while she drank a cup of tea with everybody in the living room. She thought about it when she took Monica down into the basement to see her window. Monica wanted her to bring it upstairs, where they could look at it in the light. Beth refused.

Weird and unbelievable things continued to

happen in the house on Spring Street all day. Grandad and Grandmother decided to go for a walk. And when Tom offered to come along to push his wheelchair, they said they'd rather be alone. Stranger still, Hannah and Grandmother hung out in the kitchen together later, watching soaps and weaving lattice crusts for more pies—blueberry this time. Grandmother said it was about time Hanny Lynn learned how to bake, and Hannah just grinned. While they were cozily mixing dough in the kitchen, Grandad and Aunt Iris sat chatting in the living room. They each had a beer, but when Beth checked later, both had switched to lemonade. Beth reflected that it was probably the first time since she and her mother and Tom had been there that Aunt Iris had drunk something nonalcoholic.

Weirdest of all, after the pies were safely in the oven and the aroma of blueberries filled the house, Hannah and Aunt Iris went out shopping together. Beth wondered whether Aunt Iris had been in a department store in the last twenty years and rather doubted it. They didn't ask Beth whether she wanted to come. When they returned home, they modeled new sundresses. Aunt Iris looked like a scarecrow in hers—all bones and wisps of hair like straw. But everyone went on as if she'd brought home something remarkable. And maybe she had.

The day continued to pass peacefully. Tom borrowed the laptop computer from his friend Mark and sat out on the porch reading the user's guide. Beth felt unsettled. She wandered down to the basement and cleaned her window. The polished lead gleamed like silver, and the colors in the glass sparkled even in the dim light. It was really the best piece she had ever done. What a shame it had to hide in the basement until she could get it safely home to California!

In the evening the family sat out on the porch together, drinking lemonade. At first Grandad wanted to stay inside with his air conditioner and grumbled about the heat. But Aunt Iris and Hannah each took one of his hands and begged him to join them outside.

"There's a nice breeze," coaxed Hannah.

"The fresh air is good for you, Daddy," added Aunt Iris.

"Maybe so, maybe so," he muttered, allowing them to lead him out and settle him in one of the wicker rocking chairs.

"You're much better these days," Hannah said. "You really don't need to stay up in your room so much anymore."

"You listen to Hanny," said Aunt Iris.

He looked from one daughter to the other and shook his bald head. Beth shared his astonishment. It was as if a truce had been declared after a long war. Everyone seemed so relieved not to be fighting anymore. And everyone wanted Grandad around as—what? Their peace symbol? Her toe tapped the floor to keep the glider moving. She looked around at all of them—at Grandad talking with Grandmother. At Tom telling Aunt Iris about the computer camp he had missed going to this summer. At Hannah leaning toward them, listening.

"You'll be able to go next summer, Tom," Hannah said.

"I'm glad you came here instead," Aunt Iris told him. "Though I must admit, I don't have the faintest idea at all what people do at a computer camp in the first place!"

"Oh, it's a lot of fun," said Beth from the swing. "You get to take your computer to the lake for fishing and sing with it around a campfire!"

Aunt Iris stared at her for a moment, then actually giggled. "Well, for all I know, you could be right. I don't know a thing about computers. Never touched one in my life."

Tom gaped at her. "We'll have to fix that, Aunt Iris! No one can live in the real world without a computer!"

"That's debatable," said Beth from the swing. "*You* can't live long without computers, but it's not that difficult for normal people!"

"It's funny, isn't it," mused Hannah, "the things we think we can't live without? And how, if it really comes down to it, we can after all? Sometimes it's hard, but in the end, we manage anyway."

Somehow Beth didn't think her mother was talking about computers anymore.

Aunt Iris put her hand to her eyes, and Beth hurried to change the subject. "Well, I know I couldn't live long without a glass cutter in my hand!"

"See, you're as bad as I am," said Tom.

Aunt Iris uncovered her eyes. "I used to think," she said slowly, "that I couldn't live without a paintbrush in my hand. I think I was right about that."

"What do you mean, Iris?" asked Hannah. "You haven't painted in years and years—and see? You're still here."

"Am I really?"

Beth swung gently, seeing in her mind's eye

the pile of canvases and crates of brushes and paints in the corner of the basement. In a way, Aunt Iris was right. The girl who had painted those vibrant pictures was long dead. The woman left behind without a paintbrush in her hand was in many respects no more than a shell. But did it have to be that way? Clifton Becker was dead and no one could bring him back, but the brushes down in the crates were as good as ever. Add a few new tubes of paint, and—

"Aunt Iris?" Beth began in a firm voice, before she could lose her nerve. "Listen, I was down in the basement and I found your canvases. I had to look at them, I couldn't help myself. You did *beautiful* work! The colors are totally fantastic—so lovely and bright." She shot a glance at her aunt, whose face was still and shuttered. "I was so impressed, Aunt Iris! Some of those paintings are exhibition quality. Don't you think you might, you know, be able to start again?" She held her breath, waiting for the explosion.

But it never came. Aunt Iris just sat staring at her hands for a long moment. When she finally spoke her voice was hoarse, the way it sounded after she'd been drinking. Yet there was nothing in her glass now but the fresh lemonade Beth had made herself.

"My paintings . . . after all this time. I thought mice would have gotten them. They'd have to be ruins by now."

"Not at all! Oil paints probably last forever. Some of them need dusting off—that's all."

Aunt Iris sat silently.

"Oh, Iris! You *were* such a good artist once!" Hannah reached over and put her hand on her sister's thin arm. "Would you show us your work? Please?"

"That's a wonderful idea," said Grandmother. "Iris, baby, *would* you do it?"

And Grandad rumbled his approval. "Always said the girl had talent."

"Oh, no," breathed Aunt Iris. "You don't understand."

"Come on, Aunt Iris," urged Tom. "Why not? If you'll show us some of your stuff, I'll teach you all about computers! I've borrowed Mark's laptop—that's a portable computer—and when I get it set up, I'll give you a private workshop!"

"That's a threat, not an incentive!" objected Beth. "Why don't you say that if she *doesn't* show us, you'll teach her everything you know about computers!"

Aunt Iris drained her lemonade and set the glass down at her side. Her face was pale, with dark smudges under the eyes. But the lines around her mouth seemed less sharply etched, and the wispy curls lay soft against her forehead. "Not now," she said. "I just don't think I can face sorting through those canvases now."

"I know," said Hannah brightly. "How about this? If you'll show us some of your work, Beth will show us the stained-glass window she has been working on down in the basement all summer!"

"Mom!" Beth knew she'd be as good as dead if Aunt Iris saw what she'd done.

"Why not, Beth? It's a fair trade."

Oh, great. Now what was she supposed to say? It had been her own idea, after all, to urge Aunt Iris to bring up her paintings.

Surprisingly, Aunt Iris shook her head. "I'd love to see your window sometime," she said to Beth. "But I can wait till you're ready." She turned to her sister, and her voice was gentle and sad. "I can wait, Hanny. It isn't right to manipulate situations. You just can't force people to do what they don't want to do. There's a time and place for everything."

Why did Beth have the feeling that Aunt Iris wasn't talking about art anymore?

Hannah lowered her eyes and clasped her hands in her lap.

Beth took a deep breath. "Listen, it's all right. I'll show you," she said. "I'd like to show you." She jumped off the glider. "Will you help me bring it up, Tom?"

He nodded, and together they went swiftly into the house and down into the coolness of the basement.

Her panel of stained glass was heavy. She shifted it carefully into her arms and Tom took the other end. "Careful, now," she cautioned as they started back up the stairs. No time to think now whether this was the right thing to do. Back out on the porch she lugged the window over to the low wicker table and began removing the layers of sheet and newspaper. Grandad hitched his chair closer.

The panel was two feet high and four feet long. She propped it up on the table, leaned it back against the stone wall of the house, and pulled off the last fold of cloth.

Even in the evening light, the color burst forth. Deep blue glass formed the sea bottom, with emerald and turquoise waves and crests of crystal. Beth had used many small pieces of glass to form the two mermaids who swam with the fish, long hair streaming around them. The islands rose out of the water—with gray and brown and green patterning the mountains and valleys. Beth had remained as faithful to Aunt Iris's original Notfilc painting as she could manage, except in a few details. In Aunt Iris's painting two beasts had stood guard at the entrance to a forest on one island, but Beth had etched them as a man and a woman. The man had a bald head like Grandad. On the next island she had etched a small house with a porch, though in Aunt Iris's painting the building was an elaborate palace. The roof of the little house had exploded—Beth used crystal fragments to form the shattering shingles—and she'd etched small figures of a family running out. She'd etched the prince rowing up in his barge to rescue them, but the waves around his boat were high. It didn't seem certain he would make it. On the third island the long-haired princess was held captive, surrounded by beasts. On the fourth island there was a wild garden, tangles of bright flowers, among them Beth's version of the blue iris with which Aunt Iris had signed her painting. The skies above the islands were worked in the deep purples and blues of Aunt Iris's original and dotted with her shimmering spacecraft. But the sky also showed the heavens as Beth imagined they'd formed: bursts of gold and crimson and clear crystal glass shooting sparks of fire into black space. The circles of planets hung under the spikes of yellow suns. And near the blue planet a tiny astronaut wearing a purple helmet floated, its lifeline tethered to a star above.

"Incredible," whispered Aunt Iris. Then she covered her face and burst into tears.

"Oh, Beth, it's beautiful!" exclaimed Grandmother. "Come on, Iris! What's wrong, dear?" She moved in front of Aunt Iris as if to hide her. Aunt Iris stifled her sobs, but Beth could still see her shoulders shaking.

Grandad and Hannah and Tom all leaned forward at once, as much to distract Beth's attention from her aunt as to see the detail in the window. "This is amazing, Beth, girl," said Grandad. "Funny—it reminds me of something. . . ." He shot a look at Aunt Iris. "Get a hold of yourself, Iris!"

Hannah's smile was as bright as the suns. "This is your finest piece ever, Beth! I'm so proud of you!" She put her arm around Beth's shoulders and hugged her.

"Pretty cool," Tom said, which was high praise, coming from him.

Beth left them looking at the window and walked over to Aunt Iris's huddled form. "Aunt Iris?" she whispered. "I'm sorry! I know I shouldn't have used your painting without asking. I knew you'd be angry. It's just—well, the painting was so wonderful, I couldn't help myself. I wanted so badly to turn it into glass." She touched her Aunt's bowed shoulder. "I guess it's sort of like stealing—"

Aunt Iris uncovered her face and reached for Beth's hands. "Oh, Elisabeth, no! I'm not angry. You've transformed my painting into something new. I'm honored." She wiped her face. "That painting was very special. I made it as a gift."

"Can we bring up your painting and show everyone?" asked Beth softly. "I think they should see the original. Of course, I couldn't work in as much detail in glass as you could with a brush. Your painting shows so much more."

"All right," said Aunt Iris. "Bring it up." Her voice was suddenly firm. "I want to see it."

Beth slipped inside. She returned a few minutes later carrying Aunt Iris's canvas. "Wait a minute, everyone," she announced. "If you think *my* stuff is good, take a look at this." She propped the painting on the table next to her window. "Aunt Iris was my inspiration!"

"Wow!" exclaimed Tom.

"I see now where you get your talent, Beth," said Hannah. She leaned forward to read the banner flying from the castle turret. " 'Notfilc'—oh, *Iris!* I remember now!"

"What does that mean, Mom?" asked Tom, pressing forward to see.

Hannah shook her head. Grandmother and Grandad leaned over as well, and Aunt Iris reached out her hand as if to shield the painted banner from their eyes. "You made it for Christmas, didn't you, Iris?" murmured Grandmother. "I remember how Clifton loved it."

Beth stood back as her family crowded around the table to lean over her window and Aunt Iris's canvas. They moved back and forth, gesturing, marveling aloud at the details, comparing the version of paint on canvas with the leaded glass. Beth was not surprised when she heard the crack.

The sound wasn't loud, but everyone leaped

back from the table almost in one motion and stared down in horror. A single sliver of purple glass lay at their feet.

"Meteor shower," said Tom into the momentary silence.

Grandmother had two bright red spots on her cheeks. Hannah pressed her hands to her mouth. Aunt Iris began crying again. Then the wicker rocking chair creaked as Grandad sat down, and everyone started exclaiming at once:

"That's a real shame—"

"Oh, Elisabeth! I'm so sorry!"

"Hey, I bet I was the one who bumped it—"

"Beth, honey, please forgive me—"

"I'm so clumsy sometimes—"

Beth picked up the shard of glass carefully and placed it on the tabletop. She took a deep breath, then smiled at them. "It's not ruined," she said. "Probably the seam wasn't tight enough. I can fix it. Don't worry, it wasn't anybody's fault."

"Maybe so, maybe so," muttered Grandad.

"But your beautiful work," wept Aunt Iris.

"It'll be all right," Beth said. "Accidents happen."

Grandad rocked steadily, nodding his approval.

• • •

The next day Beth received her first letter from Ray. She held it in two hands and carried it outside to the swing in the backyard as if it might leap away from her and disappear. She slit the flap hastily and pulled out the single sheet of notepaper. The left-hand edge was ragged where he'd torn it from a notebook. His writing was a dark scrawl across the page:

Dear Beth,

Jane decided to close the shop for a few weeks between evening class sessions and head for the mountains. I went along and we camped in the redwoods. Those giants are really something! I was inspired to do a new window once we got back.

I'll be teaching a Wednesday night class called "Nature into Glass." Jane will be teaching a new workshop called "Glass Portraiture." We hope you'll take one—or both—of these new classes. You're just about the best new artist I know—but you'll need to keep your hand in.

Glad to hear you've been hard at work on a new project, Babe. Give us a call when you get back and let us see the masterpiece! We hope you'll be home soon—it sounds like you've been having a tough summer, you poor kid! Hey—take some advice from Uncle Ray: Don't let the goons get to you! They're not worth it.

Love,
Ray

Beth dropped the letter onto the grass and watched it flutter across the yard into the rose-bushes. After all these weeks of waiting, this was all? A single sheet of paper? A note that filled barely half the page?

She kicked the swing up high, leaning backward to pump herself into the sky. A camping trip—with Jane? Jane Simmons was the owner of Glassworks and even older than Ray himself. She must be in her thirties. Beth closed her eyes against the thought of them together—traveling in the same car, setting up tents (or one tent?), cooking together outside, going on long hikes, talking about the beauty around them, planning new classes. She felt dizzy.

She couldn't have said how much time had passed when Aunt Iris found her sitting on the motionless swing. Her aunt walked slowly across the backyard. "Hello, Beth. I thought maybe your dog needs a walk." Aunt Iris hesitated, taking in Beth's shuttered face. "Would you come with me? Maybe we can stop off at the candy store and say hello. I'd like to taste those homemade doughnuts I've heard so much about."

For a long moment Beth stared at her aunt as if she didn't recognize her. How could it be Aunt Iris, of all people, reaching out to her? Maybe it was her imagination, but Aunt Iris already seemed to have gained a little weight. Her cheekbones weren't so sharp anymore. Neither was her voice.

Beth had to pull herself in from some dark place before she could speak. "Okay," she said finally, and was surprised that her voice sounded normal. She called for Romps, who was lying in the shade of the hedge. "Good idea," she continued in that same normal voice. "I could use a doughnut, too." As they left the yard together, a welcome breeze sifted through the trees and stirred the grass. Beth forced herself not to look back even once to see whether the letter from Ray had blown away.

When they returned from their walk, she went straight down to the basement to repair her window. The jagged shard of broken glass brought to the surface her anguish. She kept her hands steady while she cut and soldered the lengths of lead, though tears came to her eyes and dropped onto the glass.

Even repaired, the crack in the astronaut's lifeline would always be there, easy to see if you looked closely. She thought of Clifton Becker, how his death shattered so many lives in this house. Even if it were possible to repair those breaks, as Grandad tried, the cracks would still be there and would show if you looked closely. She stood back to look at the whole panel. Its soft gleam seemed to deny any cracks at all.

Maybe she should give the window to Aunt Iris as a symbol that cracks *could* be repaired, and the whole picture *could* still be beautiful and bright? *It would be a nice gesture*, she thought, but knew she wouldn't do it. She wasn't sure she even believed it. She wanted to ship her window home and show Ray and Violet. Well, Violet, anyway. The glass panel would look lovely hanging in the big living-room window of the apartment. Whenever she looked at it she would remember this summer, this house. And somehow that wouldn't be so bad anymore.

Working offered her solace. She found herself mourning the break that had severed the little astronaut's lifeline—it seemed exactly the way

Ray's letter had severed her own. All summer she'd had him in her head, and in her head he had been waiting for her. The letters she imagined he would write had sustained her through the days and nights of tension and unhappiness. She survived the summer because she imagined his strength holding her together. His love had been a lifeline stretching across the three thousand miles of America. And yet all the time, he had been camping with Jane Simmons!

Beth stayed down in the basement until dinnertime. She cleaned and polished and buffed her window, but still the cracks remained visible.

Tom carried out his threat to teach Aunt Iris something about computers the next morning. The two of them sat out on the sunporch for more than two hours while Tom showed off his expertise and encouraged her to try out the different functions. When Beth came up to call them for lunch, she saw their heads bent together over the portable computer.

"Start with something simple," Tom was urging. "Just type a simple letter or something."

Aunt Iris bit her lip. "I haven't written to anyone in years."

"Just type anything. Here, look." He leaned over her and tapped the keys:

NEW WORK BY IRIS SAVAGE
COMING SOON TO AN ART MUSEUM
NEAR YOU!!

"Silly boy," she said.

"It's not silly! Look how easy it is to change it around," he said, and he pushed another few buttons:

COMING SOON TO AN ART MUSEUM
NEAR YOU!!
NEW WORK BY IRIS SAVAGE

"Very clever," she said. "But you're still a silly boy."

When Beth broke in to remind them that lunch was waiting, Aunt Iris was shaking her head in reluctant admiration of modern technology and of Tom's mastery of it. "Clifton would have loved to write his novel on one of those things," she told Beth.

They headed for the stairs. As Aunt Iris reached for the railing and started down, Tom grabbed Beth's arm. "We'll be down in a sec, Aunt Iris," he said and pulled his sister back to the sunporch.

"What is it?"

His face was a puzzle. She recognized the look; he wore it when he was up against something modern technology couldn't solve. "I found this when I was plugging in the surge protector," he said, lifting a pile of computer magazines from the desk and withdrawing a single sheet from underneath them. He thrust the thin page of yellowed typing paper at her. "It was stuck behind the desk against the wall and I don't know what to do with it."

Even before Beth read the words typed on it, she felt the butterfly wings start flapping in her stomach.

"It's a title page," whispered Tom. "And you get only one guess which book it's from."

Beth didn't need any guesses at all.

The Beasts of Notfilc
by
Clifton Becker
Dedicated to my darling! I will love you forever.

Tom wanted her advice. Should they throw it away? Or put it back where it had been for twenty years? Should they give it to their mother?

Beth handed it back. "Toss it," she said

tersely. "We've had enough trouble from old Clifton Becker already. If Mom reads that dedication, she'll start mourning him all over again."

But just as Tom was about to ball the page up, she reached for it again. "No, wait! I guess we should give it to her. . . ." She wasn't happy about this decision, but the paper wasn't really theirs to throw away, after all.

They went downstairs. Grandmother and Grandad were sitting in the dining room while Aunt Iris dished up homemade chicken rice soup. Hannah was at the kitchen sink filling glasses of ice with water.

Beth touched her mother's elbow. "Mom?" She motioned with her head toward the pantry. Eyebrows raised, Hannah allowed herself to be led out of the kitchen. She leaned against the washing machine.

"Is something wrong?"

Tom cleared his throat, then explained how he had moved the desk on the sunporch to plug in the computer before giving Aunt Iris her lesson this morning.

Beth held out the page, brittle and yellow from twenty years of waiting. Hannah looked from Beth's face to Tom's and back again, then wiped her hands on her shorts before taking the paper. She read it in a second and her eyes filled with tears. Too late, Beth decided the best thing would have been to put it back where Tom found it.

"Thank you," Hannah said, and gave them a trembling smile. She walked back through the kitchen into the dining room.

Beth and Tom followed her and sat in their chairs. Hannah stood by hers a moment, reading over the words Clifton Becker had typed so long ago up on that sunporch.

Then she sat down and passed the page across the table to Aunt Iris. "The kids found this," she said quietly. "I believe it's yours."

September

❦❦❦❦❦❦❦ September arrived with cool winds to blow away the long summer's heat. The leaves on the trees around the house on Spring Street changed to brilliant orange. The elm tree in the backyard turned red. The roses in the side yard dropped their petals onto the grass.

Clifton's grave was in a grove of oak trees. When the wind blew, bright leaves flew down onto the still-fresh mound of earth and rustled against the granite stone.

The day set for the wedding came and went. Iris noticed that her hands sometimes went numb in the middle of the day. Shaking them to get the blood moving again seemed too much trouble. She had no enthusiasm for anything now that her heart, like Clifton's heart, was dead. The only difference was that his had stopped beating entirely and hers still pumped blood through a living body. A small difference, really. She discovered with a kind of relief that she simply couldn't eat anything anymore. Food didn't smell good now that she was alone, so why bother with it? She stayed in her room, felt the shutters of her soul coming down. Locking. Late one night in the middle of the month, when her parents and sister were asleep, she limped through the house in a kind of fog, carrying all her art supplies and canvases to the basement and dumping them in a corner. She couldn't imagine she would ever paint again.

A week or so later Hanny Lynn stood on the porch steps in the early morning light, breathing deeply. She welcomed the change to autumn and drew the cold air into her lungs as if it could fill her with new life. She knew she couldn't live here anymore under such clouds of anger and accusation. She would be leaving soon, moving on even as the seasons moved on. She was making changes. She was making plans. When to go, how best to go on from here.

6

The summer was nearly over. There was a crispness in the air now that chased away much of the humidity. The family in the house on Spring Street found it easier to sleep at night.

When Monica and Bernard came over for a farewell dinner, Hannah invited them to Berkeley for Thanksgiving. And she promised Grandad and Grandmother they'd all be back at the house on Spring Street for Christmas. After the heat of the summer, Beth had a hard time imagining Spring Street with snow on the ground. Tom and Monica took Romps on lots of walks, possibly to talk about their own future plans.

Beth's plans for the future kept changing. She decided she might as well apply to some art schools this fall—maybe even look into some in

Europe, while she was at it. Sometimes she found herself falling into the old, happy daydream about Ray and their shop, but she pushed it resolutely away. Until she saw him again, and really talked to him, she was going to try not to plan anything that would include him. Such resolutions were easier made than kept to, however. The memory of him could come upon her suddenly while she was helping Grandmother in the kitchen, doing the crossword puzzle with Grandad, or packing her stained-glass equipment away in boxes for their journey home: how Ray worked with his sleeves rolled up to the elbows, how his hands looked holding the glass cutter, how his eyes smiled at her from behind his protective shield as he shaped pieces of glass for his windows at the grinder. These memories were still powerful. Resolutions couldn't keep them away.

The tension in the house seemed to have blown away in the first cooling breezes of autumn. Hannah and Aunt Iris talked together a lot, trying to make up for lost time, like people who have been falsely imprisoned for years and years and are then set free. They could never really have back the time they had lost, but they worked at moving on. At their farewell party with Monica and Bernard, Beth heard Aunt Iris asking Monica about the Philadelphia Institute of Art, whether they accepted older students and so on. It looked suddenly as if Beth and her mother might not be the only ones in the family heading off to college.

On their last day at the house on Spring Street, Beth sat out on the porch glider with Romps at her side. She felt she had spent most of her summer sitting out here, scratching Romps's ears while she escaped the house. Now she looked around the porch at her grandparents and Tom and thought maybe Romps was the only one of them who hadn't changed that summer.

Hannah and Aunt Iris had walked to the store on the next block to buy snacks for the long drive back to California. They were leaving early the next morning. Tom had put in his order for chocolate chip cookies and pretzels. Beth wanted fruit and some animal crackers. Ray laughed at her childish taste in cookies—but never mind Ray and what he thought. Beth shifted in the glider and once more cast him out of her heart.

Footsteps on the pavement behind the shield of bushes in front of the house signaled Aunt

Iris and Hannah's return. A few seconds later, they climbed the steps to the porch.

Grandmother glanced up with a smile for both of them and handed Hannah a pot of string beans. "Would you top and tail these, dear? I want to start dinner soon."

From her seat on the glider, Beth could see past Grandad and Grandmother in their rockers, past Hannah and Aunt Iris on the wicker couch talking with Tom while they prepared the beans. She could see right through the open front door into the house, to the foot of the stairs. And it was all too easy to imagine Clifton Becker standing on the landing up there, to see him falling backward toward the radiator. She had to close her eyes against his impact. Could he *really* just have tripped? Had a terrible accident?

As Grandad would say, "Maybe so."

She'd never know. No one would ever know. But let Clifton rest in peace.

It seemed to Beth now that the question calling out for an answer didn't deal with the past anymore but with the future—with the future of their family. Could they *really* move on from here? Would they make it now, after all?

Maybe so.